"Get the police, Mag
Athena said. She was already reaching for her baton and forcing her legs to carry her faster.

"Damn! Damn! Damn!"

One man yanked Laszlo's arms behind him, the other started punching him. When Athena reached the spot, she swung her baton and gave one man two hardy cracks on the back. She heard him grunt in surprise and pain. She caught the other one on the shoulder before he jumped up and punched her in the face. She reached for her can of pepper spray.

★

"I had trouble putting down *Night Summons*—the action was so intriguing and full of surprises."

—Charles T. Tart, author of
Altered States of Consciousness

"Get the police, Magda! Two men attacked Laszlo," Athena said. She was already reaching for her purse and forcing her legs to carry her faster.

"Damn! Damn! Damn!"

One man yanked Laszlo's arms behind him, the other started punching him. When Athena reached them, she swung her bag, and gave one man two nasty cracks on the back. She heard him grunt in surprise and pain. She caught the other one on the shoulder before he turned on and punched her in the face. She reached for her can of pepper spray.

"I had trouble putting down *Night Summons*—the action was so intriguing and full of surprises."

—Charles T. Tart, author of *Altered States of Consciousness*

NIGHT SUMMONS

Anita Gentry

WORLDWIDE®

TORONTO • NEW YORK • LONDON
AMSTERDAM • PARIS • SYDNEY • HAMBURG
STOCKHOLM • ATHENS • TOKYO • MILAN
MADRID • WARSAW • BUDAPEST • AUCKLAND

To my dad, the intellectual,
and my mom, who prefers psychic things.
Also, to Mary.

NIGHT SUMMONS

A Worldwide Mystery/June 1998

First published by St. Martin's Press, Incorporated.

ISBN 0-373-26276-0

Printed in U.S.A.

ACKNOWLEDGMENTS

I would like to express my deepest gratitude to: Charles Tart for story ideas; Charles Post for the suggestion that I expand the original short story into a novel; Dorothy Wall for editing through to the end; Ruth Letner for careful comments on the text and encouragement throughout; and Richard Bankowsky for suggestions on the final version.

Special thanks go to firefighters Kim Jester, Jan Welch and Larry Rettig, who provided valuable information.

Finally, I'd like to express my appreciation to Amy Boyer, Eileen Snyder and Linda Husmann, members of my writers' group, for insights that helped bring the mystery to its final form.

PROLOGUE

"IT GROWS WORSE," Magda muttered, staring trancelike at the oval surface of the Flammari mirror. High cheekbones jutted out over dark hollows; steely gray strands glinted among dark ones. Her golden eyes were luminous, though an underlying turbulence gave them unaccustomed depth. These details she did not notice, for her attention was focused on the narrow, bronze-colored sliver of light that capped her hair like a tiara. She tilted her head. Without question her aura grew fainter each time she looked into the antique glass, the only place her past and future reflected so clearly. Though she often read signs for others, she'd never glimpsed her own fate until she gazed into this turn-of-the-century Italian masterpiece. A double-edged find for Magda, the mirror with its gold art nouveau frame had become both prized and feared for its terrible accuracy. The exceptional quality of the glass enabled her to see more than she cared to when she dared peek into its depths. She kept the glass covered with a piece of scarlet velvet and only consulted it when she could not resist.

When she first saw the mirror at the flea market, Magda had known at once she must own it but pretended indifference in order to keep the price down. Had the antiques dealer noticed the glint in Magda's eye or sensed her accelerated heartbeat and determination to possess this cloudy oval of glass with its too-fancy frame, she would have boosted the cost and refused to budge. The pout on Magda's lips, plus her visible uncertainty about whether to waste time on so unworthy an object, had the old woman groveling to close the sale. Magda knew all about bargains.

What puzzled Magda as she scrutinized her crystal-clear image in the glass were the sure signs of imminent death. She had never felt stronger in her life, yet she did not doubt that death was creeping steadily toward her. The marked deterioration of her aura indicated sudden death in the not-too-distant future.

She threw back her head defiantly. "I am gypsy," she said proudly to the mirror and stamped her small foot. "I fear nothing in this life or next."

What about Laszlo? He was her beloved and her Achilles' heel. He relied on her strength more than he knew, increasing it by his need. Laszlo was in jeopardy, especially with escalating threats to his research. If she were soon to leave his side, he must have someone to help him carry on.

"Night summons," Magda said. "I send night summons to receptive mind. Right one will come to my call. If I die, Laszlo must continue."

With a deep sigh, she covered the mirror with a hemmed rectangle of velvet. Pulling her arms close to her body, she turned around slowly three times to free herself from encumbrances. Then, arms outstretched, she sank to a sitting position on the floor. Leaning forward, she knocked on the wood at evenly spaced intervals. Satisfied that there would be no uncalled-for intrusions, she clasped her hands, elbows on knees, and breathed deeply for seven minutes. Rocking herself in steady rhythm, Magda began a low, vibrant hum. Her mind fixed on images and sent them out into the night.

PART ONE

ONE

LIGHTED WINDOWS in Suzie's small house caught Athena's attention the moment she turned her Honda Civic into the driveway. The rest of the neighborhood was still dark. Athena was pleased to arrive sooner than expected—5:00 a.m.—after covering six hundred miles, including mountainous stretches, in about twelve hours. The wild ride came in direct response to Suzie's panicked call to the P.I. office in Portland, Oregon, where Athena worked. In Suzie's words, "I need your expertise, Athena. A fatal accident has occurred and I'm afraid more will follow."

"I'd be happy to advise you if you tell me what the trouble is," Athena had said.

"Advice won't help," Suzie said. "I need your eyes, ears, and analytical skills in this place at this time. Also bring your gun." Her voice grew soft with the last word.

"I practice at the firing range, but that doesn't mean I'm ready to use it on human targets," Athena said.

"Bring it with you anyway. I know you can make a difference."

"Tell me more."

"I can't. Just a moment." The receiver hit something, and Athena heard Suzie talking to someone. Suzie cleared her throat, then spoke softly. "Come *now.* In a week, it might be too late. I'm hiring you for this job. Just a moment." Again, Suzie was talking to someone else, then said, "Tell Ted it's urgent."

Ted was Athena's boss and uncle. Athena wasn't working on any specific case at the moment, and knowing Suzie was not likely to exaggerate, Athena had said, "I'll come."

"Plane is best," Suzie said.

"Not unless I hire a private plane. Guns and gadgets in my resource kit aren't popular items in travel bags," Athena said.

"I'll also need my car and can't afford to hire one. A shoestring operation, right?"

"You got it, though I may reach into a deep pocket on your behalf. The important thing is to get results fast," said Suzie. "Must go! Bye!"

Tantalizing. Drawn by the urgency in Suzie's request, Athena decided to start the trip with the provision that she'd stop and rest if she got tired. Once on the road, the momentum of covering mile after mile and her curiosity about Suzie's SOS carried her—southward, all the way to Aston.

On the road, she'd puzzled over what Suzie expected her to do. Recent letters had held no hints of trouble. Suzie's attention tended to focus on her summer trip to Hungary and a Hungarian couple, Laszlo and Magda. Magda was a gypsy, Laszlo from noble parentage. Magda was psychic; Laszlo specialized in parapsychology. Athena would have been more impressed by expertise in ecology or international politics, but Suzie was captivated.

Frustrated by her lack of information, Athena resolved never again to accept a job without knowing what it involved, even for a friend.

As soon as Athena switched off the engine, she could no longer ignore that her right foot ached from pressing the gas pedal, her neck and back seemed fused together, and her eyelids had been fighting to close and stay closed for hours. Tempted to doze off, she stared at the glowing windows, and her mind kept moving.

Why all the lights at this ungodly hour? she wondered. Was Suzie preparing breakfast? Not likely, unless she was suffering from insomnia. She liked to sleep in as late as possible, just giving herself enough time to get to work, and she didn't expect Athena until noon. Of course, Suzie might have set out a snack and left welcome lights, but why so many?

Athena opened the car door, stretched her legs, and stood up. She walked around the car to get her bags from the passenger seat. Strange that Suzie hadn't picked up phone calls the night before or left her answering machine on for a message. Athena had tried to reach her at least four times on the car phone and quit only after 10:30 p.m.

Leaning against the car, she inhaled deeply and savored a whiff of ocean in the breeze. An unseen bird trilled a few notes, echoed by another. For a moment, Athena floated in a dream state, but a feeling that all questions would soon be answered and she could catch some sleep pulled her onward.

With handbag, resource kit, and compact suitcase in hand, Athena headed for those lights. It would be good to see Suzie, find out why she was alarmed and what she could do. She stumbled on the uneven flagstones of the path to Suzie's door but kept her balance.

Athena was going to reach for the duplicate house key under a flowerpot when she glimpsed chaos through the window. She tried the door, which wasn't locked, lurched across the threshold, and stopped in disbelief.

Suzie's body lay sprawled awkwardly on the carpet, head turned sideways like a broken doll's. Pieces of glass, porcelain figurines, a cascade of papers, musical scores, travel brochures, and books of all shapes and sizes littered the room.

Athena's heart thundered as she moved forward. "Suzie!" she called urgently, hoping to see her friend's head move, her eyes focus in recognition. "Suzie!"

Close up, Athena saw blood matted in the woman's hair, partially covering a wound on the left side of her skull. Suzie's eyes were half-closed. Freckles stood out like careless splotches of brown paint against the pasty white, almost gray, hue of her face. One leg was turned askew. A run in her stocking went from ankle to thigh, though no sign of sexual abuse was apparent.

Fighting a strong foreboding, Athena knelt amidst the wreckage and felt a cool wrist, then the carotid artery for a pulse, but her own racing heartbeats interfered with results.

"Live, Suzie. Live," she said, as she leaned closer. "I didn't come for a funeral."

Although she'd practiced CPR on a dummy, the body of her friend with a serious head wound and possible spinal injury was totally different. Suzie's chest rose and fell ever so slightly. Athena leaned her whole body forward to put her cheek close to her nostrils and was relieved to feel air blow lightly on her skin, a pause, and then more air. Shrugging out of her coat, she tucked it around Suzie's figure.

"You're on your way to the hospital, Suzie. Hang on, you hear?"

In search of a phone, Athena ran through the dining area, dodging computer disks, napkins, placemats, and dried flowers on the floor. On the kitchen wall phone, Athena punched the emergency number with trembling fingers. Papers from Suzie's message board were scattered everywhere. While the phone was ringing, she decided to take pictures of Suzie and the general devastation before the police arrived.

"9-1-1?" Athena shouted.

"Yes, ma'am!" came a snappy reply.

"Emergency—I repeat *emergency*—at 224 Cantata Lane. Woman with head injury, barely breathing. House ransacked. Send ambulance and police right away. Hurry!"

"That's 224 Cantata Lane? Hold on, please."

Athena could faintly hear the message going out on another circuit.

"Police and emergency crew have been notified."

"How long before they arrive?" Athena said.

"I can't say. We got a call a few minutes ago."

So matter-of-fact. Athena pushed for more. "Get a doctor or somebody the hell over here immediately. Can you?"

"Yes, ma'am. I need a phone number."

Athena repeated it twice and added, "If nobody comes in ten minutes, I'll call the mayor and the local TV station and raise hell."

Rechecking Suzie's breathing, Athena timed it at about fourteen breaths per minute. She was holding her own, but Athena wanted to improve her chances. "You're going to be fine, Suzie. I'm here to make sure of it." Words to soothe and encourage. Athena had read that people undergoing surgery sometimes heard what doctors and nurses said in spite of anesthesia.

She was unpacking her camera when a *thunk* sounded somewhere inside the house. She flinched and reached for the Smith

& Wesson .38 revolver in her purse while straining to detect any other noise. Better to do a quick security check of the premises.

Gun uplifted, she stepped quickly but cautiously down the hall. In Suzie's bedroom, a fluffy white cat sat on the floor, licking its paws near a window braced to allow pet entry through a foot-wide opening. Suzie often mentioned her two cats, Spook, a model of beauty, and Tigger, a scruffy, disreputable specimen. This one, definitely Spook, had probably made the noise coming in. Athena kept moving into the guest bedroom, a bathroom, and back through the living room where Suzie lay to the small dining area and kitchen.

The back door was locked. A screened porch had a door with a bolt, also locked. A quick search for a point of forced entry brought zero results. Access gained through the unlocked front door, she guessed.

Every room she scanned, including closets, had been trashed—clothes from underwear to sweaters, shoes, towels, tubes of cosmetics and skin cream, dangling earrings—the only kind Suzie wore—and dozens of loose photos were strewn all over. What was significant in the crazy whirlwind of stuff?

In the bathroom, Athena spotted a streak of blood in the sink and vomit in the toilet. Nauseated herself, she was momentarily startled by the strange woman in the bathroom mirror, the palest face with circles under deep-set black eyes and black curls standing out wildly like Medusa's, then recognized the image as her own.

"Move forward, one step at a time, and don't miss a thing," she said out loud and heard an echo.

Athena checked her pal once more. "With you in a moment, Suzie."

Equipped with the small camera from her resource kit, Athena snapped pictures of Suzie, her immediate surroundings, and the other rooms. The police would take photos too, but she might catch something they missed. Athena spotted no obvious weapon, nothing upon which Suzie might have struck her head.

On the surface, the intruder had spared no area from the rampage. Drawers and cabinets hung open; containers, including wastebaskets, lay overturned; even bookcases had lost part of their contents.

Though small, the house had spacious rooms with special features such as a bay window with window seat; the niche in the dining area where Suzie had placed her computer and printer; a walk-in pantry; and built-in shelves, drawers, and a corner display cabinet. The rooms held a mixture of antique furniture, a legacy from Suzie's aunt, and modern Scandinavian pieces in Suzie's taste. Impressionist oils of gardens and landscapes throughout the house were signed by Beth Midden, Suzie's deceased aunt. Beneath the debris, Athena saw the cheerful colors and sensed that ordinarily coziness and comfort reigned in Suzie's house.

"Coming, Suzie," Athena said, forcing herself to speed-write notes on her steno pad: overturned wine glass & spilled wine on carpet; picture of garden path on floor (fell from above?); hole in wall where nail should be; blood (whose?) in bathroom sink; vomit (whose?) in toilet; objects dumped on floor. This was not the pattern of a burglar looking for valuables.

Finished with pictures and notes, Athena tucked gun, camera, and notebook into the bottom of her suitcase away from trained and prying eyes, then redialed 911. The same operator answered.

"I called from 224 Cantata Lane ten minutes ago." It was actually seven, though it seemed twice that. "Where's the rescue team?"

"An ambulance and a police car are on the way."

She doubted it. "Speed up. This woman can't wait," Athena said and hung up. She wanted to yell, "What are you there for? No excuses. Just results."

Athena seated herself on the Aubusson carpet at Suzie's side and took her hand. Easier to move around than to confront Suzie's state. Impossible to maintain scene-of-the-crime detachment at close range. At some level, Athena still expected Suzie to jump up, peel off a plastic wound, and yell, "Surprise! Now solve the crime. All clues are in plain view."

Athena spotted no suspicious matter under Suzie's nails—fibers, hairs, or detritus—that might yield evidence; no scratches, bruises, or abrasions indicative of a struggle. She imagined her own hands sending healing rays to soothe and repair damage as she stroked her friend's arm, then squeezed and released her right hand repeatedly.

"When they come, they'll fix you good as new," Athena said.

Would they? Suzie's eyes did not see, her ears did not hear. So different from the real Suzie who listened attentively to others. The same Suzie whose light brown eyes grew bright and molten as maple syrup when she talked. Who laughed easily. Her head wound looked vicious. How badly had it fractured the skull? Could there be permanent brain damage or even brain death? Enough of that!

Athena wanted to brush strands of Suzie's straight brown hair back off her forehead. Too many times she'd seen Suzie look in the mirror, screwing her face up in a ferocious frown, and she'd taunt herself, "Plain face! Plain face!"

"It could be worse," Athena had said.

"You're attractive. You don't understand at all," Suzie said. "Some might say I'm ugly but never beautiful. This overlay of freckles is a stigma like masses of pimples or a birthmark spread all over your face. Besides that, I'm built as square as a box."

Looking at her now, Athena said, "You're beautiful, absolutely beautiful, Suzie. Do you hear me? I apologize for poor timing. I thought I'd come too soon, but I came too late to prevent this."

Athena retucked the coat around Suzie's body. How long had she been lying here? The matching skirt, top, and shoes were definitely work clothes, indicating she hadn't changed into casuals—the usual jeans, T-shirt, sandals. When she'd phoned Suzie's number, there'd been no response. Most likely, Suzie had spent the night this way, which explained the lights. Some uninvited guest had crossed the threshold.

Athena focused all her energy on talking her friend back to life.

"Your trip to Hungary is only five weeks away. I saw the brochures near your desk. You've got lots of preparation to do."

Athena paused to see if she could detect any change in Suzie when something living touched the back of her calf, making her jump and cry out in alarm. She glanced over to see Spook curling up between her ankles. The animal settled in and began a rasping purr.

"Spook, you almost scared me to death!" If only the solution were so simple—the cat did it!

Aside from steady breathing, Suzie remained inert and pale. Where were the paramedics? Why were they taking so long? Thoughts tumbled while time seemed to have slowed down, down, down.

"Suzie, you're one of the bravest women I've ever known," she said.

Suzie looked small and defenseless now, but Athena recalled their first encounter in a Paris railway station where Suzie saw a pickpocket lift the billfold out of Athena's bag. Suzie didn't know her but came to her rescue, grabbing ahold of him like a pit bull terrier, shouting, *"Voleur! Voleur!"*

Athena's first hint that something was wrong was when someone's elbow caught her in the ribs just as a woman shouted in her ear, and she'd watched the struggling pair move down the platform—a short woman gripping a thin man and stomping on his feet. The woman was shouting "Thief!" and the man was shouting "Whore!" so waiting passengers were confused about what was really going on.

That time, Suzie fought like a devil and didn't let go. That's why Athena thought whoever hit Suzie took her by surprise.

"You wouldn't go down without a fight, Suzie! Not you! You're no victim," Athena said.

Athena was the victim in Paris, Suzie the defender. They were both idiots then compared to what they knew now about self-defense. It had always amazed Athena what Suzie did for a total stranger. The guy had tried to throw her on the train tracks. Suzie held on and gave him hell until he threw down the billfold, which she returned to Athena, who hadn't noticed it was missing. What a headache it would have been to lose all her cash and traveler's checks. It would have ruined her one and only European trip. Athena wasn't having much fun until she met Suzie, who knew the places to go, things to do, and people to meet.

France was only one country Suzie had visited and revisited in her worldwide travels. She had her summers free and spent them roaming around the world. In Suzie's words, "I want to feel the pulse of other places."

At Athena's suggestion, they were planning a trip to Greece for next summer. Athena wanted to see the land where her mother was born and seek out distant relatives. She and Suzie were discussing other trips to Japan, Russia, and Egypt in the future. Something to reach for and look forward to. Suzie was a great travel companion with her enthusiasm for different cultures.

"Where are you now, Suzie? Are you vacationing in some distant land? You've got to give me the puzzle pieces I need. We were going to work as a team."

Athena shifted her legs, and Spook stalked away, twitching her tail.

Suzie was so still. No sign she'd heard a single word.

Athena shook her head. "I owe you, Suzie. I owe you. I'll find whoever did this."

From her position on the floor, Athena glared, slit-eyed, out the front window at the sky, which was beginning to lighten.

Finally, sirens and flashing lights pulled up outside. Only fifteen minutes since she'd called, but it seemed like hours.

"They're here," Athena said. "Fight your way back, Suzie. I'll take care of the rest."

TWO PARAMEDICS hovered over the body. Athena kept an eye on them while a bleary-eyed cop, reeking of fresh cigarette smoke, pulled out his pen and notebook and started firing off questions. It was too early. She was too tired. She looked at him and saw a troll in a police uniform.

"Name? Address?"

Athena replied, and he scribbled, his pen scraping on his clipboard. No time to waste now. She'd save the choice information for the detective assigned to the case.

The pair of medics lifted Suzie's head carefully to put a cervical collar around her neck. Their quick, efficient actions convinced Athena they knew their stuff.

"How'd you discover the victim?"

"Suzie invited me to come stay with her. I arrived early, but not soon enough."

"Where you from?"

"Portland, Oregon."

Keeping Suzie's head straight, the medics rolled her loglike on her side and then turned her over onto a backboard.

"How long you known the victim?"

"Three and a half years."

"Any relatives?"

"Her father's in a nursing home in Sacramento. Had a stroke and doesn't recognize her when she visits. She has cousins but I don't know any names."

One medic strapped Suzie to the board while the other inserted an IV in her arm. Next, they placed an oxygen mask over her face.

"Boyfriend?"

"Not that I know of."

The cop stuffed a piece of Dentyne in his mouth. "I need to see your driver's license and another ID."

She complied. He scribbled on.

As the rescue team carried Suzie outside, Athena said, "I'm going to the hospital."

"We're locking the house, so it would be better if you don't stay here for a day or two until we've finished. Come to the station this morning—say 10 a.m.—for a longer interview."

"Will do." Athena grabbed her purse and suitcase and went outside. The cop followed her.

Medics had placed Suzie's stretcher in a white ambulance with WESTCOTT UNIVERSITY MEDICAL CENTER, SERVING ALL OF PATWIN COUNTY emblazoned in red on the side. Another police car pulled up, brakes squealing.

"Great timing!" Athena said.

The troll disguised as a policeman was copying down her license plate number and the make and model of her car. Athena scanned assembled neighbors and passersby as she started her engine and backed down the driveway. Several cyclists in helmets, neon-colored shirts, and black stretch pants had halted astride their bikes to see what was going on. A jogger, afraid of missing something, was jogging in place. A plump, gray-haired woman in her bathrobe stood gossiping with a thin, white-haired woman in a striped housedress, who held a small dog in her arms.

Just before driving away, Athena noticed a man standing on the sidewalk in the half-light with a German shepherd beside him. He had wide shoulders and thin hips. Something about his pose and the concerned expression on his face caught her attention. The dog, restless in the flashing lights, whined and pawed at the cement when the siren started up again. The man leaned toward his dog and spoke reassuringly. He stroked its head, holding on tight at the ruff.

A neighbor out walking his dog? Someone who knew something? He didn't look her way as she followed the ambulance.

TWO

HALF AN HOUR LATER, Athena washed her face and hands and brushed her thick black hair in the ladies' room at Calamar restaurant near the Westcott University campus. She'd left the hospital after they wheeled Suzie off for a CAT scan and surgery to relieve pressure on the brain. The ER doctor said only that Suzie was in a "deep coma," and that chances of her complete recovery were "unpredictable at this point in time."

Seated again in a dark blue booth, Athena rubbed her eyes and indulged in the luxury of a yawn. Since she was expected at the police station in a couple of hours, she couldn't doze off or she'd be out for a long time.

"Tired?" the waitress asked.

"More than a little," Athena said.

For breakfast, she chose eggs and pancakes, the latter not allowed on ordinary mornings. The French vanilla coffee slid down her throat like nectar. Munching on hash browns, Athena focused on the little information she had. The case, planned as a tandem effort, had ended up solo, at least until Suzie got well. *If* Suzie got well. There was only one place to start.

Suzie worked for the psychology department at Westcott University. Suzie had described Ginger, her supervisor, with respect and fondness. So, Ginger would be first to know about Suzie's injury.

Several cups later, Athena had sketched out a plan and was ready to act on it. Leaving her car near the restaurant, she walked the block to campus. Off limits to cars, campus streets were clogged with bicycles traveling at different speeds, which meant hazardous crossing for walkers, especially those bearing heavy backpacks.

Unlike those around her, Athena did not have to rush. She

questioned a passing student, studied a campus map, and then advanced into unfamiliar territory. The landscaping reminded her of a giant park with vast lawns, pines, palms, and occasional clusters of buildings.

Rimington Hall, an elegant, cream-colored Spanish-style building with thick red-tiled roofing and wrought-iron balconies, seemed to occupy a whole block. Its main entrance faced the corner of the intersection of California and Walnut streets. A round tower with large panes of glass dominated the third story, rising above it. Athena paused to look up at seven terra-cotta heads spaced at even intervals above the entrance. Each head—four masculine and three feminine—showed a distinctive hairstyle and symmetrical features with the blank, staring eyes of Greek gods and goddesses.

Inside the building, Athena admired the grand staircase with a wrought-iron rail, which ascended three stories. The psychology department office was on the first floor. The minute she opened the door, Athena saw a white-on-black nameplate for "Suzanne Frazier." A large poster of the Parthenon, ancient columns brightly lit, adorned the wall behind the desk.

At a side desk, a woman with pale blonde hair was studying a spreadsheet. Her bright blue eyes, when she raised them to study Athena, were rimmed with red. She was turning an engagement ring with a large, many-carated diamond around and around on her finger. The woman nodded but said nothing. Through a window into the adjoining office, Athena spotted an older woman with her elbows propped on her desk.

"I'd like to speak to the supervisor. I have news for her," Athena said.

Following a few words on the phone, the blonde, still playing with her ring, said formally, "Ginger will see you. Please go in."

Ginger was in her fifties, and her light brown hair was peppered with gray. The navy-and-white jacket and dress complemented dark blue eyes. Athena noted smile lines creasing her cheeks and bordering her eyes.

"I have news that's hard to tell," said Athena, glancing through the window to see a pair of curious eyes looking in at them. Ginger reached out to close the blinds and firmly closed the door. "Did Suzie mention a friend coming for a visit?"

"Are you Athena?" Ginger asked, holding out a hand. "Suzie said you'd help with the mess we're in, but I expected her to bring you in tomorrow."

"Can you explain the trouble and give me details?"

Ginger nodded but looked puzzled. "Didn't Suzie brief you? She'll show up any minute."

"I'm afraid not," Athena said, then described the condition of Suzie and her house.

"A coma? Who would hurt her?" Ginger asked. Nervously, she touched the back of her head, the locus of Suzie's injury, as Athena had described it. "Suzie's our peacemaker. I told her to ignore the faculty feud. She couldn't. At this point, no one can stay neutral."

"I need to know what's going on."

Ginger bit her lip and raised her eyebrows. "Usually, faculty act like rebellious kids. You pick up after them, make them fill out forms at the right times, and remind them how to keep on track. Since the department became a battle zone, we live in fear. Not fair for any of us. Now I'll prepare a memo to tell everyone about Suzie's...accident. I guess it's an accident until proven otherwise. She's not just away but in danger."

Ginger dabbed her eyes with a tissue and inhaled deeply. "Sorry. I've never acted—so unprofessional. It's just that I rely on her—she's the dependable one. With Suzie away and Vicky acting like a fruitcake, I can't take much more. I'm ready to walk out."

"I came to help Suzie. Perhaps I can help you too."

Ginger leaned over and gave her a hug. "Thank you for finding Suzie. She could have been there for days."

"May I ask a few questions?"

Ginger nodded.

"Suzie knew something. She mentioned 'a fatal accident,'" said Athena, pulling a notepad and pen from her pocket. "What did she mean?"

"Steve's accident. That tragedy has troubled us all." Ginger blew her nose and cleared her throat. "Less than two weeks ago, Steve Linstrom, one of our grad students, lost control on a winding road. His truck jumped a ditch and ran straight into a tree. He was killed instantly," Ginger said. "The police discovered that his brakes weren't working and looked as if they'd been tampered with. Steve had repaired his own brakes only a few days before, so they couldn't be one hundred percent sure whose fault it was. I saved news clips about his accident and the memorial service."

"I'd like copies," Athena said.

"Of course. What a mess we had with police questioning people. Vicky Conway, the woman in the front office, was living with Steve, even expected to marry him. She's having a rough time—not only with the loss, but she spent several hours with Steve the afternoon he was working on his truck, so she's on their suspect list."

Ginger opened a drawer and took out a stack of photos. Flipping through, she held one out. Athena took a long, careful look. Steve, a large man with Nordic good looks, was sitting with Vicky at a table. In his plaid flannel shirt, he reminded Athena of a lumberjack. He was talking straight to the camera, as Vicky gazed at him with open devotion. It was a revealing picture. Looking toward them was a woman whose eyes seemed to flare with anger, though the camera angle might have caused the effect.

"Who's the other woman?" Athena asked.

"That's Dr. Briggs, a specialist in success psychology. Steve was working with her before becoming one of Laszlo Honvagy's graduate students. Some people link Steve's death with Laszlo's research project on life after death. Others blame it on the battle going on between 'the new bunch,' as they're called, and 'the old-timers' in the department. As far as the police are concerned, there isn't real evidence of foul play. Steve's death remains an accident with a hint of suspicion associated with it."

"Suzie didn't tell me about the new bunch and the old-timers."

"The new bunch have become real troublemakers. Some of them have been here for ten years now. With eight retirements in five years, new faculty outnumber old. The split causes friction, like trying to house opposing gangs under one roof. The new bunch are mostly physiologists and behaviorists, and right now they're trying to oust Laszlo, who specializes in altered states and ESP. Laszlo joined our department in the early seventies, when parapsychology seemed in tune with the times. While some old-timers support Laszlo, others vote with the new bunch, knowing they hold the future in their hands. I'm in support of 'live and let live' around here.''

''Sounds grim. You don't have a counseling program here?''

Ginger was shaking her head as she examined her fingernails. ''Only a few classes. Students interested in becoming counselors transfer to Lexford.''

''Tell me more about the conflict. What form does it take?'' An image came to mind of professors shooting at each other from behind barricades of books.

''At the last faculty meeting, Gerald Derring stated that Laszlo's research program is outdated and suggested he retire to make way for those on the cutting edge. Laszlo jumped up and challenged him to a public debate. Derring accepted. The debate is scheduled for next Friday. Can you believe it? 'A duel to the death,' Suzie called it.''

''From threats come real injuries,'' Athena said, wondering who'd threatened Suzie. ''From war games come real wars.''

''For years, I heard rumors about guerrilla warfare in other departments where professors attack and injure each other, catching students in the cross fire. Everyone suffers. I never thought it could happen to us. Where is it going to stop? It makes me frantic.''

''Can't someone in authority act as arbiter?''

''We need proof of wrongdoing,'' Ginger said. ''Suzie was documenting whatever she could. Laszlo wants to press charges but needs sufficient evidence to support his case. He'd like to topple Derring from his self-appointed position as king of the mountain. The whole thing makes me sick.'' Ginger's voice trailed off. She drooped, looking older and more careworn.

''Do you think Suzie's injury and Steve's death are connected?''

Ginger pressed her fingers to her forehead. "I thought I knew everything about everyone around here. A murderer under our roof? Impossible. Now I don't know."

"I have a suggestion," Athena said. "Suzie hired me to deal with the situation. I'd like to work as Suzie's replacement for a few days as a way to get a close-up, inside view."

Ginger frowned. "You mean work in our front office?"

"You're the only one who knows I'm Suzie's friend with a special interest. To the others I'm just here to get the job done. People will open up more if they don't know my purpose."

To Athena's surprise, Ginger laughed. "You aren't familiar with Suzie's workload—phone calls, student questions, and professors expecting computer miracles can interfere with what you're trying to accomplish."

"I'd rather work from the inside than outside. Hearing what Suzie heard, seeing what she saw could give info she didn't deliver in person."

"How are your office skills?"

"I type ninety words a minute, worked in offices while I was a student, and I'm used to taking messages. The problem is—I don't know this campus."

Ginger's eyes traveled around the room. She massaged her neck, and her mouth twisted in different shapes. Finally, she shook her head.

"Your offer doesn't mesh with campus practices. I'd get in trouble if things went wrong. Too much risk."

Not willing to give up, Athena tightened her grip on the chair arms. "My approach will bring results. I guarantee it."

"Here's a problem. Professors like to chat near the mailboxes along the front wall. From Suzie's desk, you might not catch all their words, since their voices rise and fall. People come and go. Phones ring, et cetera."

"So I'll bug the mailbox area for conversations."

Ginger eyes showed more interest.

"Sounds like you have ways to find answers for us. I've got to know what's going on and who's behind this, but I don't want the details if you do plant a bug."

"Please give me a chance."

"Steve was one of our best, though he took risks." Ginger stopped and the sad look returned.

"What kind of risks?"

"He changed his studies, shifting from working with Briggs to working with Laszlo. Suzie called it a 'high-wire act' because the feud was already on. He was taking chances with Vicky too."

"You think Steve's overextending himself led to what happened?"

"Possibly, although it's considered an accident. Now there's the question of Suzie. I want you to find out who did it. She's my best employee, bright and fun and always does an outstanding job. You know, I've had this awful feeling that the department is rushing toward a large-scale smashup. I'd hate for you to be in danger too."

"Danger is my business."

Ginger met Athena's eyes and Athena held the stare. "You're sure you want to work here?"

"Absolutely."

Ginger sighed. "Okay. The official way is to hire you through the campus temporary pool, which means you take tests and fill out forms. I'll fax a special request for your services to make it all legit. Let's try it for a few days. Next week, I can hire a regular from the temp pool. This way you get paid for your time, but since we're paying for your services, I may make demands on you, depending on work flow."

"Fine," said Athena. She'd make sure the setup worked.

"Keep me informed. Ask questions. Be careful." Ginger smiled and raised her eyebrows. "Ready for a few nuts and bolts?"

Athena nodded.

"I must caution you that Vicky and Suzie don't speak to each other these days. Vicky is one hundred percent anti-Laszlo, going back to when her dad and Laszlo were on a university committee years ago and opposed each other on every issue. Be careful with Vicky, Athena. Her father is assistant dean of Arts & Sciences and a professor in the genetics department. Her mother is a full professor in the English department. With her university ties, Vicky has clout and uses it."

"Would Vicky harm Suzie?" Athena asked.

"Last week I'd say Vicky is more likely to harm herself than anyone else. At present, I'm no longer sure. You be the judge." Ginger suddenly switched from low to high. "Suzie locks her desk. I have a spare key. She was keeping daily records of what she heard. I know there's information on her computer in a locked file, but I don't have the password."

"I'll find it."

"You amaze me. I can't thank you enough." Ginger stood up. "How about a short tour of Rimington Hall? Tomorrow you'll visit the temp office first and then come here."

Following Ginger into the front office, Athena felt a brief sense of triumph. Step one of her plan was in place.

THREE

"IF YOU HAVE questions about office matters, ask Vicky." Ginger turned toward the blonde woman. "Athena will work here for a few days."

Vicky was sorting index cards into separate piles at top speed. A great card dealer, Athena thought.

"Suzie on a trip?" Vicky tried to sound peppy. "The goddess Athena in her place."

Jokes about her name were common. "The original goddess was my Greek grandmother," Athena said. "I was named for her."

Ginger gave Athena a pointed look. "Vicky knows the department."

"Welcome to the zoo," Vicky said. "Don't believe your eyes or ears."

Turning, Athena saw a woman in a designer suit and expensive shoes standing near the mailboxes along the front wall. She was flipping through a sizable stack of envelopes and tossing most of them, unopened, directly into the wastebasket. Manicured nails and a well-shaped cap of black hair, Athena noted.

"These are faculty mailboxes," Ginger said. "Dr. Reyna Briggs, I'd like you to meet our temporary employee, Athena Dawes. A speedy typist who will do your work as needed."

Briggs turned piercing eyes Athena's way and looked her up and down. "Nice to have you with us. I'll have an emergency job in a day or two." She nodded, scooped up the remains of her mail, and seemed to glide out of the room. Except for her dress and mannerisms, she didn't look much older than the students.

"Difficult," Ginger said. "She gives us illegible scrawl and then expects perfectly typed copy. Her specialty is the psychology of success."

"She needs lots of props to be successful," Vicky said.

The picture, of course. Reyna Briggs was the angry woman in the background of the photo Ginger had shown her.

"It's our business to be kind to faculty," Ginger said.

Ginger opened the door and stepped across the hall to an open door. "This is the break room, where we have a coffeemaker, refrigerator, microwave, and a few junk food machines. A place we all love."

The worn furniture—a couch, armchair, table and chairs—offered a rest area. A colorful array of travel posters were Suzie's contribution, Athena guessed.

Ginger walked to the bulletin board and yanked down a sheet of bright yellow paper. "Damn!" she said, shaking her head. "This is what we're dealing with."

She showed Athena a caricature of a man exposing himself, only he didn't have much to show.

"This has to stop," Ginger said.

"Who is it supposed to be?" Athena asked.

"Professor Laszlo Honvagy," Ginger said.

Athena looked again. The picture showed a man with dark curly hair and huge dark eyes that seemed to ask the viewer for approval as he waved what looked like a small lollipop.

"I'll tell Laszlo about this one. I hate to upset him, but he needs to know."

"Who's doing this? Any ideas?" Athena asked.

"So far, we're not sure who produces this trash. Maybe a graduate student. I'd like you to pin it down, if you can."

"How often does it happen?"

"Something new every few days. Shall we go?" Ginger resumed her role as tour guide. "Upper floors belong to Sociology, Anthropology, and graduate students from all departments." They passed faculty offices, identified with name cards. Too many, Athena thought, as Ginger called off the names—Ben Silver, the chairman, Marcia Praeger, Bill Wolpert, and on and on.

They stopped at a glass door facing an inner garden and parking area. Athena gazed out at three skinny palm trees, a lawn, and two stone benches beside a basin with a fountain shaped like a leaping fish.

"The Rim, as we call it, is built around this inner courtyard."

"Does the fountain work?" Athena asked.

"Not for ten years. See the building on the far side?"

Athena noted a one-story, modern building, painted white with purple trim. It made a distinct statement of independence against the period style and color of the main building.

"That's Laszlo Honvagy's research facility. He worked so hard for funds. It was an old building, moved here from another site on campus and renovated with donated money, some say from adoring ladies. You should have seen Laszlo when he first came here in the early seventies." Ginger's voice softened, and she had a dreamy look in her eyes. "Women drooled. Students worshiped him." Ginger paused and then became more businesslike. "We don't do much work for Laszlo these days. He has his own building with Magda as his secretary and grad students to help him out. They used to visit us, but since the trouble started, they stay over there most of the time. We send student couriers back and forth."

"Do you know the phone number of the Research Institute?"

"Yes, I do: 257-1001."

Athena wrote it down.

Ginger took Athena's arm, and they continued walking. "Here's the department computer lab."

The sign on the door—COMPUTO ERGO SUM—amused Athena. Five Macintoshes and a laser printer occupied the room.

"Who uses these?" she asked.

"Grad students and faculty. We try to keep the door locked."

Athena noted that it was not locked at that time.

They walked on, turned a corner, and started down another long, echoing hallway. Near some stairs, Athena noticed a picture posted on the door, a large skull and crossbones reminiscent of a flag on a pirate ship.

"That's the custodian's room. Josh is only here while our regular is away on sick leave. He seems to be a gentle giant and gets the job done." Ginger studied the skull and crossbones with a frown. "He put that up the first night he worked here. Some sense of humor."

"When did he start working here?"

"About two weeks ago."

"What's this?" Athena pointed at a cement outline the size and shape of a door on the wall adjoining the custodian's office. She found it disturbing.

"They closed off an old exit here after a number of robberies. Intruders broke in from the courtyard without being spotted by the night patrol. A few years ago, it was sealed off as a security measure after we lost most of our computers."

Athena followed Ginger on down the hall to the open doorway of a classroom, which sloped toward the front auditorium-style.

"This is where the debate will be held. The room is expandable by taking down the far wall of this and several other classrooms like it. That's Professor Gerald Derring," Ginger said, softly. "Leader of the new bunch."

Athena was looking at a man in his late thirties with a receding hairline, a scraggly mustache, and signs of a former football player—stocky with wide shoulders and a flattened nose. The words ANIMAL RESEARCH were printed on the blackboard. It reminded Athena of her intro class.

"Animals in the wild act in their own best interests," said Derring in a booming voice to about two hundred students. "In our modern and controlled habitat, we humans act in our own best interests, whether that means selling natural resources or preserving forests to supply oxygen necessary to maintain a habitable atmosphere. Humans don't just resemble animals, *we are animals.*"

Athena recognized his logic. He put human life on a basic survival level of "kill or be killed."

"We are unquestionably the dominant species. If another species were dominant, its members would use lesser species for their purposes. Nationwide, we raise millions of animals for consumption, a practice that we're not likely to discontinue. Most humans want meat on their tables, don't they? So, no one who eats meat has the right to criticize the raising of animals for research purposes.''

Athena glanced at Ginger, who was listening to the lecture.

''We are advancing in leaps and bounds in our understanding of the human brain through research based on animal physiology.''

A man with auburn hair stood up and spoke.

''Russ Atkins, Laszlo's student,'' whispered Ginger. ''Watch what happens.''

Russ was as tall as Derring with muscles visible through his T-shirt. He looked capable of a fist-to-fist match with the prof.

''If we're all animals, why not treat other species as our close relatives rather than view them like so much trash to use and throw away?''

Athena heard a distinct New York City accent.

Derring raised his eyes and his hands as if to communicate with some gods on the ceiling. ''The man has asked why we don't step down from our position of dominance and let the cows, our ancestors, come to school as in India.''

A current of laughter rippled through the audience.

''Let me ask how many of you are at this time or are willing to become lifelong vegetarians?''

He counted the few raised hands and wrote the number on the blackboard.

''How many of you would agree to give up all benefits of modern civilization derived through animal research?''

There were no raised hands.

''How many think that animal lives are more important than human lives?''

No hands.

Athena recognized Derring's black-and-white, them-or-us argument.

''Are you satisfied with numbers, Russ?'' Derring said to the man still standing in the audience. ''*Numbers speak louder than words.*''

''So it's okay to kill and dissect cats, dogs, and monkeys to see how humans function? If they're so close, they suffer like humans do, but since they can't protect themselves, we do what we want with them,'' Russ said.

Moans and boos from the audience.

''Researchers follow strict protocols to minimize animal suffering. Are animals in nature free from suffering?'' Derring pointed a finger straight at Russ. ''I will ask you now, since you're not enrolled in this class, to remove yourself pronto so we can get on with important matters.''

The student turned and came up the aisle. As he reached the open space behind the seats, Athena saw that he was flanked by a German shepherd dog. He was the man she'd seen in front of Suzie's house earlier that morning.

As he approached, Ginger stepped out the doorway into the hall, signaling to Athena to follow.

''Good for you, Russ,'' Ginger said.

The dog sniffed at the hem of Ginger's skirt and wagged its tail. Athena noted its alert eyes.

''I don't think all people rate higher than animals,'' Russ said, dark eyes resentful, and then walked on. He looked more like a construction worker than a student—a Charles Bronson, or a young Yul Brynner with hair, Athena thought.

''Russ hasn't been here long and I'm not sure he can last,'' Ginger said, as he turned a corner.

Heading back to the main office, Athena glanced at her watch. Nine-forty! She had twenty minutes to get to the police station. ''I better go. The police want to talk to me.''

''Do you have a place to stay?'' Ginger asked.

''No,'' Athena admitted. ''I'll get a room somewhere.''

''I own some apartments, and there's an empty studio apartment. What do you say?''

''I say 'yes' and 'thank you.''' Athena was amazed. Such generosity! ''I thought I'd stay at Suzie's.''

''You're my guest,'' Ginger said, writing an address and phone number on a piece of paper she snatched from a nearby bulletin board. ''Tell the manager to call me. She'll give you the key plus sheets and towels, since you're a short-term guest.''

''I have to agree with Suzie. You're a great boss.''

Ginger looked pleased and Athena took off at a run, thinking of the distance to her car.

FOUR

ON HER portable car phone, Athena called the hospital for an update. Following a delay, a nurse informed her as Suzie's official contact person that the patient was out of surgery, in Intensive Care, and that her condition had been upgraded from "serious" to "fair."

"Great!" Athena said.

The police department was housed in a tan building with a brown roof on a busy street in the center of Aston. The second bit of good news was that the detective assigned to Suzie's case was a woman about thirty-five years old with a brown fringe of bangs above hazel eyes. The policewoman was the same height as Athena, about 5'8", and had the benefit of thin hips, which meant she looked good in the regulation police pants. Athena was glad to be interviewed by a woman, since communication usually seemed smoother and less stressful.

"I'm Detective Coles," the woman said. "Please come this way."

Athena followed her down a short hallway. Framed vintage photographs showed the town of Aston in the early 1900s with views of the two-man police force, sitting stiffly in chairs and on horseback. The policewoman turned into a room and shut the door behind them. It reminded Athena of a cell but there were no bars and no bed—just a table and chairs. On the table, she saw a tape recorder, lined pad, and pen.

"Please have a seat," Coles said. "What you say here will be recorded."

"Fine," Athena said. She liked Coles, who might be a good contact if all went well.

During preliminaries of name, address, and occupation, Athena showed Coles the professional card for Ted's office.

"So you're a P.I.?" Coles asked with interest.

"In training. I'm most experienced at information searches on computer. When there isn't anything specific for me to do, Ted gives me a variety of assignments. Some are real cases; some possible ones. I report on steps I'd take plus results I'd expect. Then, we discuss. I learn from him; he learns from me too. It's a partnership."

Coles nodded. "Sounds like a good method."

"Continuous education. Keeps the mind alive."

"For what reason did you come to California at this time?"

"Suzie wanted me to investigate something but didn't say specifically what was wrong. Suzie's boss Ginger told me about the trouble in the psych department. Steve Linstrom's death came up."

"I'm not assigned to the Linstrom case," Coles said. "I'll talk to a few people who work with Suzie but internal campus problems fall under the jurisdiction of the campus police. Who are Suzie's friends in Aston?"

Athena thought back. "A neighbor named Peggy was a close friend of Suzie's aunt and of Suzie's too. Suzie considers Ginger in the office a friend. In preparation for a trip to Hungary this summer, she's become good friends with a Hungarian woman named Magda, who works with Professor Laszlo Honvagy."

"Did Suzie keep valuables at home?"

"Suzie's aunt died two years ago and left her the house on Cantata Lane, along with all its contents. There are a few antiques, but I don't know their value."

Coles' eyes swept over Athena for telltale signs. Athena remained relaxed, though probing eyes could make anyone nervous, innocent or not.

"What did you notice first when you arrived at the house?"

"Lights. Every light in the house was turned on. I know Suzie likes to sleep as long as possible."

"Anything else?"

"The way things were pitched around inside the house didn't make sense."

"Why is that?"

"A robber looks in likely places for valuables rather than throwing things everywhere—unless the person wanted something specific and couldn't find it."

"Did you go into other rooms of the house?" Coles said.

"Yes, I saw the blood and vomit in the bathroom."

"You didn't lose it when you saw your friend, did you?"

Athena shook her head.

"Are you willing to take a lie detector test?"

"Of course," she said, smiling. Athena knew they weren't valid. A veteran cop in Portland had told her criminal justice class how he could lie about anything under the sun and get a perfect reading on the polygraph.

"All right," Coles said. "I'll contact you when I have more questions."

Athena told her she'd be working at the psychology department.

"Is that a good idea?" Coles asked.

"I told Suzie I'd help her. This is one way."

"Okay," said Coles. "I'll talk to a few people on campus this afternoon. Tell me if you learn anything relevant."

"Is Suzie's case going to appear in the local paper?"

"Others may be in danger, so we won't withhold information about the attack," Coles said. "Session concluded."

She pushed the recorder button on the tape machine and visibly relaxed.

"How do you like working for the police?" Athena asked.

Coles smiled. "I like it a lot. It's what I wanted to do. My father was a policeman in Sacramento. My brother is in the highway patrol. I have cousins in the L.A. police department. I'm the first woman in the family to join the police force. I chose Aston, a smaller locale with less overt violence."

"You're a detective!"

"One of my hats. I'm patrol cop, community officer, or whatever they happen to need at the time. I especially like visiting schools to talk about drugs and give safety demonstrations. You try to make a difference in teens' lives by showing them consequences before a crime is committed or how to protect themselves from being victims."

"So, I might see you around town?" Athena said.

"It's quite likely. Let me know what you find. Don't take chances on your own."

"How much longer will Suzie's place be closed?" Athena asked.

"A day or two," Coles said.

"I want to straighten it up before Suzie's back, but I won't be staying there."

"Good idea." Coles glanced at her watch and jumped up. "I have a department meeting in five minutes. No rest for the weary."

Athena felt her own fatigue, but she still had things to do. In the car, Athena put in a collect call to Ted's office. To her surprise, he was there, and she updated him on Suzie, the psychology department, and the police interview.

"What do you think of my plan?" Athena asked.

"Frankly, I don't like the sound of it. I think you should tell everyone she hired you and get straight to the point."

"I want to sit where Suzie sat, see what Suzie saw, and not have people know who I am."

"As long as I can remember, you've complained when I give you standard office work," Ted said. "Remember the insurance office?"

How could she forget it? It was her first job after graduation from college. She'd needed time to consider what she wanted to do for a real career, since no jobs were likely in French without a graduate degree. She was soon convinced she was not cut out for clerical work. As she told Ted, "I didn't get my education for that." Ted offered her a job in his office to tide her over. They discovered that they worked well together.

A few years ago, Ted joked that she'd make a good private eye.

"Why?" she'd asked.

"Every time you opened your mouth when you were a kid,

you had a question. Then you learned good logic in your French classes.''

He'd attacked French as a waste of time until she mentioned that the French considered themselves the most logical people in the world. This impressed Ted, who claimed that the mind's ability to establish cause-and-effect connections was its most valuable skill. He loved to exercise it himself. Athena sometimes called him ''Hercule'' after Agatha Christie's Poirot, who relied on pure reason to solve crimes.

''This time I do office work to get what I need,'' Athena said.

''Undercover work is risky. In this case, you don't know what information to look for or who the major suspects are. You could be looking one way when you should be looking the other.''

''It's my case. I do it my way.'' Athena knew Ted was testing her. ''I chose indirect rather than direct. Since the police are questioning people already, they're on guard. You'll see. I'll get results.''

She heard a long, low sigh and could picture him tapping his pencil on his desk. There were a few muffled words, probably in Greek, which surfaced when he was frustrated.

''Just remember—I want you back soon. I have new jobs coming up and need your help.''

''Give me two weeks.''

He groaned. ''Okay. Do it, but keep me posted—regularly.''

''Kiss, kiss,'' Athena said.

''Kiss, kiss,'' said Ted.

It was their routine closure, though they never really kissed. Ted was not a cuddly uncle.

A fit of yawning caught Athena. She had another call to make. She located the number of the Research Institute and punched the numbers.

''Laszlo Honvagy's office,'' said a richly accented voice, so low and hoarse that it gave Athena a chill.

''May I speak to Magda?''

''I am Magda.'' The way she said her name, it sounded like music.

''My name is Athena.''

"Tina? Tina? You get message. Yes?" Her voice sounded more animated.

"Right. I need to see you soon," Athena said.

"Good! Lunch tomorrow. Yes? I bring food for us. We do not meet in public place. No. I tell you. There's a grove of redwood trees. You cross footbridge from campus and go over river. There are tables. I wait there at noontime."

Athena agreed to meet Magda there. She hadn't expected it to be so easy. It occurred to her that neither she nor Magda had mentioned Suzie's name. Did Magda know about Suzie, or did she think Athena was someone else?

Time to find her temporary home and make some quick notes on people she'd met at the Rim, but first she had to drop off her roll of film to be developed. Then she'd be ready, more than ready, to settle in for some serious slumber.

FIVE

As Athena entered the psych department office, someone so thin she was almost linear, skirt swirling around matchstick legs, whipped past and out the door. She moved so quickly that Athena realized only after she'd passed that it was Vicky. Athena recalled yesterday's notes on Vicky: "High-strung. Dangerous to herself and others?"

Athena went to her new desk. Much as she liked it, the huge picture of the Parthenon, shown partly in darkness, partly in light, seemed to hover over the chair and reminded her of "Heavy, heavy hangs over thy head." Though clear yesterday, the desktop now held a schedule of professors' classes and office hours, an awesome stack of envelopes and addresses, and a pile of manuscripts. What Suzie faces every day, Athena told herself. Today, her whole plan of action seemed less bright.

Athena waved at Ginger, who smiled and waved back. She rolled an envelope into the carriage of the typewriter, one of twenty she'd address at lightning speed.

The phone rang. "Department of Psychology," she answered. "May I help you?" A woman asked for Professor Wolpert's office hours, and Athena tracked down the info. Next time she'd be faster.

With no one in the office and Ginger on her phone, the time was right to plant a bug. Her desk was close enough to the mailboxes. Taking the device out of her bag, she slid the mini-recorder down the side of her desk near the wall and pressed it against the metal where it adhered perfectly. She positioned the tiny microphone near the front of the desk, aimed at the mailboxes, then checked to see how visible her equipment was. Unless someone knew what to look for, it should be safe. Ted had ordered the bugging equipment from a catalog but found he preferred an older model, so he passed it on to Athena. The system was voice-activated and clicked off when the stimulus stopped for a full minute.

Athena had just resumed her position at the typewriter when she heard jagged, forced breathing behind the opening door. A man in royal blue shorts and saturated T-shirt ran into the office as if he were still on some invisible track. Gray-bearded and blue-eyed, he passed her and ran in place in front of the mailboxes. Suddenly he pounced on a box beneath the table. After reading the name on the label, he ripped the box open.

"My book," he announced triumphantly. "My book's in print."

Without noting that Athena was a new face at the desk, he joyfully held a volume up for her inspection. Athena read the title, *A History of Psychology as Discipline and Science,* and the author's name on the cover, Patrick MacRae.

"I've waited years," he said. "And here it is! One reviewer wrote 'Best-informed book on the subject.' My book." He kissed it, hugged it to his chest, and then leaned over to look reverently at the other copies in the box. After a moment of obvious pleasure, he grabbed envelopes from his mailbox, hefted the box of books into his arms, and walked out.

Were secretaries interchangeable parts for him? Athena wondered as she typed another envelope.

Ginger opened her door. "Here's a key to Suzie's desk and that info about Steve's death you requested. You met Professor MacRae, an old-timer on Laszlo's side."

"He showed me his new book."

"Professors live for publications and research." Ginger sighed. "Well, brace yourself. Our work-study student called in sick, and Vicky's in one of her moods."

"Why not take a leave of absence?"

"She hates to stay home alone but isn't much help to us as is."

"I'm having lunch with Magda today."

"Where?" Ginger said.

"Across the river."

"If you're seen with Magda, there'll be rumors. That's a fact."

"She's aware of that," Athena said.

"Magda is...unusual." Ginger hesitated as if about to say more but changed the subject. "When you finish the envelopes, we have a full box already labeled. Announcements for the debate must go out in the afternoon mail. I thought our student assistant could do it, but since she won't be in, you're the one."

Athena picked up the box of envelopes and moved it close to her desk, then added piles of announcements to other piles on her desk. She scanned a page:

A TIMELY DEBATE

Friday, May 8, 8:00 P.M. Rimington Hall 100
Psychology:
Unlimited Study of the Human Mind//
The Importance of Focusing Research Now

Speakers:	1. Laszlo Honvagy vs. Gerald Derring.
	(Parapsychology) (Human & Animal Physiology)
	2. Ben Silver vs. Bill Wolpert
	(Humanistic Psychology) (Neurophysiology)
Panel:	Reyna Briggs (Success Psychology)
	Patrick MacRae (History of Psychology)
	Harold Springer (Developmental Psychology)
	Doug Weil (Social Psychology)
	José Huerta (Psychology/Anthropology)

On a blank envelope, Athena typed: "Nancy Coles, Aston Police Department," and the address she recalled from the day before. If Coles came, maybe they'd work as a team. If things were as bad in the department as Ginger described, the debate could turn into more than a battle of wits.

Vicky returned a few minutes later, her eyes redder than the day before.

''Athena, Athena. How good to see an unfamiliar face. Much better than the one who's usually there. I call her Pickle Face.''

''You won't have to put up with her for a while,'' Athena said.

''She's in bad shape. I read the department memo.'' Vicky did not sound sorry or upset as she turned the ring on her finger. ''She won't die. As they say, only the good die young.''

Vicky was definitely a pain. Athena folded and stuffed, folded and stuffed.

''My fiancé died recently. He had everything going for him.'' Vicky's voice faded away. She began refiling folders and closing file drawers with a loud bang. ''He'd still be alive if it weren't for Laszlo.''

''Why do you say that?''

''Laszlo Honvagy is a black king and his lady Magda's a black queen. They're phonies, who prey on innocent people like Steve. They play around with death.''

''What do you mean?'' Athena was all attention.

''There's a price for tampering with people's lives. They've gotten away with too much for too long.''

''I don't understand.''

''One of these days, I'll tell it like it is around here.''

AN HOUR LATER, Athena was folding and stuffing, faster and faster.

''Marcia Praeger has a darling baby,'' Vicky said in a sticky-sweet voice.

Mesmerized by the routine, Athena glanced at the woman by the mailboxes with a babe in arms. All she saw from the back was the pink outfit and old-fashioned bonnet with a brim.

Gerald Derring strode in like the lord of the manor and joined Praeger.

''Oh, the little sweetie,'' he cooed, putting his face up close and kissing her. ''Isn't she precious?''

Athena would never have picked Derring as a softie for babies. Glad to be close to the gathering place, she listened to what followed.

''The gods are on our side,'' Derring said. He was not trying to keep his voice down but checked to see who was in the room before continuing. "First Steve, then Suzie. It's as if those who side with Laszlo are cursed."

Praeger cuddled the baby, and Derring moved in close with a few more noisy kisses before turning to consider the contents of his mailbox.

Athena suddenly noticed that Vicky was staring, not at them but at her, with a wide grin on her face. Did she suspect something? Athena lowered her head to her task but focused on the trio nearby.

"Laszlo's assistant, Russ, is a dumb hulk. He hassled me in class yesterday. Did you get a close-up of those muscles?" Derring said.

"How could anyone miss? He models T-shirts à la Schwarzenegger," Praeger said.

"Struts like a rooster. Thinks he makes the sun rise."

Derring had just described himself perfectly, Athena mused.

Praeger laughed. "So brave he needs a large dog to protect him at all times."

Both profs were laughing when Praeger turned and came to the front desk. Athena dropped an envelope on the floor when she saw the baby's face. Curious about how closely it resembled its mother, she did a double take. Praeger's baby was a definite throwback—a little chimp. Athena laughed heartily.

"This is Mandy," Praeger said, picking up the small curved hand and waving it at Athena as they left. The baby chimp looked at Praeger with love in her eyes and a sweet expression on her face.

"Want one of your own?" Vicky asked with a wide smile.

"I'd rather have a dog," Athena said.

"Treats it like her own child. Even takes it to class with her. The experiment has been done before, but she thinks she can do it better."

Derring came to a full stop before Athena's desk.

"I need a draft of my baboon manuscript this afternoon," Derring said.

Athena sorted through the manuscript pile and held up one on

"Hormone Stimulants and Aggression in Male Baboons" by Gerald Derring.

"That's it," he said. "Top priority."

Another prof drifted in, and Derring joined him in the faculty corner.

"Compliments on your latest contribution to the *Simian Papers*," Derring said. "Your observations were on the mark and had a ring of distinction."

"I simply followed your suggestions, and they accepted it posthaste," the other man said. He was thin with fair, bushy hair that stood up comically. "You saw my acknowledgment?"

"I did. Thank you. What's your assessment of the situation?" Derring said.

"Lahlah is wearing down from lots of little wounds to the ego," Bushy Hair said. "Trickling from a thousand pores can bring the baron down."

"Wait! We don't want a martyr on our hands. That'll mobilize his students, and we all know Lahlah's power over students," Derring said.

"Lahlah's fate is ours to choose. We will win, and he will lose," Bushy Hair said, dancing a few steps.

Derring bumped the smaller man with his shoulder, knocking him off balance, and they both laughed.

Lots of laughs in the psych department. Athena remembered her own university days when she'd thought professors with their highly trained minds were admirable people.

Bushy Hair took a detour and came straight to her desk. He was small and thin with a triangular face and such thick-lensed glasses that he reminded Athena of a praying mantis.

"Ahhhhhh! A new secretary! Welcome. I'm Associate Professor Harold Springer."

Athena shook the hand he extended, noting the clammy palm and loose grip. His eyes, magnified by his glasses, inspected her breasts too closely, and moved lower with regret that the desk blocked his view.

Athena wanted to say, "I'm not a new piece of office property.'' Secretaries never said what they thought. Instead, she folded her arms and glared at his vitals. He caught her meaning.

''Excuse me,'' he said, backing away with a flushed face.

''That takes guts,'' Vicky said, giving her the thumbs-up sign.

Athena cautioned herself to watch out. When men eyeballed women in that proprietary way, she might want to practice hits and kicks, but there were more important goals at present.

Vicky was walking back and forth, slamming file drawers and rearranging papers. She wiped the dust off her desk with vigorous, sweeping motions and then stood, hands on hips, surveying her territory. Athena could feel Vicky's turmoil in the air of the office.

Suddenly, in a barely audible voice, Vicky started talking fast. ''Just when you think your life is improving, it all comes apart. Against all odds, you've won the prize, and it gets snatched from you. Suddenly, you come alive and start enjoying life, then—*snap*—it's gone for good. No way to bring it back. When you've lost the only person you ever cared about, you wonder what's the point in going on.''

Athena had experienced losses of her own. ''I understand,'' she said.

''No one understands. Besides, I'm not talking to you,'' Vicky said. She sat down at her desk and put her head in her hands.

Having thoroughly mastered the art of folding and stuffing, Athena was going to finish well before noon. The repetitive movements had a therapeutic effect, but Athena knew Vicky would refuse to join her.

It was a relief to think of meeting Magda in the woods for lunch.

THE FOOTBRIDGE ACROSS the river was a miniature Golden Gate. She'd never seen this side of campus before. Athena paused halfway across to watch the boats. One was stationary with two fishermen plying their rods, the other a motorboat zipping along.

Athena found the redwood grove. The area was paved with redwood chips and the air was rich with the woody smell. Magda was sitting at a round wooden table under the trees. As Athena joined her, she could hear a kind of humming, and the trees seemed to shimmer in sunlight as if she were entering a magic circle of intense energy.

Magda was a small woman with a heart-shaped face, naturally tan skin, and startling golden eyes rimmed with green. Cat's eyes, Athena thought. Her steely gray hair was caught up in a large bun on the back of her head. Her dark gold blouse and olive green skirt complemented her coloring. What fascinated Athena in particular was the assortment of bracelets and more than ten rings Magda wore on her fingers. No attempt at coordination. A different concept of style.

Magda smiled, showing uneven teeth.

"Welcome to Aston, Tina," Magda said with her rich voice. "We have simple things—bread, cheese, and wine."

She took these items, one by one, from a large straw bag.

"Next time, I bring the food," Athena said.

"Next time?" Magda said, as if in doubt there'd be a next time.

Magda laughed at a squirrel halfway up the trunk of a tree. Swishing its tail furiously, it observed them with a pert dark eye.

"Little one want food. Sometime, I bring nut or raisin."

Athena liked squirrels too. She watched one scamper in search of hidden treats in the nearby grass.

Magda gave Athena a paper plate and a large knife. As Athena cut the loaf of bread and then sliced the cheese, Magda opened the wine bottle, inhaled deeply, and poured white wine into two glasses. No words passed between them, but the silence seemed full.

Magda handed Athena a wineglass. "Students give Laszlo gifts of wine."

Athena took a sip. "Delicious." She paused. "I hear you're a gypsy."

"What does gypsy mean?" Magda asked, tossing her head.

Athena's mother had sung her an old lullaby about the gypsy life: "Slumber on my little gypsy sweetheart, Dream of the field and the grove. Can you hear me, hear me in your dreamland where your fancies rove?" She'd liked the song, which hinted at a carefree life, and remembered asking her mother to sing it night after night.

"Gypsies live where they choose and do what they want," Athena said. Her favorite preteen book featured a gypsy girl named Jen, who knew how to get out of any scrape and didn't care what other people thought.

Magda raised her eyebrows. "They say, 'Gypsies are free and live outside society. How nice to be gypsy.' But is not that way. My people always scorned, hated, and accused—no matter where they go. Hitler kill my relatives in concentration camps. Mother, father, and three sisters die. For Hitler, gypsies not human. Everywhere people treat us like beasts because we have different ways. Not 'belong' anyplace."

"Aren't gypsies crafty and brave?"

Magda laughed. "My people are smart. They have many skills and scorn those with houses and fancy things. But their life not so good. No! Sometimes, I play wild gypsy myself. But I ask: How you like if people throw rocks and tell you—'Move on!'—when you stop in field by road? What life is this? Upper class envy gypsy because we feel emotion. We are not numb. We enjoy life each day with little but also free to starve. Without money we can live. They call us thieves but we survive. It change in last thirty years. Gypsies settle down. Property. Property. Every inch of land belong to someone who put fences and signs KEEP OUT. Open areas along road gone. No choice anymore."

"It doesn't sound like a nice life," Athena agreed.

"In Hungary, gypsies mix in by work and marriage," Magda said with pride. "My father was best gypsy violinist of his day. He make you laugh and cry at same time. Good man, though he drink too much. We live well. I leave Hungary at fourteen to stay with cousins in south France where I see poverty and no hope. 'Not for me!' I said. 'Not for me.' My first job was fortune-teller."

"A fortune-teller?" Athena asked with dismay.

"Fortune-telling is an art," Magda said. She looked at Athena with amusement, then threw back her head to laugh. Athena, who'd been sipping wine and feeling tense, joined in Magda's laughter.

"Anyone can tell fortunes," said Magda, wiping her eyes. "Listen. I tell truth. The person who want fortune gives you information. You watch how they dress, how they act. You listen to voice, which tell many things. I'm good at this. I can tell how they grew, how much money, what problems, what they want to hear. I know before I start. Then, I watch how they accept what I say to see if it is the right thing."

Athena was intrigued by Magda's words. What did Magda know about her? Could the gypsy read her like a book?

"Aaaach!" Magda said with distaste. "Tell fortunes and trick people. Laszlo hate fake. It spoil his studies, he say, because people think there's nothing true in psychic experience. Laszlo not know about fortune-teller. I do it to stay alive."

"How did you come to Aston, Magda?" Athena said.

"I hear of Laszlo's research and think he need my help."

"Are you really psychic?" The word sounded absurd to Athena.

"I come from tradition of psychics."

"How do you know you're psychic?"

"Depend on gift," Magda said, taking a big mouthful of wine, holding it for a moment, and then swallowing it fast. She looked at Athena intently. "You're psychic too."

Athena remembered Suzie's letter:

> I didn't realize this, but Magda says I'm psychic. That explains a lot of things that have happened to me—dreams, coincidences, déjà vus. With Magda as guide, I'm discovering a world that has always coexisted with the familiar one.

Athena went on guard. Did Magda play this game with everyone?

"I've never had any indications I'm psychic," Athena said. "I pay attention to what's going on around me—what I can see and hear especially. I use reason to understand."

"You have a radiant aura—color of lilacs. You have *much* ability."

"Aura?" Athena said as she bit into the crusty bread.

"Energy force around body. Famous psychic call human aura 'weathervane of soul.' Yours is lilac—good mix of mind and emotion—but pale. You doubt power?"

"What?" Athena said as if she'd heard an unknown language.

"Psychic—as I explain." Magda nibbled her bread and cheese. Those rings! Athena felt almost hypnotized by the gold and silver designs with multicolored stones in different shapes and sizes that vied for attention. When Magda gestured, they caught drops of sunlight and gleamed with a life of their own.

"Tell me about parapsychology," Athena said. For once she had not done advance research.

"Information everywhere. To receive is difficult. For seven years, I was Crystal Bright, the medium or channeler." Magda's voice acquired a theatrical ring and her eyes flashed. "I give weekly séances, solve crimes, appear in courtroom... My name known worldwide. Once, royalty summon me. Very hush-hush."

"What happened?" Athena said.

Magda's eyes fell and her voice got lower. "Exhausted. I do too much. Phone never stop. So much mail, I had secretary. I gave many talks and demonstrations."

"Why did you stop?"

"I overuse abilities. Long illness and so retire."

"Then you came to work for Dr. Honvagy?"

"I volunteer to help—at least, he think so. British psychics sent me to bring this man with his research methods and discoveries back to their land. They have a long tradition there of psychic research."

"Does Laszlo know you were Crystal Bright?"

"No. Better to end one life—start other. I guide Laszlo. He's genius, not psychic. Now, tell about you."

Athena shrugged her shoulders. She'd never cared for open-up sessions.

"My father died in Vietnam when I was five years old.

My mother remarried and went to live in Idaho. I finished school. Now I work for my uncle.''

Magda's eyes gained such intensity that Athena could not look away. ''I tell my secret. What's yours?''

Athena was puzzled. Not knowing what Magda wanted, it all seemed ridiculous.

''I studied French and Russian at university because reading a foreign language was a challenge like breaking a code. I broke up with a boyfriend because we disagreed on too many things. No secret life to reveal.''

''I tell you—you have gift. Learn to use or it can harm you.''

Athena remained silent. Magda regarded her with a pout on her lips. ''I see you tight closed like fist, but next time you trust me. We work together before it's too late.'' She refilled her wineglass and added to Athena's.

''Magda, I want to work with you, but maybe not the way you wish.''

''Tina, I bring you here for purpose,'' Magda said. ''Very important.''

''I came for a purpose.''

''Ha! Now you tell truth.''

''Suzie asked me to come.''

Magda looked surprised. ''How you know Suzie?''

''I met her in Paris. We've kept in touch.''

Magda looked angry for a moment. She drank half her wine, then changed her tactic with spite. ''I tell Suzie to bring you.''

Athena doubted it but was glad they were moving toward a more productive channel.

''What do you think of Suzie?''

''Sweet person—like daughter. She learn Hungarian, want to know all about my country. I love her. She special one.''

''Someone injured Suzie,'' Athena said, convinced of Magda's sincerity. ''I think the person intended to kill her. She's alive but in a coma.''

''Suzie will be fine,'' Magda said without hesitation.

"When I look for her future, I find only a delay in plans. She'll go to Hungary later than she expect."

To her surprise, Athena experienced a sudden release of pressure, which made her feel as light as a helium balloon. Why believe Magda? Magda was telling her exactly what she wanted to hear.

"Should be me, not Suzie," Magda said in a low voice, almost a moan.

"What do you mean?"

"I die soon. The cards tell, the mirror tell. Soon I must die."

"Maybe we can prevent it. Why do you want someone to come?"

Magda gave her a tormented look. "I'm not important. Laszlo is."

"You're important, Magda." Athena hated it when women put men before themselves.

"Two at risk, but I worry most for him. Grave danger. You protect. Go to his class tomorrow at noon, Athena. We have little time."

"I'll go. I want to protect you both." Athena focused her attention on the older woman. "Can you tell me who killed Steve? Who hurt Suzie?"

Magda looked startled at Steve's name. "I try but not strong anymore. Grow weak. I try." Magda breathed slowly and appeared to sink deep inside herself. The seconds stretched out while she seemed to go into a trance. "Steve killed by someone he know and trust. Different for Suzie. A person not belonging here. Someone we all know."

Athena felt a chill. Magda's voice sounded more hollow, as if another voice spoke through her. Her information was not useful. For that matter, Athena herself fit the category of "a person not belonging here."

Silent for a few more seconds, Magda took several deep breaths and raised her head. "No more. Sorry."

"Thank you," Athena said. "What do you mean by 'different for Suzie'? I need a name, a face, a sign to recognize."

"Try your psychic power, Tina. You so young and strong. Now tell me, where is Suzie? I want to visit."

"University hospital outside town."

They packed up the remains of the picnic and walked back in silence. The magic circle of energy was gone. Athena knew she'd let Magda down. Magda expected someone else, but Athena had come to help, and she'd do it.

Magda gave her a searing glance. "I invite you for dinner at Laszlo's house Friday night. You come, yes?"

"I'll come," Athena said. Progress for her or for Magda? They parted at the far side of the bridge, but Athena felt the disturbance of unvoiced murmurs that continued all too clearly. "You are." "I'm not." "I know you are." "You're wrong."

How would she describe Magda in her notebook? Proud, strong, manipulative, exotic. Suzie's friend. How reliable?

SIX

As Athena distributed the afternoon mail, a throng of professors gathered behind her. Some profs she knew, some she didn't. She listened and tried to identify speakers.

"A few minutes ago, I saw Magda flying along like a bat out of hell," said a prof well over six feet tall. Athena saw a shoe, larger than size 12.

"Magda is Lahlah's weak point—one of many." It sounded like Springer's voice.

"He pays Magda a salary when she can't even get messages right," said the tall one.

"She adds color to his office with her crystal ball," a woman's voice said, then laughed. She wore a denim skirt under an extra-long blue blouse.

"Don't tangle with Magda. She's a lioness," Reyna Briggs said.

"Lahlah prefers older women—the surrogate mother—to the lusty virgins in his classes." Derring's voice.

"Come on. There aren't any virgins anymore," said Springer.

"Sounds like you speak with authority. Have you documented this astute observation?" Derring said.

"Yes, indeed. Using Lahlah's method for manufacturing data, I hallucinate and get carried away."

"Lay off, you guys," Reyna said. "There are feminists present."

Athena tossed the last bit of advertising into a box and backed away.

"At least she delivers," Springer said in a low, suggestive tone. Athena shot him a cold look.

Birds of prey, they closed in on their mail, clutched it, and either carried it away or tore it apart on the spot. Finally, the profs left en masse.

Athena sat down and turned to the Macintosh. She liked what computers could do but was not enthused about the machines themselves. A little sign posted next to the screen had the word *KISS* in bold lettering, surrounded with mini-hearts. The computer's name?

"Okay, KISS! We work together. I'm boss," she said. She often talked to Simon, Ted's office computer.

Wondering why Vicky was so quiet, Athena looked her way. Although spreadsheets covered the top of her desk, she was engrossed in a magazine held under the desk.

Athena stared at the manuscript on her own typing stand—"Hormone Stimulants and Aggression in Male Baboons" by Dr. Gerald Derring. "APA Style" was scrawled across the top. The APA reference manual was within reach, and she scanned the specifications. Athena couldn't imagine giving male baboons injections of testosterone to see what happened. Another version of war games. Pump the critters full of macho hormones and watch them shake the bars of their cages or put them together and watch them rip each other apart.

Athena skimmed along, her quick fingers rhythmically stroking the keys. She didn't read the words, just imitated them. Derring's research didn't appeal; she didn't care how baboons aggressed, regressed, or messed. She resented his power to inflict whatever he chose on the primates.

Athena reached for the phone as it rang. Just as she hung up, a petite Asian student entered and walked up to her desk. She looked ready to burst into tears.

"I called this morning to check on Dr. Wolpert's office hours."

Athena remembered her first call. She looked at the schedule. "Two to three Wednesday afternoon. He should be there right now."

The student shook her head. "I went to his office. I knocked. No answer. I don't usually come to Aston Wednesdays. Where can I find him?"

"Is there a place to look for Dr. Wolpert?" Athena asked Vicky.

"He might be in the coffeehouse with a few favorite students or at the library or at the faculty club or at the primate center."

"You might check the coffeehouse," Athena said.

The student lowered her head. "I have to see him alone. I'll wait at his door until three o'clock then drive fifty miles home. For nothing."

As she left, Athena looked at Vicky with raised eyebrows.

"Who is Wolpert?"

"The department giant."

"Is he an exception on office hours?"

"Some profs don't feel obligated to see students. They play hooky."

"What are they here for?"

"Big careers, grant money, mutual admiration societies. Students are incidentals at the bottom of the totem pole. Research outweighs teaching ten to one," Vicky said with a shrug.

"They should be more accountable to students," Athena said.

She turned a manuscript page and saw data tables to type. She preferred words. Numbers were a nuisance. As she set the format for four columns per page, she puzzled over marks on the tables. Derring had changed his numbers more than once, since some changes were in blue pen and some were in pencil. Sometimes the difference amounted to as little as .001, but sometimes as much as .5. Revisions to improve variables, means, and probabilities? Maybe everyone did it, but were they honest, fact-based adjustments? For once, she regretted not knowing enough about statistics to pin down the significance of Derring's toying with his data.

Just as she finished one table, Athena heard some quick clicks that couldn't be echoes of hers. Vicky had traded her magazine for knitting. Vicky's fingers moved with lightning speed, and she didn't drop a stitch.

"You certainly are good at that," Athena said.

Vicky held up an extra large sweater for Athena's approval. The hunter green sweater with a raised pattern of elongated diamond shapes, front and back, looked from a distance as if it were factory-produced.

"Almost finished," Vicky said. "My parents used to call me Fire Fingers. They were disappointed that I wasn't a blazing genius."

"I admire your skill."

Vicky smiled while her needles flew. "Been doing this since I was ten years old. It burns off excess energy, as my mother used to say. I've always had too much."

Athena was just about to turn back to KISS when Vicky said, "I started this sweater for Steve. Without Steve, I've got to rework my life. Steve was like a bright flash of light. He had more insight into the human mind and behavior than all the psych profs put together, and they listened to him."

"Amazing." Athena wondered what the real Steve was like.

"Steve worked with Reyna Briggs when he first came and suggested new ways to look at her specialty. He learned everything there was to learn in her area in one year and moved on. When he was working with Laszlo, she still called him for advice."

"Why did she do that?"

"She can collect data, but she isn't much of a writer. She had to publish fast or she wouldn't get tenure this year. Steve wanted her to stop leaning on him so much."

"A terrible loss," Athena said.

"One of a kind." Vicky was sniffling. "The person responsible should pay."

"Are you sure it wasn't an accident?"

Vicky kept knitting. "The brakes gave out."

"It happens."

Vicky nodded but made a face. "Steve worked on the brakes himself. He wouldn't screw up like that. Someone tampered."

"How much do you know about cars?"

"Quite a bit. My dad always fixed our car and did repairs for friends' cars. It was his hobby to get away from academics. I was his helper."

"What do the police think?"

"They don't think. 'Accident'—case closed."

"Did Steve have enemies?"

"Laszlo's assistants were all choking with envy, because Laszlo gave Steve preferential treatment, even as a newcomer. And Laszlo knew Steve was better than he'd ever be."

"What makes you say that?"

"The people in the institute are full of extrasensory baloney. I don't know how Steve could take them seriously. He wouldn't have stayed. He got accepted into medical school and planned to go into psychiatry."

"That's no reason to kill him."

"They're hung up on death experiments"—Vicky spat out the words—"and desperate to prove their 'life-after-death' hypothesis."

"You don't think they'd—"

"They would and they did," Vicky said with conviction. "Laszlo encouraged Steve to join the death preparation group. A few grad students got together on Thursday nights for 'after-death' meetings and did exercises like rehearse chants and stuff. Some training. Look where it got him. That night, he was on his way back to Aston after taking a member of the group home to Seaward, ten miles away."

It sounded weird to Athena. "What did they do to train?"

"They practiced fixation on the self, something like meditation but with a different slant. The idea was 'If you develop Self sufficiently, you can cross over and still contact the living.' That's all Steve told me."

"It still doesn't compute."

Vicky's needles clicked like rifle shots. "Steve's truck was parked in the lot behind the Rim for hours. Anyone could have messed with it."

"Why single out Laszlo's group in particular?"

"Why stand up for Laszlo? Did he put you here?" Vicky was looking at her with alarm.

"I've never met Laszlo."

"I'll tell you about him. He wanted Steve to test his death theories, see? His research is on the rocks."

"You think Laszlo did the tampering himself?" Athena was more careful now.

"Laszlo doesn't know a thing about cars, but his students do. He could hypnotize one, send him on a mission, and the student wouldn't recall after."

"Sounds like you're guessing. What if you've picked the wrong target? How can you be so sure?"

"In any case, I'll burn in hell without Steve. I want something for what I lost." Vicky's blue eyes burned with certainty.

Athena was relieved when two profs entered the office, and Vicky decided to take a break. She was as fired up as a Thoroughbred before a race, nostrils flaring.

A few minutes later, Athena was fighting the impulse to nod over the keyboard. The wine at lunch tasted wonderful but didn't help efficient production. Athena's fingers were not striking the keys correctly and, worried that she'd lost the manuscript, she leaned forward to look. A sequence filled the screen.

C3C3C3C3 C3C3C3C3 C3C3C3C3 C3C3C3C3
C3C3C3C3 C3C3C3C3 C3C3C3C3 C3C3C3C3
C3C3C3C3 C3C3C3C3 C3C3C3C3 C3C3C3C3

"I didn't type that!" she said. Puzzled, she checked the finished portion of the manuscript. All there. She deleted the annoying rows of C3's and continued. Minutes later, she experienced the same sensation and stared in frustration at a whole screenful of C3's. What was going on?

Knowing little about basic programming, Athena considered a virus in the software or a key combination that triggered a macro. The computer must be at fault. She'd never had this problem before.

Ten minutes later, Athena was partway through the bibliography when it happened again—the sudden flurry on the screen as it filled with C3's. Tedious! She pushed the print button to test the "phantoms." They did print on the page, and she put the copy in a "Keep" file. Proof to use if she needed to call in a computer expert. Before talking to Ginger, Athena wanted a clear picture of what was going on.

"Stop driving me crazy, KISS," Athena said out loud.

If the trend continued, she'd have to review all printouts for intrusions. She was typing with less confidence now. A very long day.

Finally, Athena put Derring's paper in his mailbox and returned to her seat. She was starting to type a manuscript by Patrick MacRae on "Trends in Psychology Come and Go: A Historian Voices a Warning" when Derring entered. He went to his box, snatched his twelve-page manuscript, and approached her desk.

Athena half expected him to thank her for her work, but instead he waved a page at her. "This is a list of supplies I want in my mailbox by eight-thirty tomorrow."

Words of submission stuck in her throat. "I'm new. I don't know where things are," Athena said, batting her eyelashes to imitate helplessness.

A look of rage crossed his face. "I heard about you," he said in a tight voice. "You've got an attitude."

Athena didn't reply but typed faster. Derring stood behind her and studied the screen. Upholding her claim of being an excellent typist, she made no typos while he watched. She couldn't have sustained it much longer when he sauntered to a nearby cabinet and threw the doors open. He found what he wanted without hesitation, flung it all in an empty box, and walked off with his booty, whistling quietly.

Before Vicky returned, Springer stuck his head in the door, looked around, and announced, "No one's here!", then shut the door with a bang.

Springer's revenge. What a fool! Athena laughed.

IT WAS 4:15 p.m. Vicky had already left, and Ginger was going to leave at 4:30. Since Suzie stayed in the office until 6:00, Athena planned to keep that schedule.

"You seem to be coping well," Ginger said. "I've had an eye on you but left you alone. Vicky talks to you, which is good. Are you getting the kind of information you need?"

"Vicky told me more about Steve. I think she trusts me or she wouldn't be so open."

"Vicky likes to talk about personal and private things, as if we're all counselors. Suzie always listened to her sympathetically, until they took different sides on the faculty disagreement."

"Why does Vicky dislike Laszlo so much?"

"Dean Conway, her dad, crossed swords with Laszlo years ago. Like father, like daughter, so she's against him too. By the way, Vicky's father arranged for her to work here, so that we'd keep an eye on her. With so many psychologists around, he thought they'd know how to handle her. That's why she gets more leeway than a regular employee. She's a burden, and, recently, I've worried she might snap."

"She needs time to grieve. I'll encourage her to talk. From what I've overheard so far, Derring and his group amuse themselves by taking jabs at Laszlo, mostly gossip, but if I catch any specifics, I'll follow up."

Ginger sighed. "I hope you can. Next week we'll have a regular temp in your place, but you'll still need a home base in the department. To justify your ongoing presence in the department, I'll tell everyone you're working on a special project with our chairman, Ben Silver, to give you a screen. Silver is Laszlo's best friend. I doubt if he'll object. You'll like him."

"Has Silver come in?" Athena asked. "How can I recognize him?"

"No matter what season, he wears jeans and a blue denim work shirt," Ginger said. "You can't miss him."

"Sounds good. Thanks for the support, Ginger."

"Thank you for helping us out." Ginger gave her a warm smile.

Alone at last, Athena began looking through the large drawer in Suzie's desk where files were kept. Toward the back was a file labeled "Laszlo." Inside, she found a clipped sheaf of pages. The top one had a macabre picture of a mask in the bottom corner of the page. The message read:

Voodoo king holds ceremonies every Wednesday evening at 7:00 p.m. Bring your personal charm or fetish to share with the group. Refreshments of chicken blood and sheep eyes will be served.

On another sheet, Athena noted assorted costumes—a Greek tunic, the Arab garb of a jellaba and kaffiyeh, a knight's sword and shield, a priest's cassock, a fancy wig, and a cocked hat with plume. The words read:

COME ONE, COME ALL!

Unbelievable opportunity to hear pseudoscientist Laszlo Honvagy unveil true identities of his previous incarnations. If your present life is disappointing, don't despair. He will prove beyond a reasonable doubt that another life awaits you.

The third sheet depicted several tombstones under the rubric "Twilight of a Magician."

Laszlo Honvagy died of Ridicule on April 1. His last words were: "The more I peered into the unknown, the less I saw." An international gathering of fortune-tellers, palm readers, and mediums will take part in the funeral procession at 9 a.m. Friday. Police will cordon off Main Street, so cult followers can tear hair and beat breasts in a last spectacle of devotion. All generous donations will go to Muddy Concepts Unlimited for continued research in the supranormal.

All were insulting and absurd. How many professionals could stand an attack that continued week after week, month after month?

Taped inside the back flap of the file folder was a copy of a letter to the editor of *Psychic Review* that Suzie had done for Laszlo on March 3. Athena read the middle paragraph through twice.

...I am convinced that it is possible to survive the perilous journey of death. Some individuals have crossed the boundary intact. The requisite personality configuration includes enormous ego strength to the point of obsession. I'd like to suggest a new angle: it may be possible to enhance identity maintenance after death by disciplined practice and learned control of certain altered states of consciousness.

Feeling she'd answered a few questions only to have others emerge, Athena tucked the Laszlo folder back in the desk drawer and turned to the computer. Searching through file names used recently, Athena discovered "Excalibur," which required a password. With a vocabulary extending through many languages, Suzie had an enormous number of words at her command. Athena tried a few words: *Laszlo, Magda, aura, power, psychic, parapsychology.* No luck.

Someone opened the office door and left it open. Athena became aware of a huge man, well over six feet tall. His thin blond hair stuck out at odd angles as if he didn't comb it. He had broad features with a broken nose and an ugly jagged scar along his right jaw that raised questions about what sort of life he'd led. Strangely, his wide blue eyes looked innocent and childlike. He stood for a moment with a hand on his hip and surveyed the floor area. Early to late fifties, Athena guessed. Clothes hung loosely on his large frame. His gauntness decreased the feeling that he'd be dangerous in a dark alley.

"Name's Josh," he said, turning her way. "What's yours?"

"Athena."

He'd given her a scare, but it was only the custodian, the one with the skull and crossbones on his door.

"Nice name." He stuck out his hand, and she shook it. "Don't mean to bother. Just doin' my job. Only take a minute."

He wheeled a large waste container through the door, then headed for Ginger's office, where he claimed a wastebasket and emptied it.

Athena refocused on the computer problem. How would she ever get inside the closed files to reach the crucial information?

"Damn! Damn! Damn!" She leaned her head on her hands and glared at the screen.

Josh stopped beside the desk. "Are you awright?" he asked. To her surprise, she saw concern on his face.

"It's been a long day," Athena said, sitting up straighter.

Josh turned his head toward the open office door. Athena saw an angry glint in his pale eyes.

"Don't let 'em get to you," he said.

"What?"

"Think they know it all, but they don't know nothin'."

"I'm just tired." Athena forced herself to smile.

"I'll get you some coffee," Josh said. "Got a hot pot in my office."

Athena realized he was referring to the custodian's room under the stairs where the skull and crossbones was posted.

"I don't need it," she said. "I leave in twenty minutes."

Josh appeared not to understand, because he left the rolling container behind and disappeared through the door.

Athena tried the words *Hungary* and *gypsy* on the computer but still no success. Suzie might have chosen a Hungarian word from her new vocabulary. Damn!

"Coffee here," Josh said, setting a Styrofoam cup on her desk. Coffee powder floated on top, and the water looked tepid. A vile brew.

"How kind," Athena said, and he looked pleased. She managed to sip the wretched coffee, and Josh went on to empty the three other garbage cans in the main office. The one by the mailboxes was overflowing. Next he lifted the broom off the mobile unit and started pushing it around.

Athena could tell he was watching her. Maybe he thought he'd rescued a damsel in distress. False impression! She forced herself to take more sips of the coffee and then went through the process of closing down the computer and locking the desk.

SEVEN

"THE PSYCH DEPARTMENT is a strange place, Suzie," Athena said. "You never told me about all the kooks. I'm working there for a few days, so I can get to know people. You deserve credit for staying over the years and certainly earn your summers off. No wonder you go to faraway places."

She pressed Suzie's hand. According to the nurse, her vital signs were strong. Suzie's coloring had improved; her freckles looked natural. Her head was extensively bandaged, eyelashes just visible below the gauzy edge.

"Everyone hopes for your speedy recovery. Ginger sends her best. She misses you and needs you at the office. Ginger's been lots of help, even given me a place to stay. It's a cute little studio apartment, complete with kitchen and bathroom. I have everything I need, but I want you back on your feet, Suzie. Magda predicts you'll be well soon. I hope she's right. I agree with what you said in your letter about Magda. She's fascinating. I don't know about this psychic stuff—whether it's real or nonsense. I was never interested. I'm surprised you are. Magda says I'm psychic. I don't believe her."

Athena looked at Suzie's still, sheet-covered figure. Except for steady breathing, there was no sign of life.

"Here I am in Aston at your request, and you're not cooperating. I need the info you withheld so I can verify what I'm doing."

There were limits to one-way conversations, Athena thought.

"Suzie, I bet you're playing possum, as Dad used to tell me when I was four." It was one of her few clear memories of her father. "They probably overworked you, and you took a break. You'll be back soon, all fresh from your time off. What country are you in now, Suzie?"

Athena wondered if Suzie might relive her travel experiences or rehearse for new ones. That's what she most liked to do in letters.

"Suzie, if you don't watch out, you'll run out of places to go. You'll visit every single country and meet thousands of people. Your name will be in the book of world records. Suzie Frazier, world traveler. Come back, Suzie. Come back. Your friends are waiting for you."

A noise at the door turned out to be a gurney, transporting a patient, a middle-aged woman with bleached blonde hair, fully awake. Her first comment once she was placed in the empty bed beside Suzie was "Turn on the television."

The sound of canned laughter convinced Athena that it was time to go. She hoped that the presence of another person and auditory stimuli might speed Suzie's recovery. Nothing could be more aggravating, Athena conjectured, than sharing a confined space with someone whose television tastes differed from your own, especially if you couldn't state your preferences.

After stopping at her apartment for a quick shower, Athena was ready to scout around town. Though she'd prefer to jog and was worried about losing the habit, she needed a slower pace for information gathering.

Suzie's neighborhood was an old, established area just across the railroad tracks from the central downtown area but less prestigious than the other side, where there were many vintage Victorians. Suzie was within easy walking distance of a grocery store and a whole variety of specialty shops. The sidewalks on Suzie's side of the tracks were uneven, and Athena guessed that few walkers chose to come this way because of the high risk of tripping on the cracked and buckling cement.

Most of the houses on the four square blocks surrounding Suzie's house were small, with large yards and gardens, but special touches to individual dwellings made each unique. Suzie's house was identifiable by its yellow shutters. Athena noticed an alley behind it. She turned into the alley to examine Suzie's backyard over the fence. A yellow gate identified the spot. Entry from the back was easy, and she followed a flagstone path through Suzie's vegetable and flower garden to the house itself. Walking along the side of the house, she let herself through a gate to the front of the house. Anyone could pass through at any time, Athena realized, without any trouble at all.

Hearing water running nearby, Athena looked over to see a white-haired woman with a garden hose. She realized by the angry looks coming her way that the woman had spotted her first and wondered what she was doing there.

Athena went to stand next to her on the driveway.

"Hello! Suzie told me about you," Athena said. "Are you Peggy?"

"The name's Peggy, but Suzie isn't home, and you've no right to go traipsing through the back way," she said with a formidable frown.

"Suzie invited me. My name is Athena Dawes." She paused to see if that meant anything to Peggy.

"Athena! Suzie told me you'd be coming." She turned the ring on her hose to stop the flow of water. Now Peggy was smiling. "Come in and have a cup of tea. I'm afraid Suzie won't be back for a few days."

Peggy's house was full of lace curtains and overstuffed furniture. Tiny statues of animals and humans occupied all available shelf space. A smell of fresh polish permeated the air. A Pekingese rushed at Athena's legs with frantic barks.

"Calm down, Yuki," Peggy said in such a kind voice that the dog ignored her and kept scrabbling around Athena's ankles as if it meant to attack her.

Peggy led Athena to the kitchen and motioned for her to sit down on a chair beside the phone. She filled the teakettle at the sink.

"I saw you yesterday morning when the ambulance came," Peggy said as she put the kettle on the stove and turned the knob. "How did you find Suzie?"

Athena explained the call, the trip, and the grisly discovery.

"Such a terrible thing to happen. I've known her since she was a baby in a basket, so to speak. Her mother brought her to visit Beth regularly, and as soon as she could walk, she'd come running over to see me. She was the most friendly, cheerful child. A joy to have around. I've had the pleasure of her company over the years. On Sunday mornings, her aunt Beth used to come over for a cup of tea. Now, Suzie comes every week for a sip of Earl Grey and fresh scones."

Peggy put cups, saucers, and several selections of tea on a tray.

"I visited Suzie at the hospital about an hour ago," Athena said. "She's improving. There's no way to know how long the coma will last."

"I'll visit her and take flowers from the garden. She'll like that. I miss her a bunch. It's different when she's on a trip because I know when to expect her. She comes back with stories about where she's been, what she's done, and whom she's met. It's like a guided tour. She shows me her slides and souvenirs. I almost feel like I went along."

Peggy took the whistling kettle off the stove and poured the steaming water into a blue teapot.

"Beth used to be a great traveler too. She took Suzie on her first trip—to England that time—when she was twelve years old."

Athena followed Peggy to the dining table and took a chair that faced the street. She could just see through the lacy curtains that the light was waning outside.

"What kind of tea do you prefer?" Peggy asked.

Athena chose orange spice.

"On Sundays we always brew the tea with loose leaves," Peggy said.

Now that she was sitting across from her, Athena could see that Peggy's eyes were a bright cornflower blue in contrast with her white hair. Her figure was thin and youthful looking. Athena could imagine Suzie and Peggy at the table deep in conversation, just like family.

"Why don't you come Sunday morning?" Peggy asked with a smile.

"I'd like to," Athena said, stirring sugar into her tea. "This weekend I'm going to clean up Suzie's place. It's important to go through things carefully in case the police missed evidence. Trouble is—I don't know where Suzie keeps things."

"I know where things go, so I can help you with that."

"Do you take care of Suzie's garden and feed the cats while she's away?"

"For the last seven years, I've kept up her place every summer. The cats come tell me when they're hungry. I fed them tonight."

"Good. Now I'm going to turn detective on you," Athena said. "Did you notice anything Monday night at Suzie's place?"

"Detective Coles asked me that. I go to bed about nine o'clock every night. I did see Suzie come home about six-thirty with a bag of groceries because I was in my garden. Nothing after that."

"Do you know if Suzie has evening visitors?"

"I've seen people stop by to chat with her when she's in her yard. She doesn't entertain, if that's what you mean."

"I notice you're close to the railroad track. Are vagrants a problem?"

"There are homeless people in Aston, who hang out near some abandoned buildings. They don't do much harm—maybe a little petty theft now and then. Who can blame the poor souls?"

"Do you know anyone who takes evening walks?"

"I see Charley and Mary out walking several times a week. They've lived here longer than I have."

"Do you ever see a man with a German shepherd dog?"

"Oh yes, he comes by several times a day. He lives around here."

"Does Suzie talk about the psychology department where she works?"

"No, she goes on about things like her trip to Hungary next month. Suzie stays on the bright side when she's in company. I've seen her looking sad and worried, but the moment she sees me, she's right as rain."

Athena sipped her tea, which was cooling nicely. She put her cup down and happened to look out the window. Someone was standing on the sidewalk looking in. She turned her head away casually and then looked back. Someone was definitely there.

Peggy was talking about Suzie when Athena leaned toward her. "Don't turn your head, but someone's watching us. In a minute, I'm going outside to see who it is." Athena glanced back. No one in sight, but he couldn't be far away. "I'm leaving now, Peggy. Sorry to be so abrupt, but I'll come Sunday, and we'll put Suzie's house back in order. Maybe you'll notice something I can't see, since you're familiar with it all."

Peggy looked worried. "Take care of yourself."

Athena moved quickly out the front door to the sidewalk. Not far away, she saw a man and dog turning the corner. The dog was a giveaway. Walking after them at a brisk pace, she also turned the corner, but they weren't in view. Running the short distance to the next corner, she saw them partway down the block, going up a driveway. She paused for a minute, then followed. Russ had turned in at a small house identical to Suzie's except it was blue with white shutters. No light showed through the blinds, but now Athena knew that Russ lived almost directly behind Suzie's place with only an alley between.

Walking home to her cozy apartment, she thought about it. There was no particular reason to suspect Russ except that he lived close to Suzie, walked by her house often, and liked to look in windows. She'd have to do better than that.

EIGHT

ATHENA REACHED FOR the phone. If Ted had this much business, she wouldn't last a day. He'd have to hire a team to work for him.

"Psychology department. Can I help you?"

A raspy, unnatural woman's voice spoke up. "You'll pay for what you've done. So many deaths... Humans and animals... You don't care what you kill."

Athena's heart accelerated with the first word. "Who is this for?"

"It will haunt you like it haunts everyone who knows what goes on there, and we condemn you. You...sl-sl-slime"—it sounded like a growl. "You have no respect...no right to spoil innocent lives. You...scum. You'll get what you deserve. It won't be long. Not long..." A click ended the call.

Athena replaced the receiver slowly. The menacing voice gave a new dimension to hate. She went straight to Ginger's door. "I took a phone call just now. A woman's voice full of accusations."

"I should have warned you about those. The psych department is a target for crazies. Hate calls come in occasionally."

"Do you know who the caller might be?"

"Could be Cheryl. She's called the department on and off ever since her sister, a psych major, killed herself five years ago. The police checked Cheryl out and said she's harmless. She was in an institution for a while, but nowadays, they don't have room for all the troubled ones."

"So much spite."

"There's a male caller too. Once in a while, oddballs show up. Once or twice, we've called the police. Last year, for example, a man started punching the side of a filing cabinet and yelling obscenities. Suzie and Vicky came into my office. We locked the door and called the police."

"What happened to Cheryl's sister?"

Ginger shook her head. "Another sad story. Cheryl's sister Wendy was in one of Laszlo's classes. She put cards in his mailbox, phoned him at home, even sat outside his house in her car. He was the one and only, she insisted. He had to marry her. She said she'd kill herself if he didn't keep his promise. A fantasy. Laszlo never encouraged her. He thought if he ignored her she'd go away. Magda told Wendy that Laszlo was hers. Sadly enough, the girl killed herself, and Cheryl holds Laszlo responsible."

"Laszlo again. He seems to be at the center of everything."

Ginger shook her head. "Don't misunderstand. Laszlo is the kindest, most intelligent *gentleman* I've ever had the privilege to know. You'll understand what I mean when you meet him."

Athena wondered if Laszlo matched his reputation—worst and best.

Derring and a man in jeans and a blue work shirt—Ben Silver, no doubt—came in a few minutes later and stood in front of the mailboxes.

"These are exciting times in the field of psychology, don't you agree?" Derring said. He spoke with bravado. "We're making huge strides in understanding how emotions arise out of neurological stimulation to various parts of the brain. We're outdistancing the old psychology that was built on air, and quite erroneous, I might add."

"A matter of values," Silver said in a deep baritone voice.

"Values are just abstractions," Derring said. "We get results."

"Statistics aren't everything."

"Think of knowledge on alcohol abuse and anxiety thresholds from experiments on primates. Don't listen to Betty and her animal rights friends."

"Their arguments make sense. I went to the conference with the attitude of 'convince me,' and they did. We subject animals to whatever torture we choose because they can't defend themselves. A drug-dependent monkey at the primate center didn't choose his addiction, whereas humans get hooked on drugs of their own free will—in a sense. Social factors, such as peer pressure, are important, of course, but, in most cases, no one forced it into them as we do to animals in our research centers."

"Humans want lives free from stress and illness. Think of wonder cures made possible by medical research."

"How many billions of lives sacrificed?"

"Animal research isn't crucial for you. Consider our position."

"I honestly think that if you want to know how monkeys, baboons, or apes behave, you should observe them in the wild." Silver's voice boomed, though he was not a large man. "Aside from learning games—those too are forced on them—no research under artificial conditions can be accurate. We know human subjects often distort or falsify responses when presented with contrived situations, even if you disguise the real goal of the experiment. How can you consider creatures confined in cages or pens to be acting naturally? Would you use prison inmates as models of any human behavior besides captivity?"

"Animal rightists have enlarged hearts and pygmy brains."

"It's time to develop research techniques that don't offend the public."

"No way. We're making unprecedented breakthroughs in physiology that require the use of research subjects. It's becoming clear that we can know *everything* about how the brain functions if we continue on our present course."

Ben Silver nodded in Athena's direction as he led the way out with Derring following determinedly on his heels. Athena liked Ben Silver's point of view. It made her feel better about typing his manuscript on the inherent limitations in the winner-loser model for competition. Silver focused on humans with an eye to improving their behavior rather than justifying everything they did on the basis of animal behavior.

ON HER WAY to Laszlo's noon class, Athena saw the poster. Next to a debate announcement was a sheet, which said in large, bold letters:

WARNING!!!!

DON'T BE A DUPE.

THE GREAT DEBATE WILL BE A GIANT DEBACLE—

DON'T BE BORED ON FRIDAY NIGHT.

BRING ROTTEN FRUIT AND VEGETABLES TO EXPRESS YOUR OPINION.

The invitation would have instant appeal for some students, Athena thought. Vegetables—carrots, tomatoes, squash—bordered the top and sides of the page. At the bottom were pictures of people dozing and almost falling out of their seats, and in the lower corners hands with thumbs pointing down. The artist who'd done this was not the caricaturist who'd produced Laszlo exposing himself. Athena removed the sheet and tucked it into her notebook.

As she walked on toward the classroom, a man, looking very chic in a lavender shirt, black suit, and freshly polished shoes, stopped near the doorway and stared at Athena with a frown. He took two steps toward her, held out a hand, and said something that sounded like, "Cotty? Cotty?" His eyes searched her face.

She shook her head and said, "I'm Athena."

Regaining his professional manner, he turned and entered the classroom ahead of her. Laszlo. Why did he look vaguely familiar?

Athena sat down next to Russ in the row of seats against the back wall, which bordered on a nice wide aisle that traversed the back of the room. The German shepherd was reclining near Russ' outstretched legs. Russ glanced her way when she sat down but said nothing.

The room resembled the one where Derring had given his lecture, but fewer than a hundred students were present. Laszlo was down in front talking to a student who stood with his hand on a portable stand with a VCR and large television screen. Class wouldn't start officially for a few minutes.

"You work with Laszlo, don't you?" Athena said to Russ.

Russ nodded. "I'm one of his assistants. Why?"

This time he did meet her eyes, and she noticed how dark and cold they were. He kept them partly closed as if for self-protection. His whole manner conveyed meanness and toughness.

"Look at this," Athena said, showing him the disclaimer. "It was on the board down the hall."

Russ curled his lip. "We hunt down the crap they post," he said.

A tall, awkward student with a folder in hand poked his head in and came quickly to talk to Russ. "Petitions are ready for signature, so we're setting up a table outside."

"Can you fix this, Robert?" Russ asked, showing him the poster.

"Dan can check all over campus, especially in men's rooms where we found them before," Robert said. "I'll see to it."

Evidently, Laszlo had a band of concerned supporters.

Laszlo stepped to the blackboard and wrote: TRANCE—HYPNOSIS. Watching Laszlo, Athena guessed he was several inches under six feet tall. He held himself very straight, with almost military bearing. His high cheekbones were striking, as were his black eyes and wavy black hair laced with silver, which was thick and finely cut. She could understand why women fell for him. Why had he acted like she was a long-lost friend? It puzzled her, as did her own sense of his familiarity.

"Trance states occur naturally," Laszlo said. His voice carried with great clarity and resonance, British accent and all. "Driving on the freeway puts some people into a trance, especially those who travel the same route frequently. A driver suddenly realizes he has covered many miles without noticing any passage of time or movement along the highway. In a trance state, peripheral events are no longer important."

Laszlo was a master speaker, so intent on his message that he didn't notice when he dropped a piece of chalk and crushed it underfoot a few minutes later. He gestured frequently with his hands.

"We hypnotize ourselves," Laszlo said, tapping on his head

with his forefinger. "Without noticing, we slip from trance to peripheral awareness many times during an ordinary day. What a trance does, in effect, is put the left brain in neutral while allowing the right brain, with its imaginative powers, to do a solo performance.

"Hypnosis is a way of inducing a trance. The old myth that a hypnotist can take over the mind of the person he is hypnotizing is utter nonsense. A hypnotist merely provides a way to enter the trance state.

"Hypnosis received a bad reputation for many years because of false claims made at the end of the nineteenth century about the power and control exercised by the hypnotist." Laszlo held up a gold chain with a gold locket and swung it like a pendulum back and forth briefly before catching it in the palm of his hand. "Now that you are all under deep hypnosis, I want you to stand up, all at the same time, and say, 'God save the queen!'"

Only laughter followed. Russ' dog lifted its head for a minute, looked around, and then went back to sleep. Russ was taking detailed notes of Laszlo's comments on a legal pad.

"More recently, behaviorists have put hypnosis in disrepute by demanding objective measurements and consistent results. Since individuals differ widely in hypnotic susceptibility and response, their demands were impossible to meet. They claimed a victory, but all it demonstrated was that science cannot measure everything.

"Doctors and psychologists, such as Herbert and David Spiegel, have successfully used hypnosis to reduce pain, overcome fears, and change habits. Hypnosis does not produce fast, miraculous results but must be used repeatedly over time, as is true of other forms of therapy. We're going to watch a few cases of therapeutic hypnosis with follow-up interviews."

A murmur rose from the students as two uniformed police officers, a woman and a man, entered through a side door and went down the aisle to speak to Laszlo. The male officer talked to him while the woman addressed the class: "We've been notified of a bomb threat to this classroom."

A shuffling noise swept through the audience. Russ' dog jumped up, ears perked, and Russ put a hand on its head.

"Please listen and follow instructions. I want you to look under your seats. If you see anything suspicious that you didn't put there yourself, please raise your hand. Now, gather all belongings and leave the classroom as quickly as possible. Go outside to a distance of at least one hundred yards from the building. Any questions?"

A flurry of activity followed as students packed and left. A thin ripple of comments accompanied their quick departure.

Mouth pressed into a tight, thin line and his eyes shooting sparks of resentment, Laszlo put his notes in his briefcase, retrieved the videotape from the stand, and watched the exodus of his class.

Russ slipped his notebook into his book bag and turned to Athena. "Are you leaving?"

Athena shook her head. "Not yet." She was interested in the search method of the police, who were moving swiftly row by row to double-check. A fireman came running in to join them, another following soon after.

"I'm sure there's no real bomb," said the policeman to the fireman. "Your talent's wasted here."

Athena stood up. "Look under the lectern on the front table," she called out to the police. In a room bare of cabinets and hiding places, the small lectern on the front table might have a hollow interior, the logical spot.

The policewoman went to the lectern, lifted it slightly, and said, "Something's here all right. Everyone out! Out! Out!"

The short fireman grabbed a metal case he'd left by the door and hurried forward.

Laszlo was still at the door. "Well done," he said to Athena. Unlike Russ, his eyes were warm. She couldn't help smiling at the compliment. "Just logic," she said. She left the room reluctantly, wishing she could stay and see what they'd found.

"Think they're behind this too?" Russ asked Laszlo, as the two walked off down the hall with the dog trotting behind them.

"More intimidation," Laszlo said angrily. "The goal was to interrupt my class."

Athena noticed that classrooms close to theirs were also empty. She joined a throng of students on the lawn, who were staring at the classroom wing of Rim Hall. She could feel their eagerness for action, which would turn the present scene into a real event. Robert and a woman student were making the rounds with clipboards, asking students to sign for Laszlo. Sorry that she hadn't heard Laszlo's whole lecture, Athena headed for the main entrance.

Outside, she paused for a moment to admire the seven terracotta heads, all with faint, mysterious smiles on their faces. When she returned to the office, Ginger was waiting. Her voice wavered as she said, "I answered the phone and a deep voice said, 'Honvagy's class will blow sky-high at twelve-thirty.' Then he hung up, and I called the police. This has come up before, but I'll never forget that voice."

Athena patted Ginger's shoulder.

"Bomb threats on campus come from students who aren't prepared for exams, but I think this was different. You were in class. What did you see?"

"The police asked students to leave, then started their search," Athena said. "I stayed to watch as long as I could. Some firemen came, then they found something. I don't know what."

"That's a first. I'd better stand by to see what comes next. There goes my phone. Maybe there's more news."

Ginger was already talking on her phone when the one on Suzie's desk rang. Athena picked it up.

"Killers get what they deserve. Tell Honvagy they burn in hell," said a deep masculine voice. A disgusting sound of spitting followed, then a click.

"What do you do with hate messages?" Athena asked Vicky, who came in just as she put down the receiver.

"Give them to Laszlo," she said sweetly. Whirling around her area of the office, Vicky hummed softly and twice laughed out loud. Vicky was up to something—Athena was sure.

"Why don't they call the research institute directly?"

"Magda doesn't listen, just bangs the receiver down hard," Vicky said with the voice of experience. "By the way, I went home for lunch and brought back cookies and banana bread, which I put in the break room. Help yourself."

Vicky had dark gashes like bruises beneath her eyes but seemed to be in better spirits. "Sometimes I have the urge to bake," she added.

"You made them yourself?"

"Of course—from scratch. Nothing but the finest ingredients."

Athena accepted the offer since she'd had no time to eat lunch. She crossed the hall to the break room. Amazing how Vicky differed from one meeting to the next! A person with many masks, Athena reflected as she took a thick slice of banana bread, which looked good and tasted wonderful. Ginger entered and zeroed in on the banana bread.

"Vicky's treats are great," Ginger said. "There won't be a crumb left at the end of the day."

"Does Vicky eat what she bakes?"

"She's hyper, burns up every calorie she eats," Ginger said. "Steve was building her up. He took special care of her for a while, but I got the impression things weren't working out for them."

"He gave her a spectacular ring."

"I don't understand that. No one heard of an engagement until after Steve died. He didn't seem to have bucks for a ring like that."

Athena would add Ginger's observation to her file on Vicky. She selected a peanut butter cookie and took a bite. Thick and crunchy.

"Guess what the police found? An old book bag on the table right in front of Laszlo. It contained a capped bottle of clear inflammatory liquid, gunpowder, and a book of matches."

"Sounds like it wasn't ready to go off," Athena said.

"'Not under the circumstances,' the police said. The parts weren't connected like a real bomb would be."

"It might be a warning," Athena said.

"You're right. I'm worried that Laszlo's debate might cause a real bang. I feel it in my bones."

"Will there be extra campus security that night?"

"After the bomb threat, I'm sure the campus police will agree."

"Every person should be searched for unusual stuff before entering," Athena said. She was thinking of rotten fruits and vegetables they might find.

"Good idea." Ginger finished her banana bread and licked the last crumbs off her fingers and lips. "Back to the grind."

Athena followed her.

"Isn't Laszlo something?" Ginger had a dreamy look in her eyes. "Stirs up the lust. Suzie agrees."

Ginger must have had a crush on Laszlo ever since he came to the department. Why did Laszlo look familiar? Athena was searching for some connection, but finding none.

NINE

"WHERE'S THE BEST PLACE to go jogging?" Athena asked.

"Some people like the river," Ginger said. "Paths follow it for miles. Don't you dare jog after dark, though. Aston is safer than San Francisco, but don't take chances. I've seen women students running out on lonely country roads as late as eleven p.m. Crazy!"

Ginger left to answer her phone. Athena turned back to KISS, but she was anticipating the pleasure of a good jog. She'd also visit Suzie this evening. She typed on, wondering when to expect more C3's. They popped up soon—as inevitable as the truism that night follows day, Athena thought.

When Ginger spoke up behind her, Athena jumped. "We have a special request," she said in honeyed tones. Dr. Briggs stood beside Ginger. She stepped forward with a sheaf of handwritten pages.

"The finished paper has to be postmarked before midnight tonight in order to be accepted by the conference board," Briggs said. "My contribution is the central piece in a panel on success psychology. It's way past deadline, and everyone is waiting."

Briggs looked at Athena with a mixture of disdain and expectancy. Athena was tempted to ask why she hadn't prepared it earlier.

"Briggs' project is highest priority, so I'm asking you to stay and complete the job," Ginger said.

"Of course." Athena squinted at the first page. Briggs' linear script eliminated high and low loops for consonants. It needed a translator.

"I'll go over a page with you," Briggs said, as if doing a favor for an inferior. She read her material quickly and with passion. Good delivery, Athena had to admit as she rushed to make notations in the margins and spaces between lines to help her produce the final copy.

"There. I'll be in my office. If you have problems, just call."

Once Briggs left, Athena sat in a daze, wondering how Suzie coped with last-minute work, which robbed her of the evening.

"Shouldn't happen, but it does with Briggs," Ginger said.

"If only I could read her scribbles," Athena said. The lines hardly qualified as handwriting, for they weren't meant to communicate.

Ginger leaned toward her with a smile. "You've done a wonderful job here. I didn't think you'd manage so well. People don't realize what goes on in the department office."

"Thanks, Ginger," Athena said. She could use a bit of praise, and it wasn't coming from the profs.

"Why not take a break? Get a snack at the coffeehouse. You'll be more ready to tackle the job," Ginger said.

"I'd like to disappear for a while."

"Here's a key to the office. The Rim's deserted after five p.m., but the custodian's around." Ginger patted Athena's shoulder before she left.

Outside, Athena enjoyed the fresh air, the trees, the peace. She'd always found late afternoon colors richer and deeper than those early in the day. The quad was almost deserted. A fellow sitting under a tree was playing a recorder and getting a nice flutey sound. The campus had its own dreamy magic. She envied the students their leisure—time to chat, take in a movie, or jog a few miles before studying.

After buying a large coffee and bagel with cream cheese at the counter, she sat down at a small round table. A student newspaper kept her attention while she ate. She refilled her coffee cup to take back with her.

Inside the Rim, halls were quiet. She paused at the half-open door of the custodian's room to study the skull and crossbones. The picture was strangely irritating, as if it was stating more than it appeared to.

Back in the office, Athena wished it were morning and that she had hours of sleep behind her instead of wanting so desperately to stretch out, close her eyes, and forget the psychology department. She muttered a few names for Briggs—"birdbrain," "egomaniac," "inefficient"—while she opened a new document on the computer. A glance through the stack of pages showed there were actually two versions—the one Briggs would deliver at the conference and another to be published with the conference proceedings. Sneaky!

"A prerequisite to success is to know clearly and without hesitation what you want to accomplish," Athena typed. Hardly earthshaking, she thought.

She plunged on, but it became clear that speed was impossible as she struggled to make out the inked words on the page. C3's popped up on the screen more than once.

"CUSS, please cooperate," Athena said. Yes, that was the best name for the computer. From now on it would be CUSS; KISS sounded too nice.

Athena was struggling to concentrate, but it didn't help her go any faster. She had to puzzle out each word as she went, and some were impossible. If she called Briggs, the woman would stand at her elbow and dictate the whole paper, which wasn't an inviting prospect. Why not type words she could decipher and leave gaps for those she couldn't? Briggs would have to fill the gaps, and she wouldn't like it, Athena was certain.

Words seemed to dance on the screen. Athena was typing page six when the screen went blank. A message popped into view.

CODE 3: ALONE. ALL ALONE HERE. VERY COLD. VERY STILL.

She reread the words several times, then massaged her temples lightly with her fingertips and rubbed her eyes. Too strange. She couldn't help thinking, What's going on? Who's playing tricks? She printed a copy of that message before deleting it. The regular screen came back with the manuscript in progress.

Why not blame CUSS? CUSS was sending stupid messages to confuse her and complicate things.

"You wretched piece of junk," Athena said. Grabbing a blank sheet of paper, she drew a quick outline of CUSS. She showed herself, a tiny cartoon character, climbing up the machine on a rope. Then she drew another picture of herself standing on top, gargantuan in size, while the machine had shrunk. If only a drawing could change relationships.

"How are you?" said a deep voice. It was Josh.

"Hanging on." Athena showed him her cartoons.

"I like 'em," he said, eyes shining. "I got pictures too."

"I saw your skull and crossbones."

"That's nothin'." He rolled up the sleeve of his plaid shirt and showed her a snake tattoo that stretched from his elbow to his wrist. Snakes were not Athena's favorites, whether alive or merely represented, but the quality was impressive.

"Very good!" Athena said.

"That's not all." He unbuttoned his shirt and a sweaty smell became more noticeable. A huge dragon tattoo stretched across his chest. He moved his shoulders back and forth, and the dragon danced.

"Got that in 'Nam," he said.

For his large size, his chest was amazingly thin, and his ribs stood out clearly. Lowering his shirt from his back, he turned so she could see a lion's head on his back. He was a walking art exhibit.

"Good show," Athena said, though she'd never liked tattoos.

"Got a picture there." He pointed to his buttock. "Won't show you that one." He laughed.

To Athena's relief, he rebuttoned his shirt.

"That's not all I got in 'Nam." Josh leaned over and parted his hair to show a large, ugly scar. "I got this," he said, pointing to his nose. "And this," pointing to his jaw. "Used to be a good-looker and smart fellow before 'Nam. After this," he said, pointing to his head, "I lost it. So, I get dumb jobs. But this is the last. No more after this."

"I'm sorry it happened, Josh," Athena said. Looking at the huge, sad man, she decided to tell. "My father died in 'Nam. I was five years old."

Josh's chest heaved suddenly, and a tear raced down his cheek. "Too many fathers gone. Too many sons. Everythin' spoilt."

His voice gave out. Athena's eyes told him how she felt.

Josh seemed to change gears. He slapped his big hands against his thighs. "Them's the breaks. Some days aren't good, but what the heck! I still got some work in me. Lots to do today."

"You take care," Athena said. "You're a good person, Josh."

"Not good 'nuff," he said, shaking his head as he exited.

Athena attacked Briggs' project with more determination. It was like trying to find words in a cryptogram. She forced herself to move along and produced the strangest bunch of words and gaps she'd ever put on paper. No joke! She carried it down the hall to Briggs' office with the original.

"Your paper as written," Athena said. "As you correct, please print. Then you'll have the final copy sooner."

Briggs looked furious. "There'll be more work all right."

"I'll be waiting," Athena said in her sweetest tone.

"What kind of imbeciles do they put in offices these days?" Briggs muttered.

Athena left Briggs scowling over her own mess and went down the hall for a drink from the water cooler. She heard a slight noise and saw Josh.

"Come to the tower room," he said urgently. "Sunsets are special."

"Okay. I like sunsets," Athena said. "Let's hurry. I can't take long."

Josh had a hard time climbing stairs. Athena noticed how he dragged his feet but was determined to lead her to the top. The last set of steps resembled a ladder with an iron rail embedded in the wall for support. Once up, Josh gave her a hand.

The tower room was the highest place in the building, with continuous glass all the way around. Student desks stood spaced at intervals and facing in different directions. Each had pictures and distinctive knickknacks to define personal space.

"Look," Josh said, making a sweeping gesture with his arm. "Didn't I tell you it was beautiful?"

The tower room offered a panoramic view of campus and sky. Sunset had passed the point of fiery splendor, and colors were muted. The sky was a pale blue and pearly gray. Pinkish clouds unfurled like banners. Some were thin as veils, just a pale pink film; others were high-built clouds with a rich rose color, often lined with a darker edge. Dark mountains, outlined in crimson silhouette, were visible from one side of the tower. The quad with green expanses, broken by tree clumps, stretched out on the far side.

"In 'Nam, used to count sunsets," Josh said. "Never knew if we'd see another. VC often attacked at night."

"What was Vietnam like?" She'd read about it when she was in her teens and trying to understand what her father might have experienced.

Josh shrugged. "Depends where. White beaches and blue, blue waters of the South China Sea. Couldn't walk there though."

"Dangerous?"

"Bunkers, barbed wire, and minefields. Off limits."

"Were you mostly on the beach?"

"Only at first. Inland looked peaceful—peasants working in rice paddies and children playing with water buffalo."

"What was the jungle like?"

"Thick with bushes and trees 'til you couldn't see light—or the enemy either. They'd hide anywhere. Heat made it like hell. And stink and rot and sickness and death all over. Lots of fightin' and bodies blown to bits. My buddy stepped on a mine. Heard him scream and started runnin' to get out of range. A moment later, he was in pieces and blood all over. That's where I got it too."

"You came back."

"Never knew what we were doin' over there. Why couldn't we let 'em have their rice and jungles? Why torture us? Why torture them? Best thing we did was get the hell out."

"You made it back alive." She thought of her father who hadn't.

"Only half alive. Lost my youth, my energy, my dreams. Lost what mattered most. Anyways, I'm outta here by the end of next week."

"You're leaving?"

Josh nodded. "Health going down. I'm countin' sunsets now, for sure."

"Thanks for sharing a lovely sunset, Josh."

"Sunsets are to share." Josh was watching her from the corner of his eye.

It made Athena nervous. They were enclosed in a sort of capsule, far from anyone else in the building. Colors were fading fast.

"Must go, Josh," she said cheerfully, moving away. "Hope to see you before you go."

"Yeah," he said. "Yeah. I'll see you."

Her last view was of a giant silhouette against the darkening twilight sky. She had a feeling there was more to Josh than anyone realized.

Reyna was standing at Suzie's desk with her arms folded. "The only post office open until midnight is in San Francisco," she said. "I have a long drive to make."

"I understand," Athena said, feeling more mellow after the sunset scenery. Briggs' revision was not only easier to read but betrayed a severe case of inability to spell. She felt sorry for Reyna, whose life must be a web of pretenses with a persistent fear of falling. Success was a balancing act. What would she do to stay aloft?

Reyna walked to the door and turned around. "You seem to have time to flirt with Frankenstein," she said nastily. "I hope you understand that time is crucial. I'm going out to have a bite at the coffeehouse. Think you can wrap it up soon?"

Athena nodded. What she didn't say was, "It depends on your writing." The minute Briggs left, she put her head down on her arms and laughed silently. Flirt? *Flirt?* Briggs didn't know what she was talking about. Flirt with Frankenstein! Ted would enjoy that.

As soon as she opened the file folder, Athena saw the faces Briggs had sketched on every page—a looped nose, two angry eyes, and a turned-down mouth. Briggs was no artist but the message was clear. Athena was ready to walk away. She reminded herself that she'd asked Ginger for the job and received repeated warnings about Briggs. To blot out the abominable faces and lessen the insult, she pasted a Post-it square over each one, page by page, before continuing.

The office seemed hot and stuffy. They'd probably turned off the air supply to conserve energy. Now that she could see what Reyna was trying to say, Athena typed along more steadily, performing ongoing editing of spelling and sentence structure. Suddenly the computer screen filled with C3's again. Athena printed it for proof of malfunctioning, then typed: *Go to hell, CUSS,* and deleted it along with all the C3's. Her computer angst was back. Why these interruptions? Why all the same? Had a computer operator set this up? She'd question Ginger the next day.

CUSS's screen went blank before a message appeared: *To Whom it May Concern: I Was Young and Had Plans. Who Stole My Life from Me?*

A trickster at work somewhere, Athena was convinced. Was he acting on behalf of Steve, or was Cheryl sending computer messages about her sister? Athena printed the message. Disgusted, she wanted to flip CUSS's "off" switch, but she was determined to complete the job.

Half an hour later, Briggs opened the door. "Is my manuscript ready?" she asked in a strident voice.

"Not quite."

Briggs slammed the door.

"So kind of you to stop by," Athena said.

What she was working on would not be final until Briggs proofed it and made corrections. However long it took, she'd do it, in spite of CUSS, in spite of Briggs.

"Sorry, Suzie," Athena said. "No visit tonight."

TEN

TERROR CRAWLED DOWN Athena's back and tingled in her toes. The ground she was crossing had once been a rice field but was now pitted and uneven. A voice in her head said, "Minefield! Hurry! Watch out!" At any moment, she might step on a buried explosive. How could she know where to step and where not to step? Just a matter of luck.

Looking down, she was surprised to see military garb and a huge weapon, which she knew was an M-16. Looking off to her right, she could see other soldiers moving across the field, just as she was. We're bait, she thought. If we don't get it from the ground, we'll get it from the bushes.

As she watched, a soldier nearest her, a good fifty yards away, raised his hand to greet her. The name Bailey came to mind. Nice guy—Bailey. Seconds later a roar and a boom filled the air. Athena dropped down flat on the ground as earth and stone rained down on her. She looked in Bailey's direction, where the earth had opened up. If Bailey was injured, she'd better help him. For his sake, she had to find out. Still keeping low to the ground, she moved toward the spot where he'd been. First she noticed a couple of pale, wormlike things. Fingers, she realized with a sinking feeling. She moved toward the explosion area, passing a bloody arm with a fragment of uniform adhering to it. Horror choked her as she saw a boot full of blood. No body—just parts strewn around. Athena fought an impulse to vomit. She had to stay alert to keep alive.

The trees meant safety, but that was deceptive. They looked like a beautiful oasis because their dusty green seemed to promise an umbrella. The enemy might be anywhere, but with cover, she'd feel better. It was hot and humid to the point of suffocation. As Athena moved toward the trees, she saw others moving, on the right. Another explosion far right. She prayed with every step that she'd make it.

Closer, closer, closer to the dense jungle vegetation. As she walked the last few yards, a head and shoulders suddenly popped up over the top of a bush. Military garb. Not ours! Danger! His mouth smiled. He thought he had her, but she was quicker. The force of her shots threw her backward, but not before she saw half the man's head disappear, leaving a bloody mess. He fell into the bush with the fresh wound exposed.

I just killed a man! Athena thought with a start.

She flinched and was partly awake now, in a middle zone. Josh's stories of Vietnam had stirred old images from accounts she'd read in high school. She'd finally put them away when she began having nightmares like the present one. Athena didn't want to feel so much sympathy for Josh. She didn't want to speculate about whether Josh had met her father sometime or someplace in that distant war. She didn't like being so suggestible that people could get under her skin.

WHEN ATHENA ARRIVED at work Friday morning, Vicky was throwing the morning mail at faculty mailboxes in a game of "hit the basket." "Hello there!" Vicky called out as she stooped down to retrieve a piece that had landed on the floor.

Ginger's office was empty, though lights were on. Athena unlocked Suzie's desk and put her purse in a drawer. She caught herself repeating with delight, "Last day! Last day I do this. After today, I'm independent again." She'd work on what she knew and follow up on leads.

Ginger had said that "Fridays tend to be slow," a pleasant change from Thursday. Athena enjoyed the thought of having dinner with Magda and Laszlo that evening. Exchanging information directly with them would give her a clearer view of past incidents and how to prevent future ones.

"That bitch!" Vicky said. "I can't believe what she did!"

Vicky beat a folded copy of the *Psychologist* against the edge of Athena's desk as if to punish it. "Briggs published Steve's paper with her name as sole author. She printed his paper word for word without giving him credit.'' Vicky was shaking her head. ''She's not going to get away with this. Oh no! I'll see the bitch roast in hell.''

Athena had no fond feelings for Briggs after last night. She hadn't gone home until after 10 p.m., then found herself too exhausted to sleep until after midnight.

''Steve did the research. He did the thinking. I put it on computer from his notes,'' Vicky said. She was circling round the office, face puffed up with emotion. Athena could imagine smoke curling from her mouth.

''She robbed him. I'll kill her!'' Vicky flew out of the office, and Athena heard her hammering on a door down the hall. She stalked back. ''Not there! I can't wait to stuff it down her throat.''

Vicky walked the length of the office and back. ''Briggs needed more publications for tenure. Once they accepted Steve's article with her name on it, she had to dump Steve so he couldn't expose her.'' Vicky was talking so fast, it was hard to follow. ''Who else's ideas has she devoured?''

''You're jumping to conclusions,'' Athena said.

''What do you know? Mind your own business.''

Athena was glad to disengage. With Vicky one couldn't win.

''No nonsense today, CUSS,'' Athena said firmly to the computer. ''We have work to do, and I need your cooperation.'' How many people talked to their computers, she wondered as she started another manuscript. How endless it seemed—another and another and another—all in the same format.

Vicky distributed the rest of the mail, sat down at her computer, punched in, and typed like a demon for a couple of minutes.

''What do you think of this?'' Vicky asked Athena.

Athena saw that it was typed like a telegram or fax.

R. BRIGGS—

CONGRATS ON YOUR ARTICLE IN CURRENT ISSUE OF *PS.* WHY NOT MY NAME TOO? I DID THE WORK.

STEVE

"Some letters are best not sent. Don't you wonder what'll happen after she gets it?" Athena asked.

"She's not going to get away with it."

"She already has."

"No she hasn't. My name stands for Victory as well as for Vicious, that's what. This time I've got her." Vicky clipped the note to the front of the journal and tossed it in Briggs' box. "The bitch will regret what she did."

Not reality based, Athena thought. How far would Vicky go for vengeance? Did Vicky make Suzie pay for what she knew? With luck, Briggs would stay away from the office long enough for Athena to pull out the note and get rid of it.

Ben Silver came in with Patrick MacRae, the one who'd just had his book published. MacRae looked upset.

"Laszlo's research lab at Aston is first rate," MacRae said. He spoke in a high, excited voice. "He's a popular teacher, a dedicated researcher, and has authored more books and articles than any of us. How can they get approval to sever his Research Institute from the psych department without his consent?"

"Laszlo is fighting. He's gathering evidence for a harassment suit," Silver said as he collected mail from his box. "They've characterized his research as 'counter to department interests' and plan to take a vote."

"Let's be real. Laszlo has tenure. They can't oust him."

Silver scratched his head. "Old, dependable structures like tenure could tumble any day. Laszlo isn't popular with any of the higher-ups."

"Laszlo's a loser any way you look at it," Vicky said importantly.

The professors ignored comments from the sidelines.

"I don't understand how young Ph.Ds, who haven't distinguished themselves in either teaching or research, can redo the department to correspond with their limited vision," MacRae said.

Silver shrugged. "They have better credentials—Princeton, Duke, Stanford, Yale—than we had. I mourn the value of what we're losing. I'm fighting tooth and nail for Laszlo, but change is shaking the whole university. Derring and company are shrewdly jumping in to take advantage.''

Engaged in their discussion, they moved toward the door.

''What can I do for Laszlo?'' MacRae said. ''If they force him out against his will, they can do it to any of us.''

''I think they're going to make life so miserable for us that we'll all retire early.'' Silver went through the door ahead of MacRae.

As soon as the door shut, Vicky spoke up. ''How can anyone take Laszlo's magic tricks seriously?''

''Have you been to Laszlo's classes or read his books?'' Athena asked.

''I wouldn't give that charlatan a minute of my attention.''

Athena put her full attention into CUSS, and when the first screenful of C3's appeared, she wasn't surprised. She tried to ignore Vicky's hovering.

Vicky didn't see Briggs come in because she'd crouched down to search for something inside the lower drawer of her file cabinet, which was packed with coffee cups, assorted tea bags, and packages of candy, chips, and cookies.

Athena cleared her throat noisily, but Vicky didn't respond to the cue.

Briggs strolled to her mailbox, froze for a moment, then whirled around and headed straight for Vicky's desk, rounding the corner for a direct confrontation.

''Someone wants to see you about something important,'' Briggs said in a sharp, ringing voice.

Vicky looked up to see Reyna standing over her, rocking on her heels. Reyna was about the same height as Vicky, but, for a moment, she towered over her. Vicky shot up to her full height, and Reyna thrust the note under her nose.

''You're the only one who'd think of this. You're a twisted wire; this time you've gone too far,'' Briggs said in a voice that hissed with anger.

''You stinking plagiarist,'' Vicky said with equal strength. She twisted the ring on her finger, around and around, as if it empowered her. "You can't even write your own papers. Others do the work. You steal the credit."

As Vicky stepped forward, Briggs propped herself on the desk, as if she'd fall down. Her face was white, but her eyes burned. Athena guessed she'd recover quickly.

"This time you don't get away with it," Vicky said. "This time you're going to answer for what you did. You're a thief and a murderer."

Reyna gathered her dignity and stood up straight. "I paid Steve for that research. He got graduate credits, and he gave me permission to use it."

"Sure! You got rid of him so he couldn't tell," Vicky said. "You're going to answer to my father, the dean. There's a price for plagiarism. I have Steve's original paper on a computer disk."

"Wait a minute," Reyna said. "Who do you think you are? You're the one who's out of line. Where'd you get that fake engagement ring? Certainly not from Steve."

Now, Vicky reeled back and leaned against the filing cabinet as if to brace herself.

"I'm going to tell you something, whether you want to hear it or not. Steve never loved you. He felt sorry for you and then regretted it. I'll tell you a little secret—Steve loved me. I sent him into Laszlo's camp as a spy, and he told me anything I wanted to know."

"You sucked his blood. You devoured his brains," Vicky spat out.

"Steve thought you were a miserable, sniveling, spoiled bitch with the brains of a squirrel. He couldn't wait to get rid of you, but you wouldn't let go. You had a stranglehold. And *you* destroyed him, Vicky, you stupid parasite. You weren't worth Steve's little fingernail."

"Oh!" Vicky moaned with a sharp intake of breath. She was crying and cringing as if physical blows were being delivered.

"That's enough!" Athena said to Reyna, stepping in between them.

Reyna pushed past Athena for a last shot as Vicky headed for the door.

"Don't you *ever* play games with me again, you hear? I know the score. I'll make sure you never work on this campus again," Briggs said.

Ginger was coming in as Vicky went out.

"What happened?" Ginger said.

Looking shaken but not defeated, Briggs took her mail and left.

"Rough stuff," Athena said. "I'd better find Vicky. I'm not sure what she'll do."

Athena checked the halls on the first floor, then climbed the stairs to the second. She thought she could hear something on the third floor, as if a door had slammed. She went farther up. One thing she'd noticed about the third floor was that the hallways did not gleam. She was trying to decide which way to go first when she noticed the stairs up to the tower room and looked up. Of the two doors at the top of the stairs, one was closed and one was open. She could see a ribbon of sky. Vicky had probably gone that way. The stairs were so steep, they were like rungs on a ladder, and she had to rely on the metal handrail. From the fresh air coming through the open door, Athena guessed it gave access to the roof.

As she pulled herself up, a bit breathless from the effort, she saw a balcony, and Vicky was standing up on top of the rail. Just a slight motion would send her hurtling to injury or death.

"Not this! Not this!" Athena knew she had to connect with Vicky.

Facing the quad, Vicky had her arms outstretched, and her left hand grasped a large metal hook embedded in the wall at her height. The ring was gone from her finger, Athena noticed, and wondered what she'd done with it. Vicky's bare feet were balancing on a two-inch-wide balcony rail. The meager outline of Vicky's body showed up shadowlike through the loose, tapered skirt and top, and her spread-eagled stance reminded Athena of an angel she'd once cut out of an old Christmas issue of *McCall's*. Vicky looked poised to take off as if her light body would be airborne, an illusion Vicky might share at her own risk.

As Athena stepped out on the balcony, it creaked under her

weight. Vicky glanced down over her shoulder. Her cheeks were streaked with tears.

"It's you," Vicky said through tight lips.

"Just me."

"Last time, Steve persuaded me not to jump. I want him to come."

"I'm not Steve."

"You're probably a psychologist like the rest of them."

"Not me."

"Psychologists and counselers look at people like they care. It's an act. Steve had it down perfectly. He looked at me like I was a miracle."

"You *are* special, Vicky," Athena said, wishing the height of the balcony didn't bother her so much. She couldn't look down and tried to focus on how she'd reach Vicky in a split second if the woman decided to go over the edge.

Vicky kept in motion on the rail, moving her feet and swaying back and forth in a way that made Athena nauseous.

"Steve thought he saved my life." Vicky shifted her grip on the hook and waved her free arm. "I let him think so. He let me think he cared until the last. I needed someone to care, so when what seemed real turned out to be another fucking game, it was the end."

"I understand." Athena did. She'd been disappointed in men she loved more than once.

Vicky was crying again.

Athena licked her dry lips. "Steve did something good when he saved you."

"Well, are you going to save me?"

"I want to help, if I can."

"You can't. Nobody can, now or ever."

Athena spotted two students peering through the smoky window of the tower room, the floor of which was below the balcony, though it extended much higher to the dome, as Athena had seen last night.

"You have lots of years ahead. There will be good times to compensate for the pain you are suffering now," Athena said.

"Why? Suppose I don't like the setup? Suppose it's rigged against me?"

"It can change. You can change so your life looks different to you."

"Are you my fairy godmother? Can you make good things happen?"

Athena recalled her mother's words. "The road of life winds through mountains and valleys. No one knows what's around the bend. The point is to continue the journey."

"You've got to be a shrink. Positive thinking is a narcotic to keep people from seeing what's really there."

"Rose-colored glasses are better than black. I'm talking about old-fashioned virtues of patience and perseverance. You don't want to die."

"When I want to, I will. No one will stop me."

"Albert Camus asked the question—why don't we all just commit suicide when the going gets tough? He used the Greek myth of Sisyphus, a man condemned by the gods to keep pushing a huge rock uphill, only to have it roll down to the bottom. Then, Sisyphus starts over, and it happens again, but he goes on with his task. We have to keep on."

"Sounds awful."

"I don't think it's all repetition. Why not look at life like an adventure? You have to stay around to see what happens next."

"In my case, it can only get worse."

"The sun feels good up here. The air smells fresh."

"People have spoiled the air and the sunshine forever."

"Are you going to jump?" a voice called from below.

"Sure! Will you catch me?" Vicky called, dancing on the rail.

It worried Athena that Vicky was enjoying the attention. A crowd had gathered. Sweat trickled down Athena's sides from her armpits to waist. Her palms were damp; her stomach ached.

"We have a nice view. From here you can see pines and palm trees. It's like a giant park."

Bicycles were passing in the street. Pedestrians on the far side of the street had noticed Vicky and Athena on their high perch and stopped to gawk.

"Ha!" Vicky said. She turned her body and stretched her right hand over to catch hold of a hook just as she let go with her left hand. "You know what I see when I look at the campus?"

"What do you see?" Athena noticed Ginger, looking up at them from the main entrance.

"I see mountains and valleys of steaming shit."

Athena laughed in surprise. "Shit?"

"All the lies and hypocrisy that flow through the campus could create new land formations."

Athena laughed again. "So, what's new?"

Tension seemed to be draining away. Vicky was no longer crying.

Honking at bicycles, a fire truck came down the street in their direction. The huge truck stopped, and three men jumped out to look up at them. One had a megaphone in hand.

Vicky gestured with her free arm. "Move back. Move back."

Athena hesitated but then did as Vicky requested. Vicky let go of the hook, ran three steps along the rail, and jumped gracefully to the balcony floor. Clapping sounds rose from below.

"You're a circus star!" Athena said. She hadn't been sure which way Vicky would go, but now she felt the uplift of relief.

"Regional champion of the balance beam when I was twelve to fourteen with trophies to prove it." Vicky smiled proudly and looked like an impish little girl, though her reddened eyes betrayed trouble.

"You had me fooled," Athena said, holding back anger.

"I fooled Steve too."

"I'll bet you fooled a lot of people."

"What I said, I meant. To tell the truth, I feel better on a bar than anywhere else when I'm under stress."

"Heights don't bother you?"

"I don't notice, because I'm in complete control."

"After you," Athena said, gesturing toward the stairs.

To her relief, Vicky took the suggestion. When they were both at the bottom, Vicky tugged on her arm.

"You know why I came down?"

"Tell me."

"Your laugh. You laughed with me, not at me."

"I took your side against Reyna," Athena said as they descended another set of stairs. She thought Reyna had overdone her attack on Vicky, though Vicky invited it.

"She's a super bitch."

"I agree," Athena said. Now that Vicky had calmed down, Athena decided to ask her on the off chance she'd know something. "I have a favor to ask. Do you know what C3 means? Is it a symbol the department uses?"

"C3. That was Steve's sign, which stood for Code 3. Code 3 was his name in the death prep club."

Athena felt elated. A breakthrough.

"You've seen it on the computer, right?" Vicky said.

"Did you put it there?"

Vicky hesitated and then nodded.

"Why?"

Vicky laughed. "They're waiting for messages from beyond the grave. Suzie was excited about it. You should have seen her, thinking she'd got the prize."

Athena sighed. "Did you put whole messages on the computer?"

"Only C3's."

That solved part of the problem, but if Vicky was telling the truth, someone else was getting into the act.

"Do you know who put messages in the system?"

Vicky shook her head slowly but looked guilty.

"How do I get rid of the C3's? They're a nuisance."

"You have to figure that out," Vicky said impishly. "The computer is very intelligent. Why not communicate with it through the Dialogue file? You can talk directly to the computer, and it answers you."

They were both laughing as they went into the office, although Athena felt like yanking that silky hair hard. Vicky was a naughty little girl.

Ginger hugged Vicky. "I called your father. He's coming to get you in half an hour, and you're officially on leave."

"Great! I get a vacation with me, myself, and I. Such fun."

Vicky started gathering what she'd take with her.

Ginger signaled to Athena that she'd talk to her later. More upset than she showed, she returned to her desk with obvious trouble concentrating.

"I can't wait to hear what my dad says about my escapade. Professors can't figure out what their children need. He may understand the complexities of genetics, but he doesn't have a clue what I'm about."

"He does care about you," Athena said.

"First and foremost, he is a professor, and his hallowed profession consumes him utterly," Vicky said in the clipped tones of a scholar. She snatched a Kleenex from the box on the desk and blew her nose. "My father has time for faculty and students every day. Since I'm not helping to pay his salary, I'm not worth his precious time. When I call his office, his response is, 'Now what?' Anything I could want or need is unreasonable. My mother can explicate a literary text from start to finish but knows nothing about her own daughter and doesn't want to know."

"You understand your family," Athena said.

"Family is a joke. Understanding doesn't help. Life is hell when no one's there for you. You're empty enough to shrivel up and blow away, and no one would even notice."

Athena found the Dialogue file Vicky had mentioned.

"I'm going to talk to the computer," Athena said.

"Go ahead. People in the psych department love it."

Athena read the command: "Ask me a question."

She typed in, "Are you lonely?"

CUSS replied, "What makes you think I'm lonely?"

Athena: "You said you were lonely."

CUSS: "Did I say that?"

Athena: "I have proof."

CUSS: "Proof is inaccurate. Perhaps you are lonely."

Athena laughed and turned to Vicky with questioning eyes.

"The program builds on your words with basic language patterns," Vicky said. "You have to keep it simple."

Athena knew that Dialogue was not advanced, compared to more recent computer capabilities. Simon, the computer in Ted's office, lagged behind the times. Not being a computer aficionado, Athena was pleased with this glimpse into a new dimension.

Athena typed in: "Are you sending messages?"

CUSS: "I send messages requested."

Athena: "Who sends messages?"

CUSS: "The operator sends messages."

Athena turned to Vicky. "Can other department computers talk back like this one?"

"Only if they have the program."

"Can they all send messages?"

"They're all interconnected," Vicky said.

A tall thin man with glasses and sparse hair came through the office heading straight for Ginger's door. He nodded to Athena but ignored Vicky. His mouth turned down severely at the corners, and he seemed to stomp his feet for emphasis. He went into Ginger's office, shut the door hard, and they began to talk.

"See what I mean?" Vicky said.

Athena did. In her opinion, he didn't look impressive to someone who didn't know he was dean.

"Dad and Steve used to argue for hours about whether parapsychology had any merit. Dad said something odd after Steve died. He said, 'Why didn't the psychic messengers warn him?' Like Dad won the argument."

"If Steve was a spy like Reyna said he was, why did he adopt Laszlo's teachings?"

"Laszlo brainwashed him."

The conversation in Ginger's office didn't last long. Ginger was shaking her head at him, and he got to his feet. He stood and she sat, their eyes locked in some kind of understanding. Then he was back in the office.

"I'd like to express my gratitude to you," he said to Athena. Vicky was making faces behind his back.

"Come on, Vic," he said and marched out with Vicky in tow.

As she answered the phone, Athena thought of Vicky, blowing hot and cold, spoiled and deprived at the same time. What was her role in the whole mess?

Ginger came out of her office. She looked ill.

"I was so worried," she said. "I told the dean that Vicky is not welcome back here. She has disrupted operations in the department in every way by dating grad students, taking sides with professors against other professors, refusing to cooperate with coworkers, and turning the main office into a stage on which she performs."

"She's difficult."

"She's more than difficult. She won't be coming back."

"Briggs gave her some hard punches, but she provoked it."

"I don't even want to hear details. Enough is enough," Ginger said. Her hair, usually neat, was disheveled, and she looked older. "I'm going home early today. Why don't you leave about three this afternoon? There shouldn't be much going on, and the faculty can get into the office with their keys."

"Good!" Athena said. "I stayed until ten-thirty last night with Briggs' project."

"You'll get time and a half for working after hours. Also, the dean will send you a check."

"A check?"

"In appreciation for bringing Vicky down off the balcony. You can expect a large check, I think. He is generous, when he chooses to be."

So, finances were improving. She'd been worried about surviving through the next week.

"Here's a key to Ben Silver's office. You may use Ben's office anytime except when he has posted office hours. He cleared off the small table near the window for you. In case you're curious about faculty matters, I'll just mention that all confidential papers are kept in my office," Ginger said.

"Thanks, Ginger," Athena said. It amused her that Ginger thought she'd go through his files. Of course, she had done similar things on other cases in the past.

ELEVEN

AFTER GINGER LEFT, Athena looked up Conway in the campus catalog: David V. Conway (1965), Professor of Genetics, Assistant Dean of Arts and Sciences. B.A., Stanford University. Ph.D., University of California, Berkeley. It looked like Conway had been on campus since 1965. Well established. Nothing to fear. Of course, there were people above him with more power than he had.

Only three faculty came in: Praeger and Mandy, Wolpert, and Springer. A pity that Briggs had shown up when she did, Athena thought. She might have prevented the catastrophe by removing the note herself.

A steady flow of students delivered midterm papers to MacRae's mailbox and left. Phone calls were few, and Athena was enjoying her last hours on the job.

When the office had grown very quiet, Athena tried to access Suzie's closed file "Excalibur." *C3* and *Code 3* did not work. A big let down. Another try: *Code Trois* and then *Coda Tres.* The last one took her through the magic portals. Athena realized immediately that she'd found some gold.

"Messages from Steve?" was the title at the top of the page. The question mark showed that Suzie was not the dupe Vicky thought she was. Athena wondered if she'd told Laszlo about these supposed messages. Suzie had listed the time and date for each one.

4/15 10:40 CODE 3. LOST/I FLOAT/NO TIME OR SPACE/

The next one was familiar.

4/17 3:10 CODE 3. ALONE/ALL ALONE HERE/VERY COLD/VERY STILL/

Others were new to her.

4/18 8:33 CODE 3. CHANGE OCCURS/TOO SOON TO TELL/
4/20 11:04 CODE 3. TELL!...TELL!...TELL!...TELL!
4/22 4:11 CODE 3. CAN'T RECALL/REQUEST REPLY/ WAITING/
4/23 11:00 CODE 3. LOSING TOUCH/CAN'T GO ON/
4/25 9:22 CODE 3. WHIRS AND STIRRINGS/NO LONGER ALONE/
4/26 5:35 CODE 3. I AM HOME/NO WORDS DESCRIBE/
4/27 3:51 CODE 3. FINAL CONTACT/WORDS = [0]/
4/28 10:14 CODE 3. MISSION COMPLETE/SIGN OFF/ CODE 3

The last entry was the date of Suzie's accident. Had Suzie discovered who was sending the messages? Strangely, another batch of messages followed, also attributed to Steve, but in an entirely different tone.

4/20 5:50 It Wasn't Right to Spoil My Future Bright.
4/21 5:01 I Grew Too Wise, You Organized My Demise.
4/23 4:38 In Time, You Too Will Suffer for the Crime.
4/24 5:34 Justice! I Worked for You, You Worked Against Me.
4/25 4:55 Some Don't Forget. They Squeeze You to Death.
4/27 5:13 No Way to Repay for Life Stolen Away.
4/28 4:20 I Fell Too Soon to Leave My Mark. Guilt Will Burn You.

Intent on the printouts, Athena heard someone clear his throat loudly right behind her and turned the page facedown. Josh stood there, grinning and looking self-conscious. He had his hands behind his back.

"Didn't mean to scare you. Got somethin' for you," he said.

He stood still for a minute to prolong the suspense. Athena was shocked by his appearance. He'd deteriorated noticeably since only the day before. Skin hung from his face, and his eyes were rimmed with red.

"Didn't wrap it or anythin' fancy," he said, "but I want to give you somethin' special."

He held out a small, carved statue of a deer, made of redwood or coated with reddish varnish. Delicate and detailed, the deer looked sideways with a startled expression. It was the way an animal looked when caught by headlights in the middle of the road late at night.

"I like it very much, Josh," Athena said, taking it in her hand.

"It reminds me of you." Josh propped himself against the door frame, as if he needed it to stay on his feet.

Though the deer image wasn't one she wanted to project, Athena had to admit he'd seen her at her worst. "Did you carve it yourself?"

"My son did it when he was in high school. He was exceptional in everythin' he did."

"This carving is well done. Are you sure you want to part with it?"

"I got others. This one seems to have your name on it. I got somethin' else right here." He held out a single piece of paper on which he had drawn a series of pictures.

Athena took it from him. She recognized herself by the dimpled chin and dark eyes. In the picture sequence, a spindly-legged Athena grabbed the computer console off the desk, carried it through the open door, and after balancing the machine briefly on a wrought-iron balcony, threw it forcefully over the edge. Amazingly light, CUSS arced through the air before hitting the pavement and bouncing high, its empty screen an open mouth. Then, glass shattered and the case split open. Computer keys scattered over a wide radius. Fountains of microchips fanned out on the pavement to glitter like sequins in the sun, leaving the computer an empty shell. The pictures were far better than an amateur effort.

Athena fought memories of her recent experience on the balcony and smiled. ''You helped me beat the computer for sure. I can't thank you enough, Josh. You amaze me.''

Josh smiled faintly but looked deathly ill. Sweat stood out on his forehead, though it wasn't hot.

''These are special things.''

'''Cuz you're a deer and a dear—both ways.'' He turned and blundered out as if he had trouble guiding his movements.

She was both touched and bothered by Josh's show of friendship. He was casting her in a role that wasn't right, yet she hated to hurt his feelings.

Athena put ''Messages from Steve?'' in the file folder marked ''Laszlo.'' She'd take it with her for weekend study. Retrieving her mini-recorder and bug from the side of the desk, she felt content that she'd gathered plenty of information to digest.

On her way out of the building, Athena took the route past the computer lab. Russ' German shepherd lay in the hall by the open door. Pausing to look in, she confirmed that Russ was the only one using a computer at the time. Using just two fingers, he was inputting information at top speed.

TWELVE

"WELCOME! WELCOME!" Magda said, her eyes bright. "Come in."

Magda looked striking in a long dress with abstract designs in orange, light olive, dark olive, and gold. Golden combs in her gray hair, two gold necklaces, several bracelets, many small gold rings, and an ornate ring with a large ruby completed her attire. She smelled like cinnamon and cloves.

Athena noted the pallor of her skin and the deep shadows under her eyes. "Are you well?" she asked.

Magda looked at her keenly for a few seconds before she laughed. "I never get sick in my life."

Athena recalled a serious illness mentioned by Magda at the picnic. She evidently changed stories to suit the occasion.

"Laszlo not back. We wait. I'm glad you come to my farewell party."

"Your farewell party?"

"You understand. I already explain."

"You have many years ahead."

Magda shrugged. "Please have seat. I get wine for us. Look around. Your eyes will like."

Athena knew right away that Magda was responsible for the fascinating decor. The furniture and fixtures warmed the white walls and cathedral ceiling of the vast room. Cane-backed chairs and a sofa sported plush red-orange cushions. Tall lamps, topped with emerald green shades of stained glass, stood on brass bases. The pattern in the carpet of green leaves, red-orange berries, and yellow birds tied it into the color scheme. Gaudy to some, Athena preferred to call it "bold" or "exciting." Colors and patterns were energizing.

Two oversized wall hangings depicted an Egyptian king in profile, wearing an elaborate, extended collar, short white skirt, and sandals and an Egyptian woman with upswept hair and a white tunic holding a seven-stringed instrument. The resemblance between ancient figures and modern ones was unmistakable. The woman musician was Magda, the king Laszlo.

Magda returned with glasses of wine. "You see? I create atmosphere."

"It's lovely. You are talented."

"You work for psych department. How you like?"

"I was there a few days. I'm glad to say I'm finished."

Magda sipped her wine with gusto. "Psych professors." She made a noise of disgust. "Awful people, I think."

"I worked on the computer mostly, but some profs were difficult."

"Russ and Dan do computer. Steve was expert. I don't use computer. Try to learn but impossible for me."

Not knowing how to use a computer was like not knowing how to drive a car, both essential for the contemporary world, Athena thought.

"I don't drive car." Magda fixed her eyes knowingly on Athena.

"Like cars, computers can be fun once you get used to them. They make life much easier."

"No luck. I'm out of my time. I need you to help us."

"Perhaps I can. Perhaps I can't." Athena wasn't sure what Magda wanted. "Suzie called me in to help someone. I want to find out who injured Suzie."

"Suzie wanted to know all about my country."

"Suzie knows many languages, but she found Hungarian difficult."

"Such interest she has. We have fun together. She like daughter. Very psychic. You can be daughter too. I teach you psychic things."

"I'm concerned about what's going on right now in the department."

Magda looked at her cagily. "You help us, we help Suzie. Laszlo like you, Tina. You look like his sister Katya. She die when she try to leave Hungary. Laszlo make escape alone. A young boy alone. Sometime he dream at night, and I hear him call, 'Cotty! Cotty!' He wake up so upset. He dream he run through empty building—no furniture, nothing—and he can't find her anywhere."

A family connection. Athena realized that it worked both ways. She recalled an old photograph of her Greek grandmother Athena and other relatives, one a man who looked like a younger version of Laszlo. Her relative would have been much shorter, and he was a fisherman. He and Laszlo had features in common—the cleft chin, the dark coloration, the shape of the face. Though Ted had a stockier build and lighter hair, he could be Laszlo's brother.

"Laszlo talk about Tina, Tina, Tina." Magda sounded bitter.

"I went to his class. You heard what happened."

"You knew where bomb hid," Magda said, a knowing look in her eyes.

"A guess. I'm training with a private investigator, so I'm more observant than an amateur."

Magda leaned so close that Athena had to fight the impulse to move away. "Laszlo's in danger. He need someone to guard him. Can you? I pay. Laszlo's safety most important."

"His grad students are very concerned. They're trying to protect him."

"Something happen any day now. I feel it."

The front door opened and Laszlo entered with a large bouquet of assorted cut flowers in his hand. His thick hair, black with only a few gray streaks, black eyes, and strongly delineated face made him look like a flamenco dancer, Athena thought.

He smiled. "I'm lucky to dine with two charming ladies."

Magda gave him a kiss on the cheek and took the flowers. She disappeared into the kitchen. Laszlo continued on down a hallway. Returning with first a bright yellow vase to place in the center of the table then several platters of food, Magda called, "*Le dîner est servi. Bon appétit!*"

Laszlo reappeared to fill Athena's glass. "A week ago, Suzie was here with us. I told her Budapest is the most beautiful city on the Danube. At the beginning of the century, when my grandfather and grandmother, the Count and Countess Honvagy were first married, Budapest was a center of social activity. They went dancing, to the opera, and to the theater regularly. Huge parties at the Honvagy estate lasted all weekend. I told Suzie to see Budapest, not as it is now, but to imagine the former glory before it lost the sparkle. Cafés were full of artists and intellectuals. Everywhere one found music and laughter."

Magda set another dish on the table. "You know nothing about the real Budapest," she mocked. "You dream a city. Pulse of Budapest is in gypsy music. You hear my father play violin, you never forget. Music of the soul—storm and sweet. First, it moans that we suffer and die, then skips along to celebrate life."

"You see how Magda keeps me in touch with my homeland," Laszlo said with amusement.

"I'm your paprika, yes?" Magda said. Raising her eyebrows provocatively, she stood behind him, arms loosely around his neck. Such a small person, less than five feet tall, but powerful nonetheless, Athena mused.

"*Igen, drágám,*" Laszlo said, hugging her back. "You add spice and color to my life."

Athena recognized *drága* (darling or dear), which Suzie had used in recent letters. Suzie seemed to be with them.

"Suzie ready for lessons soon." Magda wiped her hands on her apron.

Based on repeated accuracy, Athena did not doubt that Magda read her thoughts. She found the pork cutlets in thick sauce a bit rich for her taste and concentrated on the salad. The talk flowed, as did the wine, and she was enjoying herself.

"How did you get interested in parapsychology?" Athena asked.

"I hoped to legitimize the study of intuitive and spiritual phenomena. Materialistic Americans deprive themselves of wholeness. They give lip service to freedom but are terrified of going beyond concrete and obvious sensory data to discover full consciousness. I don't mean drugs. Drugs provide a shortcut to altered states of consciousness but are unnecessary and can be dangerous. We all have psychic powers to be recognized, explored, and strengthened. Only a few individuals are extremely psychic. Someday, doubters will see the value of right-brain activities and realize that not all results can be measured by the familiar yardstick.

"One day soon, a man or woman with the genius of Freud, the training of a scientist, and the vision of Michelangelo will change our models of mental activity to include psi function. I thought I was the one."

"How did you find out about parapsychology?"

"My brother, sister, and I lived with nannies, governesses, and tutors on my grandfather's estate. I was four years old when my mother and father died in a railway accident while on vacation in Switzerland. I was eight years old when my grandmother led my sister and me into hiding in a small peasant community, hours before my grandfather and older brother were arrested and executed in Budapest during the final Communist takeover of Hungary. Grandmother said my father had visited her in a dream the night before with precise instructions on how to protect his children. I was the only male to survive.

"My grandmother spoke of psychic experiences as everyday occurrences. She described regular visits from my grandfather, including how he looked, how he acted, and what he said. At every meal, she set a place for him at our small table. She talked to him in my presence, and I thought I saw him with a full beard and mustache, sometimes in military dress from his younger days and sometimes in his dark red dressing gown. I believed that my father and grandfather were with us in some form and that as I grew older and wiser, I would have access to that adjoining world."

Laszlo's story sounded rehearsed but genuine. It reassured Athena to know why he followed his line of inquiry. "Did you question people who claimed to be psychic?"

"I believed them. My sister, six years my senior, described her dreams and insights about people around us. I musn't leave out Abba, our faithful nanny, and Marthe, the peasant woman with whom we were in hiding for two years. Both women told folk tales, full of supernatural elements. These were the origins of my interest in parapsychology: the psychic lives of my grandmother and sister and the traditions of my country. Prior to Communist rule, Hungary remained preindustrial and semifeudal, so we were not indoctrinated with the scientific method. As a result, I feel certain that other types of knowledge and ways of knowing are valid. Psychic investigators Nandor Fodor and Sandor Ferenczi were also Hungarian."

"Are you psychic?" Athena asked.

"No, I regret to say. What I have is the necessary detachment to scientifically investigate psychic phenomena."

Magda had heard Laszlo's story many times before and did not appear to be listening. The phone rang, and she left to answer it. Her voice rose rich and low in a rapid flow of Hungarian words.

"Now we can talk together." Laszlo took a long-stemmed daisy from the vase of fresh flowers on the table and handed it to Athena. "I thought when I saw you that my sister had come to visit me. You look like her."

"And you look like a distant relative of mine, who appeared in an old family photograph. I don't even know his name. Most men in my mother's family were fishermen."

"So, we each have doubles. Tell me more."

"Amazing as it is, I think we should discuss the present danger in the department. As a matter of fact, I came to Aston at Suzie's request. I believe she was gathering evidence for you," Athena said.

"Yes, we were devastated by the news of her accident. Magda and I visited her at the hospital Thursday night."

"I went by briefly this afternoon. She has not changed."

"Magda says she'll soon recover," Laszlo said with confidence.

"I hope she's right."

"I have examples of harassment that you should see," Laszlo said. "Come into my study."

The sober atmosphere of Laszlo's study indicated that Magda had no power there. Along one wall, built-in bookcases full of volumes rose from floor to ceiling. On a massive cherry-wood desk with a mirrorlike polished surface stood an antique bronze paperweight of a mermaid and a calendar for scheduling activities. Athena could imagine pens and pencils lined up perfectly inside the drawers and papers filed away neatly. In personal matters, Laszlo was a perfectionist.

He took a folder out of his top desk drawer and opened it. "These came directly to my home address about a week apart. Have a look. I'll also set up a tape for you to hear."

Athena took the manila folder from him and looked at the first page.

(Hector's thoughts prior to Achilles's attack)
Why debate, my friend? Why thrash things out?
I must implore him. He'll show no mercy,
no respect for me, my rights—he'll cut me down.

The passage from Homer's *Iliad* thrilled Athena. She'd studied the ancient Greek masterpiece in a university class. Considering Greek classics to be part of her heritage, she'd paid special interest to the plays and epics.

On the next page, she read:

—and Achilles went for him, fast, sure of his speed
as the wild mountain hawk, the quickest thing on
wings, launching smoothly, swooping down on a cringing dove,
and the dove flits out from under, the hawk screaming
over the quarry, plunging over and over, his fury
driving him down to beak and tear his kill—
so Achilles flew at him, breakneck on in fury
with Hector fleeing along the walls of Troy...

It was certainly a stunning description of male fury and desire for triumph. A powerful threat.

"You know the story?" Laszlo asked.

"Very well," Athena said. "Hector is overcome by fear as he waits for Achilles outside the walls of Troy. The goddess

Athena...Athena does not help Hector in his hour of need.'' Athena did not want to include the fact that the goddess contributed to his defeat. ''Achilles kills Hector and defiles his body for days until the gods protest.''

''A terrible vengeance.''

''Do you have any idea who sent these pages?''

''I'm afraid Derring thinks he's Achilles, and I'm Hector. Derring minored in classics at Princeton. Everything points to him, but without proof of origin we're back to zero.''

''We'll get proof,'' Athena said. ''You can count on me.''

Laszlo looked pleased. ''Listen. These came on the phone, and I recorded them.''

He activated the recorder and watched her. There was a click, a whirring sound, and laughter followed.

It started as high, silly laughter, but definitely male, and sounded suspiciously like Harold Springer, Athena thought. She looked up at Laszlo and saw his distress. He hit the desktop with the palm of his hand.

''We'll have the last laugh,'' Laszlo said.

After a pause on the tape came more laughter—a whole group laughing in concert. It didn't last long, because he'd obviously hung up. The final segment was a deep, resounding laugh—a basso profundo. Strange, how the laughter constantly changed. Whereas most people laughed in short bursts, this laughter went on and on. The tone became sinister, almost a snarl, before Laszlo hung up.

''They attack from every possible angle,'' Laszlo said. ''It's intolerable.''

''They're so careless that it's easy to document them,'' Athena said.

''Do whatever you can.'' Laszlo stared at her intently as if trying to read her mind. ''There's more to this dispute than the existence or nonexistence of special mental powers. I'm defending the existence of the human soul against twentieth-century barbarians disguised as scientists. They are culturally and intellectually bankrupt.''

Distanced now, his eyes glinted with frustration and disgust. He needed an affirmation.

Athena took a deep breath and thanked her university days for the words to answer at an appropriate level. "Without souls we're doomed to dust. It seems to me that different belief systems should be able to coexist without one side trying to destroy the other. Using words to cut like swords or real weapons to injure others renders any cause unjust."

Laszlo was looking at her again with interest. He opened his mouth.

Magda spoke up from the doorway. "Laszlo's ancestor Miklos was famous swordsman. He keep family tradition."

"I'm defending everything I've worked for. The Research Institute means everything to me."

"I tell him—return to Europe now." Magda's tone of voice was deep and spectral. "In England, they welcome his research. He refuse to do sensible thing."

"I chose California. I've created a unique research facility. I can't take it with me."

"Too late then." Magda turned her back. "Soon nothing left."

"Not while I'm alive."

"Don't listen. Wait and see." Magda disappeared from the doorway.

"I want to help," Athena said.

"You've seen the posters they put all over campus?" Laszlo asked.

Athena nodded. "Have you seen what Suzie found in her computer?"

"Suzie said she had something."

"I have it in my car. It's a collection of computer messages."

"Interesting!"

Athena went outside to retrieve the folder. As she came back in the front door, Magda took her arm. "Come. I show you my room."

Athena handed Laszlo the file and said with emphasis, "Don't trust what you see. Suzie questioned the source and so do I."

Magda's room, predominantly ruby red, contained stacks of

magazines on the floor, yards of folded material piled indifferently on a table with a sewing machine, a small television set, a red couch, and a small table with two chairs.

"A friend gave to me," Magda said, indicating a large print on the wall. Done in bands of red and navy blue, the print depicted a stylized queen of hearts joined at the waist with her upside-down image as on a card face. Round breasts were ringed with undulating bands of color. The overall impression of passion was appropriate for the queen of hearts, and for Magda.

"I tell your fortune," Magda said. She sat down behind a round table and shuffled the cards that waited there.

Without enthusiasm Athena took the seat across from her.

"Cut, please."

Athena cut the deck twice and waited. Technique interested her more than the result.

"Tina, I am sister soul. Trust me."

Rings sparkling, Magda laid the cards out gracefully and studied the pattern. They were splendid antique cards with lush pictures of brightly clad figures and symbols with special meaning. A gypsy tarot deck.

"No good." Magda took a rasping breath. "Danger for you."

Athena watched with detachment.

"One is not as he seems," Magda said decisively. "He trick you. He take you away and keep you. Watch out for Magician."

"Who's the Magician, Magda?" Athena thought of Russ, whom she needed to investigate and would like to know better.

"Cards give only indications. I fear for you."

"I'm not afraid."

"You do not trust cards. You do not trust me." Magda swept the cards aside and glared at her. "I tell truth. No one listen."

Magda stood up.

"I show the mirror of my soul." She walked to the wall and removed the red velvet cloth draped over a mirror so old it had lost most of its silver backing, impairing its reflective power. Magda stood before it as if entranced.

"Here I see my aura for first time. Now is gone. I send night summons for help. I thought you come to my call."

"Suzie asked for my help. I came because I was worried about her."

"My time soon finish. I know this."

"Fight it, Magda. Why not refuse?" Athena was exasperated by her passivity, if in fact she had real information.

"Gypsies say each person born with number of days in one hand," Magda said, still gazing at her murky reflection. "Each die in her way, in her time. No one says is too soon, only say time has come. That's fate."

The Greek work was *Moira,* and Greeks mentioned it too. Athena had always rebelled. "I don't accept it. You can stop it from happening."

Magda stepped away from the mirror. "I'm tired now. We talk and have lunch on Monday. Come to institute in morning, yes?"

"That's fine." Athena was ready to leave the room, which had started to oppress her with its ringing brightness.

Magda waved slightly with one hand. She looked old and depleted.

"Thank you for telling my fortune," Athena said and gave Magda a hug. Amazed at the surge of energy, like an electrical current, through Magda's body, she pulled away. Magda's strength was puzzling.

"Stay away from Magician! Listen to advice," Magda said, eyes darting back to the mirror as if she couldn't resist it.

Athena found Laszlo still at the table, gazing at Steve's messages. He resembled the Egyptian king in the wall hanging, a king in danger of losing his kingdom, Athena thought.

"If these were real, they'd be priceless," Laszlo said. "The first set corresponds closely to information I want to receive from someone who passed over. If possible, I'd like to know who did this."

"Any idea who might mimic the process?"

"Anyone connected with the institute—even enemies know enough."

"Vicky put the C3's into the system," Athena said.

"Then anyone could do it. The second group of messages is menacing, a different sender, wouldn't you say?"

"Definitely. I'll get more information on these for you."

"Counterfeit messages to lay a trap—unworthy of Steve," Laszlo said. "Steve was one of those rare minds one sees only a few times during a generation. We will mourn his loss for the rest of our days."

Athena had to risk it. "Vicky thinks you engineered Steve's death."

"Vicky is a despicable creature. That's the worst from her yet. Never! Never! Never would I condone the death of a student." Laszlo hit the palm of his hand on the tabletop, making the dishes dance. "I treasure them. Students are the minds of the future. Steve was like a gifted son. I was strongly opposed to the formation of the after-death club. Robert suggested it, based on a conjecture of mine. I told him not to but didn't actively prevent it. The interest was there. I will regret it forever."

Athena planned to question Robert, the gangly student with petitions.

"Vicky no longer works in the department. Ginger decided today."

"Reason to rejoice, but it hardly dulls the brunt of the storm. Now I think we should clear the table," Laszlo said with a faint smile.

He stacked the nearest dishes into a pile before carrying them to the kitchen sink. Athena did the same.

"I'll wash. You dry," Laszlo said as he rolled up the sleeves of his cream-colored shirt, still immaculate at the end of the day. "Magda loves to cook but she will not clean up afterward. This is how I pay for my supper."

Athena caught the dish towel he tossed her way. "You don't mind?"

"Why should I? Everything worthwhile has a price, you know. If I don't pay what's due, my debt will grow and create an imbalance. Then I'll lose what I care about. If you don't cultivate your garden, the flowers languish and die."

They worked, side by side, for a few minutes.

"Will you come to my class on Tuesday? I think you might enjoy it."

“I love to learn new things. My experience in the psych department at Westcott has been enlightening.”

“Ready to open a new vein and allow yourself psychic experiences?”

“I'd rather watch someone else and find a logical explanation.”

“Magda told me you drive her crazy,” Laszlo said, and they laughed.

Athena was impressed by how carefully he handled each dish and glass and how thoroughly he scrubbed them. In many ways, Laszlo was remarkable, especially for a man of his generation.

THIRTEEN

THE RECORDED FACULTY chatter from the main office was playing on the tape deck, and Athena was taking notes. Some exchanges she'd heard before; a few were new.

"The best strategy is to make sure the debate doesn't take place," Derring said. "Laszlo will gain an advantage. We all know how he projects to an audience and oozes charisma."

"The debate's ready to roll—scheduled and publicized," a male voice said.

"Why not up the ante?" Derring said in a spooky voice. "If the handicap becomes too great—if Laszlo's vanity is likely to suffer—he'll cancel. I've thought of some strategies to accomplish that purpose."

He moved out of range, so whatever his plans were, they were lost to her—details she needed to know.

Athena listened twice to Derring's words in another conversation with several people.

"How can we be most effective? We've got to attack the core of Laszlo's program," Derring said. "It's obvious his heart's in his Research Institute. D.C. and I have discussed ways to clean out the psychic mud in our department. D.C. thinks it can be done. The Big H is cheering for us too, but he's always saying 'Cover your tracks. Cover your tracks.' With him on our side, it's a piece of cake. Imagine our brave new world. Lahlah no longer siphons off students. No more embarrassing tie to nonsense psychology. Excellent prospects of being taken seriously as the state-of-the-art center for behavioral and physiological research. A few more superstar colleagues and major research grants, and we're on our way."

"Laszlo is protected by tenure," said a woman.

"Our effort to dethrone the prince might not come to term, but it's a gesture Laszlo can't ignore. He's barely hanging on," Derring said. "Why doesn't the guy just go for greener pastures? Suckers somewhere would pay for his brand of educated ignorance."

Athena was sick of the sound of Derring's voice. Derring wasn't super smart, because he couldn't keep his mouth shut. He stood out like a lighthouse on a flat shoreline. Nothing new there. Derring, the instigator, but did others carry out the dirty work? She'd find out who they were—grad students? Faculty swinging with departmental politics to save their jobs?

For a change of pace, Athena examined the photos she'd taken the morning she found Suzie. Spreading them on the table, she could plainly see that only top drawers and shelves had spilled their contents. Lower ones were undisturbed. To read them more thoroughly required a memory of what Suzie's place was like before the storm. Peggy had said she'd help.

Athena laughed out loud when she looked again at Josh's cartoon sequence of herself throwing CUSS off a balcony. A great victory! At least she wouldn't be using the computer regularly, though she'd agreed to uncover the inner workings of the messenger service.

"Stop making promises," Athena said to herself.

The balcony reminded her of Vicky. Vicky and her fake engagement ring. Vicky must have known Steve wanted to separate, not bind. Could she have cut the brake line, then shifted the blame because she couldn't cope with the aftermath? Reyna Briggs and the plagiarized paper. Briggs had a lot to lose. Suppose Suzie had discovered the real reason for Steve's death. Who'd silence her? Was Suzie supposed to die? The wound was too serious to assume otherwise.

In the afternoon, Athena went shopping. She walked to the downtown area and roamed through several used bookstores and clothing boutiques before going to the grocery store. Yearning for Greek food, she bought feta cheese, stuffed grape leaves, and baklava. In search of cucumbers and tomatoes, she saw a group of people surrounding a woman with a baby. Without hesitating, she went up to greet Marcia Praeger and Mandy. Mandy was precious—cute, shy, and loving. With her arms around Praeger's neck, she hid her face shyly from the curious crowd. Hard not to be touched by the chimp baby. How could a caretaker not be emotionally hooked? Eventually, Praeger would send Mandy back to a primate cage and the deprived life of a research subject. A sad fate after tender, loving care.

Athena was overdue on jogging. She threw on a pair of green shorts, a T-shirt, and laced her shoes up tight. Circling the campus, she parked near an access to the river path. Other joggers and cyclists were out, but not in great numbers.

The river world was magic—temperature midway between hot and cold, glints and shadows on the water surface, a stately procession of tall trees that stretched as far as the eye could see, periodic bridges spanned the water.

Rats scurried near the water's edge. The hour of the rat, she thought. Athena wasn't fond of rats, but she decided to count those she spotted as she skirted the river. She'd reached seven when a cordial voice said, "Good evening!"

She turned her head and saw Laszlo. He looked splendid with long, muscular legs that were usually hidden by designer pants.

"I love to run. It was my sport in my Oxford days when I discovered I had strength, speed, and durability. I won some important races."

Athena smiled. She found it difficult to talk and run, but he didn't.

"How far do you go?" Athena asked with effort. She could feel the sweat running down her face.

Laszlo looked cool and calm. She could tell he was shortening his stride to hers.

"I run three miles out to the last footbridge over the river and then I turn back. See you later."

He moved off then, leaving her behind. Athena watched his figure receding. She'd never guess that the man in the elegant suit lecturing before his class had once been a champion athlete. Though she'd promised herself to build up more, she usually settled for two miles at a stint. It kept her feeling fit without demanding time or energy she'd rather use in other ways.

SUNDAY MORNING, Athena was savoring the taste of the freshly steeped Earl Grey tea and the not-too-sweet taste of scones with apricot chunks. Peggy had been describing how she and Suzie's aunt Beth had shared seeds, slips, and gardening tips over the years.

Peggy was the liveliest senior Athena'd ever met. She hoped she'd have as much vitality when she reached the mid-seventies range.

Peggy cleared the table of cups, plates, and crumbs.

"Before we tackle the mess next door, please take a look at these pictures. Tell me if anything stands out—something that isn't Suzie's."

Peggy wiped her hands and took the photos eagerly. Her keen blue eyes raked over each. "What a jumble! I'm glad Suzie won't see it this way."

She thumbed back through and tossed a photo on the table.

"This one's odd. I've never known Suzie to leave detergent there. Her washer and dryer are hooked up on the back porch."

Athena studied the extra-large family-size orange box, teetering on the edge of the refrigerator top—obvious if you knew the resident's habits.

"Shall we check?" Athena asked.

"Let's do."

Peggy was already walking out the door. Grabbing her resource kit, Athena followed. Peggy unlocked Suzie's door with her spare key.

"My God!" she said on viewing the living room firsthand.

Athena noticed that the police had shifted some material around. Her eyes refused to turn to the spot where she'd found Suzie. She headed for the kitchen, pulled on surgical gloves, and reached for the large box. Peggy hovered at Athena's elbow with an avid look on her face. For her sake, Athena hoped the box was important. It would definitely make Peggy's day.

The box was too heavy and awkward to contain soap powder. She placed the box on the floor so the two of them could look inside, where a hammer rested, up-ended, with something crusted on its head.

"Good for you, Peggy! Here's one of the missing keys to the crime."

Athena lifted the hammer to make sure it was dried blood. It was. A major clue.

Peggy beamed, obviously thrilled. "I'd like to do more. Guess I'll get to work on the mess."

"Don't do too much until I join you." Athena put in a call to the police, and, to her surprise, Nancy Coles came on-line.

"Do you always work Sundays?" Athena asked.

"Once a month. You found the assault weapon? I'm on my way."

Under Athena's eye, Peggy stacked like items in piles on the floor—sheet music, envelopes, papers, books, maps, travel brochures.

When Coles did come, she couldn't stay and chat.

"Good job finding this," Coles said as she popped the giant box into a white plastic bag. "We missed it."

"I did too until Peggy noticed it. Hope you find prints all over," Athena said. "Did you get the invitation for next Friday night?"

"Sure did. I'll try to come but can't guarantee it," Coles said as her radio spat out static and then launched into a description of the location of an overnight burglary. "I'm off. Thanks again. Call me next time you make a find."

A little while later, Tigger and Spook thumped their way through their entry to watch the cleanup. Tigger followed Athena around with loud meows.

"What does he want?" she asked Peggy.

"He likes to have his head scratched."

"Anything to stop the noise."

The cat turned its head this way and that as Athena raked her fingernails through the area between and around the ears. Tigger was not a youngster and sported proofs of battle throughout his mangy fur that thinned to nothing in some spots.

"Old warrior," Athena said, and he purred in contentment, a deep rumble, then turned his head again.

When he finally stalked away, she got back to the work at hand, so glad that Peggy knew where everything went and where the vacuum cleaner was stored. By the time they left, Suzie's place had regained its former air of charm and comfort.

"Finished!" Athena said to Peggy. "I couldn't have done it without you."

"Now it's ready for Suzie to come home," Peggy said, her blue eyes troubled.

"Why don't we clean up and go visit Suzie?" Athena suggested. "I planned to go today."

Peggy perked up. "I'll get some flowers ready. Suzie loves fresh flowers."

In Athena's car, Peggy explained that she didn't drive anymore because her peripheral vision was deteriorating.

"Have you visited Suzie yet?"

"I kept saying I'd go, but didn't," Peggy said. "No bus to the hospital."

"You should have told me."

"I visited Beth every day after her cancer surgery," Peggy said. "They thought they'd got it all. I don't like hospitals or doctors. I want to stay healthy as long as I can. Then, when it's over, it's over."

"I understand," Athena said as they pulled into the parking lot.

With two large vases of choice flowers from Peggy's and Suzie's gardens in her hands, Athena led the way to Suzie's room.

The blonde woman was no longer there, but a woman with white hair occupied the other bed. Like Suzie, she was hooked up to tubes and cords and in a very deep sleep.

Peggy took a deep breath and seemed to say a prayer. Then she moved a small vase of flowers off the bedside table to make room for the giant ones Athena was carrying.

"I always talk to Suzie as if she can hear me," Athena said as she sat down in one of the chairs beside the bed. She expected Peggy to join her but she didn't. "Peggy is with me, Suzie. We cleaned up your house. It looks great now. It's ready for you to come home. Come back soon, Suzie."

Peggy was staring out the small window as if her life depended on it. Her neck and back looked rigid.

"You're going to have tea with us someday soon, Suzie," Athena said. "It's a date. We're counting on it."

In deference to Peggy's stress, Athena cut the visit short.

"I can't stand to see Suzie like that," Peggy said as they drove away.

Athena noticed no change since her Friday visit. A depressing sight.

"The woman in the other bed was Doreen Vincent," Peggy said. "We were best friends in grade school. She's exactly my age. In junior high, we drifted apart. She was with the popular crowd. Old friends are going fast these days. I'm not ready yet. Not by a long shot."

"Wouldn't you hate to know in advance?" Athena was thinking of Magda.

"Damned right, as my husband used to say. I watched my husband and Suzie's aunt Beth fade away. Now, I take it a day at a time and enjoy it to the max. It's the best way to live."

AT DUSK, Athena was hanging around the corner, hoping she'd see Russ out on his evening walk. Eventually, she did; he and his dog turned in the other direction. She stayed almost two blocks behind, knowing that she could lose him at any time. Outside some houses, he would stop and look in the lighted window. When she was able to reach the approximate point, she could see that there were people inside doing things—a family having dinner, a couple having an argument, some friends chatting around the table, a quartet of seniors playing cards. Russ was watching people together. He was not interested in lighted windows to empty rooms or houses where no one was home. The stops he made were all related to people. Had he seen Suzie through the window that night by herself?

Athena decided it was time to intercept him. She quickened her steps until she was only a block behind him, then half a block. Suddenly, Russ and his dog crossed the street and disappeared. Athena could see no trace of him when she reached that point.

She did find the cut-through, a sidewalk that went through to another street midblock. Too late to join him casually as if she just happened to be out and just happened to be going the same way. Russ was gone.

Frustrating man! Distance-keeping was his specialty. What did he have to hide?

"I SURVIVED THREE DAYS of clerical," Athena reported to Ted on the phone. She could tell he was miffed that she hadn't called more often. "I met students and overheard the young profs talking. They're conspiring like crazy against Professor Honvagy. I saved a woman in the office from throwing herself off an upper balcony. You know how I love heights. She's the dean's daughter and on the border where sanity's concerned. The office computer was coughing up messages from the dead man, Steve Linstrom, though someone obviously put them there for Suzie to discover."

"Haven't you been busy? Any hard evidence?" Ted asked.

"Peggy helped me locate the hammer used to hit Suzie on the head."

"Well, that's progress," Ted conceded. "But don't forget to come back."

"I'm trying to do four major things: Find out who hit Suzie, who killed Steve, protect Laszlo from threats and injuries, and save Magda from the grim reaper she expects any day now."

"It's your case, but you need to draw the line. Overcommitted leads to incompetent—a huge drop in effectiveness."

"I've never been around so many people predicting catastrophes. It's like having a storm, an earthquake, and a flood occur simultaneously."

"You don't have to be everywhere at the same time," Ted said. "What's the larger picture?"

"There's a running battle taking place between factions in the faculty. One gang is trying to push the other gang off their turf. Of course, instead of knives and guns, they use threats, tricks, and insults.

"And hammers," Ted added. "Don't get hurt."

"For eggheads, these guys fight dirty. They don't have any

respect for the other person's research and ideas. Some of them couldn't care less about students. I'm finally convinced that Laszlo is legit. He believes in what he preaches. They want to take away his power over students and send him off—anywhere but here."

"I can tell from your voice—you're having a good time," Ted said.

"I am," Athena admitted. She liked the challenge of the many-headed hydra she was trying to overcome. She was learning more psychology and a little about parapsychology. She'd met a number of people with interesting stories to tell, and some whose stories she hadn't heard yet—RUSS, which rhymed with CUSS. "You guessed it. I am."

"Well, I'm not, so fix it all up and hurry on back."

"I hear you," Athena said. "Kiss, kiss."

"Kiss, kiss," Ted said.

FOURTEEN

A NEW WEEK, a new phase on the Westcott campus, Athena thought. The purple and white Research Institute looked inviting in the midday sun.

"Magda's not back," Russ said. He was sitting in Magda's chair with his feet propped up on her desk, revealing holes in the bottoms of his sneakers. "I'm Russ, and my pal's Missy."

Missy poked her head around the corner of the desk to inspect Athena. Athena beckoned to her and patted the dog generously.

"You're Tina?"

"Athena."

"A name with a past. Magda told me to show you around. We even have a museum here. How about it?"

"Fine." Athena loved museums, and she was interested in what sort of tour guide Russ would be.

He dropped his feet to the floor, stood up, and rubbed his hands on the back of his jeans. "Right this way."

She liked the inside of the institute, which was as modern-looking, spacious, and well designed as the outside. There was a skylight over the front office with a lovely patch of azure sky visible. Shafts of sunlight also cut through the front windows.

"These pictures," Russ said, referring to radiant images on the walls in the front office, "were taken by the Kirlian method of photography."

Two of the enlarged, framed photographs were of leaves, shown in silhouette but edged with brilliant multihued rays of light emanating outward. In other pictures hands were featured, a large and a small one, each showing the contrast of dark outlines surrounded by blazes of light.

"What you see illustrated is the aura projected by living things," Russ said, as if talking to a class. "To get a picture like this requires a flat metal plate with an electrical attachment. The unexposed film is placed on top of the plate and the object to be photographed on top of the film. By passing high-voltage electricity at low amp through the plate, you get this kind of result. These pictures were made in Honvagy's lab in 1972. At that time, there was an attempt to correlate energy charges of living things with the corona discharge that surrounds them like a halo—the aura. Changes do occur, but the Kirlian method caused controversy. Skeptics doubt that auras reflect energy from the object and claim that uncontrolled electrical flashes like lightning are produced by the method."

Missy was looking up at Athena with questioning eyes, and Athena stooped over to pat her head and back. She responded immediately with a grateful look and a slight tail wag. Russ' eyes softened.

"Follow me and I'll show you our testing rooms. We perform a variety of experiments here, repeating old ones and trying out new methods in order to better test psi abilities."

Russ passed through a ray of sunlight and his auburn hair flamed with a golden halo for an instant. Athena found him attractive, muscles and all. She wished he were not so hostile and distant. He spoke like a recording.

A narrow bed with an elaborate panel of dials and gauges behind it and a printer extruding green paper occupied the first room.

"Our EEG machine to measure and record brain waves."

"Can you tell if someone is psychic?"

"Psychic brain patterns are often erratic or so I've heard."

Athena patted Missy again, as the dog hovered close with clear intentions of getting more.

The room next door revealed a rectangular table with a vertical partition in the middle and chairs at either end.

"We test psi here. Two people sit at either end of the table. As you see, there's a barrier to prevent direct communication. The sender tries to mentally transmit information to the subject. The subject then indicates what the sender transmitted. The old-fashioned method relies on Zener cards or regular playing cards."

From a drawer in a small cabinet, Russ extracted a stack of cards with circle, square, star, and triangle patterns.

"The sender sees a card, then sends information to the subject. The subject chooses from her deck a card identical to the one the sender saw. In other games, the subject predicts the order of cards to be drawn or of dice to be thrown. The experimenter does not take part in the process but observes and records what happens and then figures out the statistical significance."

Surprisingly, their methods adhered to scientific standards, Athena thought.

"Magda should be back soon, so I'll shorten the presentation. At the end of the hall is a soundproof room for the Ganzfeld technique, involving partial sensory deprivation. The subject relaxes in a comfortable chair while wearing eye coverings and describes out loud everything that comes to mind—thoughts, feelings, and images. At the same time, a person in a distant room tries to send messages to the subject."

In another small room, Russ pointed out several black boxes. "These are random number generators, which test the subject's psychokinetic ability—the influence a subject can exert to make lights move clockwise or counterclockwise. The experimenter correlates the actual movement to the subject's effort to control the pattern."

"What sort of results do you get?" Athena asked.

"There have been hundreds of papers published. Magda has binders with all articles by Laszlo or associates, if you'd care to look. In fact, we have the largest collection ever assembled of books and articles on psychic matters right here in the institute."

Russ opened a large door to a library room with twelve large shelves of books, six smaller ones with periodicals, and many drawers of microfilms and documents. At a light table an Asian man was viewing and selecting a few slides from a box holding hundreds and making notations on a pad. He looked up and nodded at them.

"Hi, Dan," Russ said before closing the door.

"This way to our museum of psychic artifacts." Russ opened

a side door to a long, narrow room with a display of paraphernalia from the past. He flipped on the light.

"Missy, sit. Stay." He pointed to a spot beside the door. "She might knock something over, so she stays out."

On a small round table by the entrance stood a statue of a head segmented into locations of different human characteristics. The area beneath the left eye was labelled LANGUAGE, a point above the nose was designated as INDIVIDUALITY, and above the left ear was an area tagged ACQUISITIVENESS. There were patches for: EXCITABILITY, SPIRITUALITY, and FRIENDSHIP. Wouldn't it be nice if human psychology were so simple that any problem could be remedied by massaging the proper area of the head? Athena thought.

Underneath the bust was inscribed "PHRENOLOGY, 1832-1932." Beside it was a table with a metal contraption, identified as the "LAVERY ELECTRIC AUTOMATIC PHRENOMETER (1907)."

"Phrenologists believed that the conformation of the skull, including bumps and roundness, indicated the character and mental capacity of the individual. The brain segments shown here were believed to control personality and ability. The machine was for charting bumps."

On the wall behind the statue, a drawing of a segmented face on which different characteristics were written bore the label "PHYSIOGNOMY—the art of judging character based on facial features."

"In some Asian countries, physiognomists still interpret a person's nature and recommend behavior consistent with the personality according to one's face—not so different from some psychologists," Russ said with a shrug. "Chinese physiognomists base their assessments on more than a hundred locations on the face—for example, down the center of the face or in the brow area. They interpret each sign by prescribed rules according to the shape, size, and features on the face. The area between your eyebrows holds the key to your ability to hold an important job or rise to social prominence."

The displays fascinated Athena. She looked into a glass case full of ivory dice and dominoes.

"Dominoes are used for fortune-telling in China, Korea, and India. The dominoes lie facedown on the table like cards. You shuffle them and draw three, which convey messages to interpret. You see the two sets of dots on each domino? The numbers indicate the message, for example 6/6 is the luckiest domino, associated with happiness, success and so forth, while blank/blank is the worst indication you could receive. Each number combination corresponds to certain types of events. For example, 6/1 indicates a wedding or a solution to your problems."

Athena laughed and moved on to a display of tarot cards. There were several identified types—Renaissance, the Golden Dawn, Mythic, and Thoth. In each set, pictures were beautifully and imaginatively done, depicting the major and minor arcana in a distinctive way. The images on the Mythic set reminded her of King Arthur's times while the Thoth collection was abstract and eerie.

"Carl Jung believed the major arcana of the tarot to be archetypes stored in the collective consciousness," Russ said after a silence during which he watched her examine the cards.

The card that particularly drew Athena's attention was the Renaissance "Priestess," which depicted a woman with a rose in one hand and a scroll in the other. That was the role she wanted most.

"The Priestess is the keeper of mysteries and hidden knowledge. Her wisdom is creative and intuitive. She can predict change, reveal secrets, and illuminate problems."

The description corresponded to Athena's hopes in her university days—to be all-knowing and wise, to have special knowledge that enabled her to help others—except that she wanted to use reason to achieve it.

Magda popped her head in the door. "Time for lunch," she called.

"You haven't seen it all. You should come back," Russ said.

Athena noticed a section on dreams and recalled that the French philospher Descartes, the creator of the scientific method, had written about the important role of dreams and intuition as a bridge to knowledge, linking the known and the unknown. She wanted to come back.

"You did a great job of explaining," Athena said.

"All Steve's, word for word. My memory takes it in and gives it back as I got it."

"What I'm curious about is why you chose psi research."

Russ suddenly met her eyes, and she felt burned by his glance.

"I'll tell you." His voice became less formal and distinctively New York. "The regular education system stinks. Students suck up standard stuff in the field of choice. Like soldiers, they march to old tunes and bark out expected answers on command. A bunch of clones. All molded by middle-class values. I'm outside and always will be. Parapsychology is an alternative. I like the psi stuff because it's not your regular stiff neck, nose-in-the-air kind of study. It's more risky, more tied in with questions about cosmic connections and different ways of doing things. I wouldn't want to sit all day and listen to richies complain about what's pinching them in the crotch or the ass, even if I could get rich that way."

Rather an earful. Magda was standing at Athena's elbow.

"It's time," Magda said, pulling her away. "We go now."

Walking across the quad to the Carousel restaurant with Magda at her side, Athena felt as if she'd known Magda a long time. Once again, a circle of protective energy seemed to surround and bind them. Magda pointed out a red-winged blackbird high in a pine tree as a symbol of a magic world.

Since outdoor tables were full of students and professors, they found one inside. The interior was arranged around an atrium, which was open to sunlight and contained a Japanese-style garden.

Once seated, Athena glanced at the menu and decided on a chef's salad. Only then did she realize that Magda was scowling at her.

"What's wrong, Magda?"

"Laszlo see you by river," Magda said.

"I went jogging there. I didn't expect to see him."

"Tomorrow night Laszlo go again. You be with him."

"I don't think I can run as fast or as far as he does."

"Too dangerous for him alone. You watch him."

"All right." It bothered Athena that Magda was still glaring at her.

"Laszlo call you 'miracle woman.' Laszlo is man who care for his research more than anything else. When he live in England, he marry for a few years. Two sons live there with his ex-wife. He never marry again."

Athena could not imagine why Magda was telling her intimate details. It wasn't Laszlo's private life, but his public life that concerned her.

"To be with Laszlo is like being mother to a child. He want me there for him always. Where we go...other women want him. They do anything. I never see a woman not crazy for Laszlo. I joke at first, but now joke is old. I tell you, other women always around. They call house. They send mail. They stop him in street."

"I have no personal interest in Laszlo. I'm here as a professional. I'll do what I can to protect him, but a trained bodyguard could do it better."

"There's more." Magda's eyes glinted with a purpose unclear to Athena. "In long life with many loves—some better than Laszlo—I go places, try different lifestyles. When I come to Aston, I think...this is death. If I stay, I die. But I stay. Stupid thing I do. Laszlo become my day and night. Now if another woman win Laszlo, it bother me."

Athena picked at her salad. "Why do you say this?"

"I know Laszlo. He must have woman...always. He talk of you, Tina. You make him think of Katya. He has regard for you."

Athena laughed. "There's nothing now, and there isn't going to be."

Magda held up her hand. Her rings winked ominiously. "I am jealous woman. I'm angry. I'm not angry. I need you to help us. It make me furious. When Laszlo come, I hear, 'Tina-Tina-Tina.'"

"I'm your friend first, Magda."

"We are friend-enemy. Is always this way with humans. Never trust anyone but yourself, Tina. In final hour, there is only self.

By old ways, I refuse to give up Laszlo. I poison him, and you too. I poison you too.''

Anger smoldered in Magda's eyes. Athena felt a chill. She glanced at her wineglass with sudden doubt, sensing the unspoken words.

''You have nothing to fear. I'm here to help both you and Laszlo. I'll be here a few more days, then I go home.''

''Against my will, I put Laszlo in your keeping. He need you after I go.''

''You'll rise from the ashes like the mythical phoenix. You're the one for him. You understand his native land and language and his field of study. I'll watch you too, because Laszlo needs you.''

''Danger. Beware of Magician. Tomorrow night come to our house at seven o'clock. You run with Laszlo. I pay you now.'' Magda pulled a check for five hundred dollars out of her purse. ''Save him.''

''If you want security, why don't you hire a bodyguard?'' Athena didn't feel comfortable taking the check, but Magda thrust it into her hand and closed her fingers over it.

''Laszlo say no.''

''Why are you so worried now?'' Athena asked.

''Every time he go by river, I am in fear. Every minute I pray he come back. I see river swallow him. I tell him. He laugh at me. The specialist in psychic things does not believe me. You are my hope.'' Magda was shaking.

Athena sat for what seemed like a long time with her eyes locked into Magda's. She felt the older woman's agony over Laszlo, the cold wind of death already blowing on her, the chill of danger to herself. She imagined for the first time the terrible burden of being psychic, knowing something would happen but not knowing enough to prevent it.

The special moment passed. Athena poked at her salad and realized she'd lost her appetite. She wished that Magda didn't complicate the picture with power games that drained so much energy.

''Come to institute,'' Magda said. ''You're with us now.''

''I have errands to do.'' Athena didn't intend to yield to Magda's control. ''I'll come tomorrow.''

PART TWO

FIFTEEN

ATHENA WOKE UP before her alarm went off. Only a week ago, she'd arrived in Aston to find Suzie unconscious. Only a week ago. And it would be terrible to leave before Suzie was back on her feet, though she wished to head back to Oregon on Sunday.

Her second thought was of the dream she'd had that night—not a nightmare but highly embarrassing. She laughed as the details came to mind.

She was on a narrow bed with Laszlo kissing her passionately. They were naked, their legs intertwined. She was hot and ready when she noticed his research assistants observing and making notes. She reached for a sheet to cover them but discovered that she was attached by electrodes to a machine registering her physiological reactions with swings of the needle.

"Don't worry, they're professionals," Laszlo said and continued his attack on her body. More like experimental research than lovemaking. No doubt Magda's suggestions had triggered that dream.

Kicking off the sheet and bedspread, Athena got up to take a shower.

THE MINUTE Athena walked through the door of the institute, Robert pounced on her. "Welcome! Welcome! my dear Athena. Why don't you take our test to measure your psychic aptitude?"

"Do I have a choice?"

"Many do it for fun. We have different sets of questions." He handed her a booklet. "You can see how simple it is."

Athena's eyes roamed down the page.

When I was a child, I enjoyed stories.	Yes.	No.
I still enjoy stories.	Yes.	No.

I identify with characters in stories. Yes. No.

"The first one just tests your imaginative ability," Robert said. "The second part is more to the point." He showed her where it started.

Do you believe in life after death? Yes. No.

"Why not?" Athena said. "I'll take both parts just for fun."

Athena sat at the far end of a table while Russ scored psychic questionnaires at the other end. He didn't look her way.

Athena took a moment to appreciate the dark purple carpet underfoot and the skylight above the room. Nice touches. Then she picked up a pencil and started in on "How Psychic Are You?"

I often have nightmares. Yes. No.

She thought of her recent one of Vietnam and the many she'd had as a teen. They didn't come "often" anymore, but when they did, they were powerful.

"Hi, Tina!" Magda called as she came out of an office and sat down at her desk by the front door.

Athena waved but kept marking answers.

I recall dreams clearly. Yes. No.

Athena marked "yes" and read the next question.

Have any of your dreams come true? Yes. No.

She couldn't think of any that had, thank God!

"Roos, you know you have hole in jeans?" Magda called to him. She was slitting envelopes and putting their contents into colored file folders.

"Nothing I'm ashamed of," Russ said irritably.

"You need girlfriend. She take good care of you," Magda insisted.

Was Magda trying a little matchmaking? Athena wished she'd quit.

"I haven't taught Missy to sew yet," Russ said.

At her name, the dog at his feet lifted her head and wagged her tail. He leaned over to scratch her ears gently.

"Missy just dog. You need real woman to fix for you."

"Missy's the best there is...happy to be with me. She'll never run out on me, and she doesn't care about the size of my salary."

"Real women work. Bring you money."

Russ dropped his pencil and looked out the window. "Cut the crap about real women and real men, Magda. What do you know?"

"Better than you, Mr. Scientist, since I'm three times your years."

"And I'm three times as smart as you ever were or will be."

Magda wasn't the only insensitive one, Athena thought.

Magda pouted and shook her head. "No humor. I try joke with you. Get light, Roos. Steve always the joker. He laugh when I tease."

"Jeez. Steve, Steve, Steve. You talk about Steve as if everyone's gotta be like him. I'm different from Steve. I'm as good as he was, if you could see it."

"You come three month ago."

"No one knows I'm here except Missy." He rubbed her ears, and the dog yawned and trembled at his touch.

"All take time, Roos."

"Till all the crap freezes over."

"Don't be mad, Roos. I say, Get light. Have better life."

"I take break." Russ stood up and Missy jumped up joyously with her eyes on him. "Back in few."

The door slammed after him.

"Strange one," Magda said for Athena's ears. "Trust nobody but dog. I think he have hard life."

Athena watched Russ stalk, stiff-legged, across the courtyard like an angry tomcat while Missy loped happily toward the grassy border.

I sometimes pretend to be someone else.	Yes.	No.

Athena wondered if her stint in the psych department as an undercover detective would count. She hadn't changed her name. In the future, she'd try all sorts of identities if it helped her get information.

Laszlo opened the door of his office and addressed Magda from the doorway. He was frowning. "Did you find the file with Adamian's original research materials as I requested?"

"Not yet."

He moved closer to the desk. "Adamian is making a fuss. He didn't keep a complete copy and can't understand the delay. There's a publishing deadline he's trying to meet. I promised I'd return it right away."

"I find," Magda said.

"I'm surprised that you've let this go in view of its importance."

"I assist you always, Laszlo," Magda said, wide-eyed.

"*Drágám.* My dear," Laszlo said, giving her arm an affectionate squeeze before he disappeared back into his office.

"I look for file many times," Magda said out loud for Athena's benefit. "I use special sense, but all blank. Adamian's research gone. Laszlo say my fault it's gone."

Athena continued with the test.

Have you ever experienced telepathy between yourself and another person?	Yes.	No.

She and her uncle Ted often understood each other without the need to say a thing. Did it count if it was someone you'd known for so long that you could predict what they'd say or do?

A few minutes later, Laszlo stepped out of his office and closed the door. He was no longer frowning.

"I'm going to class, Magda," he said. "Maybe Athena would like to come with me?"

"I'll come in a few minutes." Athena marked a few more answers and closed the test booklet.

Laszlo's class was in a small seminar room down the hall from the main office. Two rectangular tables were pushed together in the middle with rows of chairs on either side. Dressed impeccably as usual, Laszlo was erasing the blackboard at the far end of the room. As soon as she entered, Athena felt the charged atmosphere.

Russ, Robert, Dan, and another male student sat on the right-hand side of the table. Athena joined the two women students at the end nearest the door. Two unknown male students faced Laszlo's clan from the left-hand side of the table.

"What's it like among the fairies?" a student on the left said to Russ.

"You'd know more about it than I do." Russ was cutting an apple into sections with a penknife.

Laszlo met Athena's eyes and nodded at her. She could tell he was pleased to have her there. He seemed to be waiting to start his class. Russ munched his apple sections and dried his hands on his decrepit jeans.

"Our subject today is another of the neglected cognitive processes—intuition," Laszlo said. "Intuition comes from the Latin verb *intueri,*" he wrote it on the blackboard, "meaning to look into or beyond."

Athena noticed that Russ' eyes were fixed with intense dislike on the student across from him who'd mentioned fairies. The student ignored him.

"Intuition leads to direct knowledge without the one-two-three process of logic, which breaks down perception. Intuition makes possible a simultaneous perception of the whole, a putting together, such as we find in art or creativity. Intuitive perception works through the unconscious, for example, in sudden flashes of insight."

A loud, long farting noise issued from the left side of the table.

Laszlo turned and put a hand to his ear. "'All aloud the wind doth blow,' as Shakespeare said. Another poet called the wind 'the trumpet of prophecy.'"

Laszlo's students laughed, but the two on the left, where the sound had come from, did not join in.

Laszlo continued. "Intuition is not confined to a small number of the population but is an ability we all have. If neglected, it may become weak or inoperative."

"Why waste time on an abstract notion like intuition?" the student on the front left said.

Athena remembered a book in French by Gaston Bachelard that dealt with abstract concepts such as "creativity" and "awareness." No one questioned his assumptions and conclusions, for he'd written highly respected books without tangible proof to back up his comments. Some cultures appreciated mental reflections more readily, she thought.

"Philosophers and psychologists over the centuries have considered it worth discussing," Laszlo said, looking amused.

"Well, I don't."

"Can you support your objection?"

"Anything that can't be observed and measured is baloney."

"You are entitled to your point of view. So far, no single belief system has satisfied everyone or remained dominant over time, which shows the value in diversity. If you cannot agree to consider ideas with which you disagree, I suggest we meet in my office later."

The two students on the left stood up at the same time and left. Russ glared after them.

Laszlo smiled. "Some prefer not to tax their brains with what isn't obvious. For others the great mysteries of our existence are honeycomb."

The remaining students clapped for Laszlo. Athena guessed that the departed ones had undermined the class many times in the past.

"Mark Hansen, who was supposed to present a paper on Jung's interpretation of intuition, has not appeared, so we'll continue our discussion without him. Jung described intuition as a clear, unbiased, naive awareness, which helps us see beyond the physical surfaces of things and become aware of invisible connections and associations. Intuitive people receive much of their information from unconscious perceptions in the form of images. Images generated by intuition can help in decision-making.

"If you feel trapped in a rational dead end, intuition will continue unconsciously to seek outlets and possibilities to help you out of your impasse. Jung also spoke of intellectual intuition, meaning undirected thinking, which flows with images or associations."

Admirable, Athena thought. A veteran teacher, Laszlo had not been bothered by the shortcomings of his students. He also had panache.

AFTER CLASS, Athena decided to stop at the main office and see Ginger. She hoped she hadn't left Ginger stranded by finishing the clerical when she did. Now that she knew what to look for, she was eager to snoop in faculty offices for incriminating material. For that, she'd need Ginger's help.

Two new faces looked at her across Suzie's and Vicky's desks.

"Hello, can I help you?" said a short blonde girl, who sat where Athena had last week. Athena wondered how she'd get along with CUSS.

The other woman, a carrottop, was calmly and happily reconciling budget sheets. Refreshing to see. Vicky's grief and frenzied activity in that space had vanished, and balance was restored.

"I'd hoped to talk to Ginger," Athena said. She noted that Ginger's blinds were drawn.

"She's in a meeting," the girl said. "Do you want to leave a message?"

"Please tell her Athena stopped by."

"I have an envelope for you," the girl said.

Athena took the envelope, which had Dean Conway's address stamped in the upper left corner. As she was leaving, she came face-to-face with Harold Springer. She was taller by at least an inch.

"The woman warrior," he said, saluting her in mock respect and then brushing by so there was more body contact than she liked.

In the hall, she spotted Derring walking along in a purposeful manner and decided to follow him at a distance. What did Derring do with his out-of-class time? As it turned out, he was heading toward the coffeehouse. Athena crossed the quad where a crew was setting up a platform for a free concert. She hung back as Derring proceeded through the coffee line and then sauntered to a table to join Dean Conway. As she paid for her own cup, she saw that they were engaged in an animated conversation.

At a small table some distance away, she tore open the envelope from the dean and found a check in the amount of one thousand dollars for "saving my daughter from harm." Hard to think ill of Dean Conway, though he definitely shared responsibility for his flaky daughter. She glanced up to see that Springer had joined them. In a few minutes, a short, plump man, who looked like a high-level administrator, took a seat at the table. Was he the Big H mentioned by Derring on the tape? Athena was sorry not to have a bug at their table to catch their voices. Were they plotting Laszlo's fate?

AFTER SPENDING an hour in Ben Silver's office while he was in class, Athena felt she'd asserted her freedom and wandered back to the institute.

"What do you do when you find someone who's definitely psychic?" Athena asked Robert.

"We conduct a taped interview with the person. Would you like to see some interviews?"

"Sure." Athena's curiosity was growing. She followed Robert to a small room next to the museum entrance where there was a television and VCR. He opened a cabinet, eyed the tapes, and pulled out a video.

"This is a recent tape. I did the interview Friday before last."

He turned on the TV, slipped the video in the slot, and suddenly the screen was full. Athena gasped. Suzie's face was right there—

in close-up. She looked worried. Athena was fascinated to realize she'd hear unshared secrets. "I thought I knew her," she mused.

"Suzanne Frazier, please tell us about your early psychic experiences." Robert and Suzie were sitting side by side on white chairs.

Suzie hesitated, but then words came rapidly. "I remember walking along a busy street in Sacramento with my mother. She had an umbrella because it was raining. I think I was about four years old. Suddenly, I got frightened. 'Mommy,' I said crying. 'That man's hurt.' I pointed to a tall man in a navy blue coat walking ahead of us. 'What do you mean?' my mother asked, shaking me by the arm. 'Car hit him,' I said. 'Nonsense!' my mother said. 'You can see there's nothing wrong.' I kept crying, so my mother took me into a drugstore to buy medicine she used to keep me doped up. When we went back on the street, an ambulance drove up with the siren and lights. Mother hurried me away so I couldn't see the accident, but I knew it was the man in the navy blue coat lying in the street."

"You had many experiences like that," Robert said.

"I couldn't tell people, because they...didn't understand. They weren't interested or sympathetic. They thought I was crazy." It was obviously hard for Suzie to talk about these things. "I developed a strategy for survival. I listened to what they said and only told them what they wanted to hear."

"Difficult for you," Robert said.

"After a few mistakes, I stopped telling my parents. They weren't open to my 'flights of imagination' and tried to redirect me. My mother would say, 'You are what you do. Let's see results.' My father, an engineer, said, 'Trust your common sense. Ignore your feelings.' Common sense was not my forte."

"What else do you remember from the early days?"

"I used to see people who disappeared, or a building would emerge in outline at a particular location, even if another one stood on the spot, as if I could tell where a house stood in the past. Probably pure fantasy."

"Or retrocognition," Robert said. "What about other members of your family?"

"My father's mother believed in astrology. She consulted cards to get answers about her life, though she never explained what she read in the cards that directed her actions."

"What else do you remember?"

"Dreams come often and even repeat. I wake up afraid."

"Tell us about your dreams," Robert said.

"Not my own dreams most of the time. They're about people I don't know and places I've never been. It's as if I'm a witness for things that may have happened or are going to happen. I get an impression that I'm eavesdropping on other people's lives—like crossed connections on a telephone system."

"You don't know how to use your gift," Robert said.

"It's a curse. It interferes with my life. Something from outside can get in, and I can't stop it. If you don't like what's on the radio, you turn it off. I try to ignore what happens but I never know when it's coming and I can't make it stop. Day or night, I'm suddenly seeing and hearing things that have nothing to do with me. I want to be free of it."

"From what you say, you have great psychic ability. Some would envy you."

"There's no advantage. It drives me nuts." Suzie put a hand to her head exactly where she'd been hit. A close-up shot revealed the anguish in her eyes.

Did she know somehow what was to come? Athena wondered.

"I understand that you're learning about control from an experienced psychic. Once you know how to manage it, you'll derive many benefits."

"I want to find out how to make it go away," Suzie said without the slightest hesitation.

At that point the camcorder shut down and the screen was empty, but shortly, a woman with blonde hair and blue eyes appeared on the screen with Robert. Marisa, as she was named, explained to Robert how she'd often seen colored lights around other children's heads. When she told playmates, they made fun of her unmercifully for the rest of the school year.

Athena had no interest in other psychics. She rewound the tape and watched Suzie's interview a second and third time. She'd never glimpsed Suzie's hidden self nor had she credited Magda's assessment of Suzie's psychic abilities. Until now she'd kept a distance from psychic claims, which contradicted her own experience and made her acutely uneasy.

Robert reappeared in the doorway. "I have other videos, if you're interested, that give a stronger, more positive twist on psychic experience. Psychics who work with psi instead of against it can attain exceptional results. I heard that you came to Aston because of Suzie and found her unconscious on the floor. The interview I had with her was not up to our standards, because she denies her talent. We'd never show it to a class."

"You chose the right video for me. I won't forget it."

Robert smiled broadly and seemed to relax. "We want to make sure the debate on Friday night goes smoothly. Would you like to join our Psychic Protection Squad and help catch trouble before it happens?"

"You can count on me."

"Psychics Unlimited meets this Thursday night to pay a special tribute to Steve. Will you come?"

"Sure. I want to learn all I can." Most of all, Athena needed to pin down answers to questions instead of stir up more questions.

She pictured herself in a race with Time, who had nothing to do but run forward at top speed, while detours and obstacles turned her path into a twisting snake.

SIXTEEN

IN PREPARATION FOR her role of vigilante, Athena had clasped a utility belt, packed with items chosen from the resource kit, around her waist. She'd tried slipping the Smith & Wesson .38 into the largest pouch but decided it would be too cumbersome, so she left it behind. The wealth of devices she owed to Ted. If it weren't for his fascination with gadgets and compulsion to own and try them out, she wouldn't be a walking safety system.

Magda was watching her demonstration of the extendable baton, which opened out and locked into place to form an effective weapon. Under Ted's eyes, she'd practiced hitting a dummy by using a double-handed grip, as if it were a broadsword, to increase the clout. She was confident that she could effectively inflict damage if she had time to slip it from its holder. In one pocket was a pair of lightweight mini-binoculars, in another a can of pepper spray, and in another a cellular phone. Magda looked pleased with the array.

"You call me when you get halfway," Magda said. "Again when close to home."

"You should hire a track star to keep up with Laszlo."

"Maybe he listen to you, Tina."

As Laszlo came to join them, he made a face to show he didn't share Magda's concern. Athena doubted she'd have any influence at all.

Laszlo's house was half a block from a cut-through to the river path.

"I'm supposed to keep an eye on you at all times," Athena said as they walked toward the river.

"Magda exaggerates," Laszlo said. He continued as they did a few warm-up exercises. "She's jumpy lately, as if the sky's going to fall any minute. If I listen to her, I'd stop running altogether. Then I'd really lose my mind. Running is my safety valve. I've covered this route thousands of times without a mishap.''

''If you go as fast as you did the other night, I can't keep up as promised. Will you slow down so I can do my job?''

Laszlo was considering it without commiting himself. He obviously resented the restriction.

''In that case, I'm giving you this beeper to carry with you.''

He grinned at her like a young boy.

''If you spot trouble, push the button.'' Athena pointed to it. ''To deactivate the signal, push it two more times. Otherwise, it keeps emitting beeps that will help me find you.''

''Will you promise to beep me if *you* have trouble?'' Laszlo's eyes sparkled.

''Sure.'' It's aggravating not to be taken seriously, Athena thought.

Running in place, Laszlo clipped the small square to his T-shirt. ''Ready?'' he said. She nodded and they started off down the path. He stayed with her during the first phase.

''How do you feel...about the debate?'' Athena asked as they skimmed along companionably. She was aware of the extra burden around her middle.

''I welcome the challenge. I requested a debate in order to voice my convictions to the wider public. I think they'll back me up. If the crowd supports me, I win, as I see it. Do you know I was chosen as the most popular professor at Westcott in 1980? A lot hinges on what happens Friday night. If I discover I'm wrong and have lost my base of popular support, I'll revise my plan to stay in California.''

They moved along in silence for a short while. Athena lapsed into perceptual mode, noting the color of the water, the rowboat with two young boys in it, and the small number of joggers and bikers along the path.

''Have I sparked your interest in parapsychology?'' Laszlo asked.

''I still...have trouble...bringing it into focus.''

''Parapsychology arose in nineteenth-century Britain in protest to Darwin. If we accept the consequences of Darwin's ideas, we are material beings, descended from animals, and no different from other creatures except in the level of our intelligence. The original founders of the Society for Psychic Research were scientists and scholars. Early attempts to obtain proof of survival after death seem laughable today. You've seen the museum exhibits. We've refined our methods; and yet, the question remains open. Those who are disposed to believe, do. Those who doubt continue to doubt. Is life after death merely wishful thinking or do we have incontestable proof? I believe I've compiled evidence sufficient to convince the most hardened skeptics—if they paid attention. They do not."

A full-fledged lecture on the go, Athena thought, but Laszlo didn't suffer from a shortage of breath. For him, it was like taking a leisurely evening stroll.

"Most humans since our cave-dwelling ancestors have wanted to believe in life after death. We want to know for certain that loved ones await us and that existence continues in another dimension. Most religions hold, as a central belief, that the 'soul' survives the death of the body in some form. For both Eastern and Western cultures, death involves the separation of the soul from the body. How could so many people across the centuries remain convinced of life after death if it had no basis whatsoever?"

"It does...make you...wonder."

"Still, I can't imagine Derring and his bunch saying, 'You've opened our eyes. Your work has enriched our understanding of the mind. You've convinced us that humans have souls.' They aren't troubled by a knowledge of history or the soul quest that haunts young people. The ever-increasing dominance and expansion of technology, the new god, does not satisfy the longing for meaning."

They moved on.

"A question...how do you explain...that some people are very psychic...and others not at all?"

"That's a major problem. Psychologists like Derring want to prove humans are basically...machines. I try to show that some individuals are very different. Their sensitivities should be respected.''

Athena liked Laszlo's British accent. She could follow his arguments and was impressed by his candor. However, she couldn't quite overcome the feeling that a discussion of such scope ''on the jog'' bordered on the absurd.

Laszlo suddenly ran ahead, circled back to her, then ahead, then back, literally running in circles. She was tiring while he was still eager to go.

''Go ahead!'' she said.

They were approaching a bridge, and she'd intercept him on his way back. As Laszlo accelerated his strides along the path, she eased to a brisk walk and hoped he wouldn't go all the way out where she couldn't do much for him if he needed her. For a while, she could still see the figure, ever smaller, moving in the distance. She used the binoculars to watch until the path turned and he was out of sight.

Athena liked the hour, a time when the transition was unfolding from day to night. A host of starlings on the other side of the river rose from a tree in a cloud and then resettled noisily in the same tree. Though twilight birdcalls were often appealing, so many created an unwelcome cacophony.

Time to call Magda. She punched the number and waited. Magda picked it up on the first ring.

''How goes?'' she asked.

''So far, all's well,'' Athena said. ''I lost sight of him because he wanted to go faster, but I gave him an emergency beeper so we can keep track.''

Magda made a sound in her throat. ''Maybe nothing happen tonight. I don't know. I feel sick all over. You go with him Thursday night?''

''I'll go,'' Athena said, mostly to reassure her. She didn't look forward to it. The night before the debate would be the most risky of all.

''Next time, you take bicycle. Too bad I forget this time.''

''Sure. Right now I'm waiting for Laszlo to come back.''

''You call again?'' Magda asked. She sounded jittery. It must be a huge strain to know so much but not enough, Athena thought again.

She agreed to call back and broke the connection. From a viewpoint on the bridge, she looked down at the water. Some little creature was swimming. She could see its dark, sleek head parting the water but had no idea what it was.

As the light started to fade, Athena lifted her binoculars to watch for the running man. She'd been getting lots of mileage out of the gear in the resource kit. For any occasion so far, whatever she needed was right there on hand and by testing it, she was learning what worked and what didn't for future outings.

"Ted, your equipment is first class," Athena said. She'd have to remember to tell him on the phone.

A cyclist came into view and grew steadily larger. A couple of joggers passed. Another cyclist. Athena was getting worried and could imagine Magda, even more anxious. Fifteen minutes passed. Finally she saw him. What an elegant build. Those long, muscular legs. Built to run and obviously loving it.

Athena stretched and started running in place. She crossed the bridge to the other shore and joined him. He beamed at her. She knew he'd just covered a few miles, but was ready to talk. This time, his words were not as even and clearly articulated.

"When I chose to specialize in parapsychology, my adviser, Dr. Wakeman, said I'd be 'sacrificing a successful career for a lot of frustration.' I intended to prove him wrong by developing a foolproof method to verify psychic readings. He didn't understand the challenge I saw. He preferred the well-traveled path."

Athena's challenge was keeping the pace. "You've done well," she gasped. Her stop had made it harder. The belt had gained in weight and felt constricting.

"Students come to me initially for training in methodology. I'm a perfectionist in research design. Most of them go off for advanced work in practical areas. They stay in touch. I dream of bringing them all back. I see a building the size of Rimington Hall devoted entirely to psychic studies. My former students would form a think tank and research team. Together we'd amass a bank of evidence to blow the skeptics off their foundations."

It sounded to Athena like Laszlo wanted to be a cult leader, directing and blessing the activities of his group. She was not enjoying this part of the run. They seemed to be the last joggers left by the river.

"I always quicken my pace in the final stretch," Laszlo said.

"Go ahead!" Athena said. Laszlo sped up, and she fell behind again. She reached languidly for her phone to tell Magda they were nearby. In the dimming light, she focused on punching the right numbers. With Magda on the line, she said, "Looks like we'll be there in a few minutes. We're not far from the cut-through."

She didn't hear Magda's reply because she could just make out two men approaching Laszlo. Roughly the same height and build, they moved in synchrony. He slowed to try to avoid them, but one man threw himself into Laszlo, knocking him so that he flailed to avoid falling down. Laszlo pressed his beeper.

"Get the police, Magda! Two men attacked Laszlo," Athena said. She was already reaching for her baton and forcing her legs to carry her faster, though she felt shooting pains of protest throughout her lower extremities.

"Damn! Damn! Damn!" she said. Laszlo, marathon man, had put distance between them.

One man yanked Laszlo's arms behind him, the other started punching him. He was struggling, kicking out his leg to block his assailant. His foot made contact with one attacker, but the other grabbed his leg and twisted it, pitching Laszlo to the ground. Both were down punching him when Athena reached the spot. She swung her baton and gave one man two hardy cracks on the back. She heard him grunt in surprise and pain. She caught the other one on the shoulder before he jumped up and punched her in the face. Stars exploded in her right eye. She reached for her can of pepper spray.

"*Vamos! Vamos!*" someone shouted. She managed to connect her baton again with the butt of the man who'd hit her. He turned, and, while she sprayed in his general direction, he landed a punch in the stomach that doubled her over. She heard the baton skittering on the pavement but no splash followed.

Laszlo was groaning on the cement. Athena knelt beside him. She pushed the button on his beeper twice to stop the racket.

"How is it?" she asked.

"Not good," he said in a halting, breathy voice.

"Help's on the way."

With darkness falling, she caught sight of a flashlight. A short person was half-running down the bank toward them. Athena knew it was Magda. Her prediction had come true.

SEVENTEEN

ATHENA EXAMINED her first shiner in the mirror. Her right eye, peering through a slit, changed the outside world into unidentifiable shapes and colors. Surrounded by ugly discoloration, the eye was not for the public to view, she decided. After putting on a flesh-colored eye patch, she added a hat with a large, flexible brim tilted over that side of her face.

Her eye, sore tummy, and aching leg muscles were minor compared to Laszlo's injuries. As in Suzie's case, she'd been too far away to prevent what happened. There'd been trouble on the river path before, a policeman said, so the question of whether this was random or planned remained. If the attackers were hired by someone on campus, it would be hard to prove.

On her way to campus, Athena took inventory, finding progress on who hit Suzie and who killed Steve nonexistent. Most likely, Laszlo would cancel the debate, diminishing further threats to himself and Magda.

At the office, Ginger told her that the institute was closed for the day and Laszlo's classes cancelled.

"Laszlo has a cast on his ankle. He also has two broken ribs, a black eye, and a slight concussion. Magda says you saved his life," Ginger said.

"Don't tell faculty my role. They aren't supposed to know about me."

"Ben Silver knows. He's glad you're here. Now our dirty linen will be displayed to town and campus. We have criminals in our midst."

Athena took a deep breath. "I think it's important to search several faculty offices right now."

Ginger frowned. "I hate violating rules."

"Haven't you gone into faculty offices when you needed something?"

"I'm authorized."

"I'll be careful. I have gloves and a camera. I won't remove a thing, just look for relevant items."

"I want to allow it, but give me a minute to think about this."

"I also need access to Suzie's computer, so I can clear up a problem."

Ginger sent the two temps, Emily and Sandy, to the dean's office and told them to take a break before coming back.

Athena sat down at Suzie's desk. CUSS was already up and running. She called up an empty screen. Assuming that Vicky had created a C3 macro, she tried various key combinations. She wished Vicky were there to provide information. Being a talkaholic, Vicky would let things slip. In fact, without Vicky, Athena felt a major ingredient in the discord was absent.

Faculty came and went with mixed expressions of concern, mirth, and hostility, as if Laszlo "got what he deserved." The thought of Laszlo's pain, Magda's anguish, and her own discomfort made their responses repugnant to Athena. A few profs greeted her, but, caught up in their own concerns, no one commented on her floppy hat. At present, this worked to her advantage.

"Did you hear about Laszlo?" Springer asked Wolpert.

Athena could hardly test letter combinations for listening to their exchange.

"Most people have enough sense to stay off the river path after dark." Wolpert gave him a conspiratorial smile.

"I guess Laszlo had an encounter last night," Derring said a few minutes later when another young prof came in.

"Met up with banshees."

"The prince of parapsych bites the dust." Derring laughed.

They're all mad, thought Athena. She'd love to place a few strategic blows on Derring's head and shoulders with her collapsible baton, which she'd recovered with the aid of Magda's flashlight.

Reyna Briggs sped in and confronted Derring. "You're going too far, Gerald. You're going too far."

"Me?" Derring said with mock innocence. "Me?"

After many efforts to find the macro combination, it turned out that *z-y* obligingly produced C3's in quantities.

"Got you!" Athena said to CUSS as she deleted the feature.

There was a number combination too, so she started another search.

Athena was pleased when Ben Silver arrived, and Ginger emerged from her office to talk to him.

"The debate will take place whether Laszlo is there or not." Silver had shed his usual calmness. His face was red; his gestures abrupt. "They're not going to get away with acts of violence while I'm chairman. Instead of the vote on Laszlo's separation from the department next week, I'm going to suggest that we sweep out all gang members and start afresh. They're a disgrace to the profession, not worthy to be our colleagues, no matter where they got their Ph.Ds. I'll bring down the whole university structure before I let them take over this department. This matter goes before the Academic Senate. I'll get lawyers. Athena, I understand you're gathering evidence against them. I'll need that information. We'll use all our resources to fight back."

Ginger put a calming hand on his arm. He was working himself into a frenzy and foam was visible at the corners of his mouth.

"You're a fair and considerate chairman, Ben. I'd choose you over all others we've had. You're the best."

Doubt flooded his eyes. "Not true. I was chosen to be a peacemaker and keep the boat from rocking. I almost let them get away with murder. I'm ready to speak in Laszlo's place at the debate."

"Magda told me that Laszlo plans to appear, no matter what shape he's in," Ginger said. "Let's hope it doesn't get out of control. Feelings are so strong."

"I'm ready to punch in a few faces myself," Silver said. He paused and seemed to gather himself by an effort of will. "Under the circumstances, we must be prepared for the worst. I don't believe Laszlo's assault was a random event. They want to destroy him. Do you realize that Laszlo was teaching at the university when they were still in grade school? Their allegations against Laszlo can't be substantiated. They say he drains departmental resources, but Laszlo has been self-sufficient and found independent funding from the time he came."

"They're good with the baloney," Ginger said.

"Their scapegoating of Laszlo is totally unjustified, and I'll see that it stops. Too many of us thought we couldn't block their strength."

"I'm glad you're chairman right now," Ginger said.

"These are the worst of times for the department. The children are trying to cut down their parents and lay them in their graves. It's not over yet. Not yet."

Silver left, and Ginger stood looking over Athena's shoulder at CUSS.

"How's it going?"

"I found one, but there's another," Athena said. Suddenly, C3's blossomed on the screen. "See! The culprit is *91*."

She eliminated it with relief that it wasn't any harder to find.

"Good for you!" Ginger said. "I've figured out a way to cover your presence in certain offices. We have a rating sheet for custodial services. I want you to carry a clipboard and evaluate the categories listed."

"I'm willing. According to their schedules, Derring, Springer, Woolpert, and Briggs should be on their way to classes about now."

Ginger pressed the master key into Athena's hand. "Don't spend too long in one place. Here's the clipboard to make you look official."

Within minutes Athena was in Derring's office. She was instantly awed by the atmosphere. Every surface—desk, window, floor—shone. Everything was immaculate with no miscellaneous clutter anywhere. The stillness and cleanliness conferred an almost religious tranquillity.

"Probably dusts his bookshelves," Athena muttered as she forced her good eye over title after title. She lifted a gloved finger to follow her progress across the backs of books. He had a lot of them. She finally found the *Iliad*, opened it, and saw passages underlined in red ink.

> Achilles...dashed toward the city, heart racing for some great exploit, rushing like a champion stallion...

Derring had not only underlined it but written "Yes!" in the margin. Athena found the section, copied and mailed to Laszlo, in which Hector awaited Achilles' attack. Derring had outlined that excerpt with a black felt-tip pen.

Laying the book open on the desk next to a fancy nameplate bearing the inscription DR. GERALD DERRING, she snapped two pictures, then replaced the book on the shelf. To use her camera to advantage, she had to remove her eye patch. A glance at her watch told her she was taking too long. Derring kept detailed notes of daily appointments and calls on his desk calendar. Initials, times, and phone numbers became part of Athena's photo record as she turned pages back to April 15. Glances into desk and file drawers confirmed his all-pervasive tidiness. On that point, Derring and Laszlo were in accord.

Athena checked the hall before closing Derring's door and moving quickly into Wolpert's office. This prof was a fan of Salvador Dali, judging from a series of the artist's surreal prints, including his drooping clocks. Wolpert was not meticulous. Wadded balls of paper—failed shots—surrounded his wastebasket. Minor clutter marred his desk. What interested Athena were the many minisketches on notepads, random scraps of paper, and even his desk blotter. She could almost see his nervous fingers in constant motion. He did not like to see blank spots.

Unlike Dali, Wolpert was a realist with an eye for shape and proportion. Athena took pictures of fruits and vegetables akin to those on at least one anti-Laszlo poster. What she could not find were sketches of people. Wolpert's fancy seemed confined to objects, including the trash can and a chaotic pile of paper clips.

Athena waited for two students to pass before opening Springer's door. She almost closed it again in alarm. Chaos!

Every surface was overloaded with stuff, mostly books and papers stacked at precarious angles. Every chair carried a burden. More than absentminded, Springer was non compos mentis, Athena thought. How would he ever find lecture notes, student papers, or research data? Odd for a scientist to be so disorganized.

If proof of guilt were there, it was buried forevermore. She pulled out a desk drawer to observe a tangle of tapes, labeled as psych lectures. Not wishing to dig around, she closed it and tried the top middle drawer, which was crammed with papers and envelopes. She tried to shut it, but it stuck. Shoving the mess of paper back in she saw a sliver of black plastic. The tape proved to be "Laugh Along with Us" and promised "rollicking fun." Athena moved it in line with an envelope addressed to Dr. Harold Springer. Click! She had what she needed. Luck was on her side.

Athena tucked her gloves and camera in her handbag. She'd decided not to investigate Briggs' office because she'd already been there. Her frowning cartoon faces had been too rudimentary to indicate artistic skills, nor was her writing skill equal to the posted messages. If Briggs had something to conceal, she'd do a better job. These jokers were so self-confident and unimaginative that they hadn't bothered to hide evidence.

Clipboard in hand, Athena closed Springer's door. She took a deep breath when she saw Springer and Briggs coming her way.

"I oppose any form of physical violence," Briggs said in a ringing voice.

"Look on it as an accident that...tipped things in our favor."

"Henry's advice was classic. He said, 'Smooth as silk. No broken feathers.' This hardly qualifies."

Too engrossed to notice her, they almost bumped into Athena. Who was Henry? She hadn't noticed a Henry among the faculty.

"IT WAS WORTH IT," she assured Ginger when she returned the clipboard.

But was it? Her pictures answered minor questions and weren't admissible evidence in court. At most, she'd started a trail for law enforcers.

Walking down the long hall, she saw Russ and Missy. Missy

eyed Athena soulfully. She patted the dog firmly on the head and along the spine. Missy grinned at her with her tongue lolling out. Athena turned her good eye toward Russ.

"Athena!" he said as if they were friends. "Goddess of wisdom, arts, and war. What was it like to spring fully grown from the head of Zeus?"

"I don't recall." Athena was surprised by his sudden warmth. She'd always liked the roles assigned to the goddess. In grade school, she'd pretended to have unlimited physical and mental powers.

"Wisdom and war—quite a combination. You've come to the right place, Athena. Here we have wisdom *at* war."

"So I've noticed."

Russ moved closer. "I heard about what happened last night. You saved Laszlo's life. Much credit to you. Wish I'd had the chance."

"So do I. They deserved worse than they got. How did you hear?"

"Magda called Robert from the hospital last night." Russ smiled impishly at her. "I hear you're a dick."

Athena made a face and then winced, because it hurt her eye. She loathed the term.

"I wondered why you kept eyeballing and following me that way."

Another reason to make a face, but she didn't. "I need to talk to you," Athena said.

Ignoring her comment, he continued. "In junior high, I fell for the world of the private investigator. I liked the ones who took jobs no one else would and sniffed out the bad guys against incredible odds. They always triumphed in the end, doing their bit to make the world better. Read all the books I could find until I got past that stage. A nice myth."

"I'm still in that stage," Athena said with an edge to her voice. "I like the job."

Russ lifted her hat and with a gentle touch peeked under her eye patch. "Looks familiar."

Waving a paper in the air, Robert was bearing down on them. "Another poster to kill. It turned up last night."

Athena looked at the fancy picture of Laszlo in nineteenth-century dress. His incisor teeth were long and sharp. The logo read: PSYCHOLOGY PROFESSOR LASZLO HONVAGY THRIVES ON STUDENT BLOOD.

Robert looked at Athena. "Are you with us? We have to comb the campus and pull down every copy we find."

"I can't go right now. I'll work with your group at the debate, if it takes place." Athena's leg muscles still ached from last night's strain so that any walking was unpleasant.

"It'll take place all right," Robert said. "We've gathered data to support Laszlo, and we'll distribute it that night. It's accurate and convincing. Through our efforts, we'll make sure Laszlo is here to stay."

"Time for the poster search," Russ said. "Let's get on with it."

Russ found Robert a bore, Athena guessed.

"Oh, before I forget—there's a meeting of Psychics Unlimited tomorrow night," Robert said. "Will you come, Russ? You too, Athena."

"Maybe," Russ said stiffly.

"Sure. I'll be there," Athena said.

Russ and Missy walked away. Robert hung around as if he wanted to talk.

"Why did you start the after-death club, Robert?"

"It offered an opportunity to explore from a different angle. The kinds of exercises we did were strengthening for the inner self. There was nothing harmful at all. In fact, we all felt refreshed and invigorated after a session. There was no emphasis whatsoever on dying soon, if that's what you're fishing for."

"You wouldn't set up computer messages as if they were coming from Steve?"

"No way!" Robert said, looking insulted. "I'm dedicated to authentic evidence. None of our people would do that. Laszlo is very strict about the standards we keep."

"Any idea who might tamper?"

"Not a clue." Robert had a guarded look, as if a thought had suddenly occurred to him.

AT THE police station, Athena answered questions about Laszlo's attackers of the night before. Coles wasn't on duty. Lieutenant Ramirez was pushy and seemed resentful at Athena's assertion that Hispanics were involved.

"Tell me again what you saw," he said. "We need more details."

"I told you. It was getting dark. I was some distance away. Most of the time they either had their backs to me or I was reeling from their blows. They had stocky, muscular builds. One had a mustache, one didn't."

He set her up with a stack of thick binders of repeat criminals. The more she looked, the less certain she was that she could identify them. She was near the end of the second binder when she got a shock. She turned the page and found them both looking at her—Geraldo and Fernando Lopez, twin brothers, who'd been charged with petty theft, armed assault, and served time in juvy hall, though obviously without changing their way of life.

"I know I've found them," Athena said. She'd carried the binder to the front office.

Ramirez looked interested until he saw the pictures. He got a strange look on his face. "Damn! They just can't stay clean."

Athena looked at him curiously, and he added, "Known those guys since we was toddlers. Lived on the same block. Used to play together. When they got older, they got tougher too. Mom told them not to come around our house anymore."

Athena put an envelope with the tape of faculty conversations in Coles' mailbox.

Ironic, Athena thought as she left the station, how one kid from the neighborhood became a cop and others became criminals.

OUTSIDE THE hospital room, Athena heard voices. Looking in, she saw Suzie propped in a sitting position. She and Magda were deep in conversation. Athena hadn't felt so elated since she arrived in Aston.

"*Köszönöm,* thanks, Magda." Suzie's voice was strong and, except for a six-inch square bandage on her head, there was no sign of her ordeal. "The most frequent words I'll say when I get there are *nem értem*—I don't understand."

"You remember what I teach." Magda gave her an affectionate smile.

Athena chose that moment to enter.

Suzie looked puzzled. "Athena! What are you doing here?"

"You asked me to come," Athena said, faintly surprised by the less than warm welcome. She gave Suzie a hug and then sat down on the bed's edge.

"Your vacation," Suzie said. "That's right. You came early. You must have been surprised when I didn't meet you. I'll be out of here as soon as they do a few tests on me."

"Don't worry, Suzie. Just take it easy." Athena looked at Magda, whose expression said *caution.*

"Have you met my friend Magda? Do you know I'm going to Hungary?"

"You told me in your letters. Are you still going on that trip?"

"I can't wait," Suzie said with her old determination. "Magda was telling about Hungary. Tell us more, Magda."

"I talk about my father's violin. His band play in Grand Hotel dining room where chandeliers sparkle so nice. Many tables with white cloths and mirrors all around the room. Floor polish all shiny like gold. Sometime, my sisters and me dance while orchestra warm up before guest come. We love the music so much."

Magda danced in the small space between beds and sang a strange but appealing melody that made Athena want to dance with her. Suzie watched, her eyes wide with interest, and a smile playing on her lips.

Magda continued, a little breathless. "With sisters I go to hotel kitchen early afternoon. Wonderful smell of honey bread and pastries. Sophie slip me pieces of bread when chef not see. Matyas, the chef, learn cooking in Paris. He get angry if workers not slice meat and vegetables just right or keep his sauce simmering as he wish. Mean man, Matyas. He tell us to stay out of his kitchen.''

"Tell about Budapest.'' Suzie sounded like a child asking for a story.

"Proud city for elite people of Europe. Parks, streets with cobbles where I love to walk, museums, statues of heroes. I love Budapest. Many things gone now. I give Suzie directions on where to look.''

Athena could easily understand Magda's love for a great city. She loved Portland's graceful landscapes—buildings, parks, and statues—embraced by emerald hills and cut by converging rivers. Etched in her earliest memories, Portland and she had grown together, the grand city changing before her eyes. She could not imagine being uprooted as Magda had been and not allowed to return for a whole lifetime.

"Tell us about your trip to the country, Magda,'' Suzie said.

"I have cousins in the country,'' Magda said with a nostalgic smile. "They grow apricots for the brandy. Hungarian brandy, *barackpálinka,* is best in world. Every year, sisters and I go for harvest and festival after. We have apricot brandy for breakfast. Taste so fine! It warm body and wake up mind. Also bacon and bread off giant loaf. Best breakfast ever. Best days of my life.'' Magda looked younger and more alive.

Maybe signs improved once Laszlo had survived his ordeal, Athena thought.

"What about Imre?'' Suzie said. "Don't leave him out.''

"The year I was thirteen, I go visit cousins by myself—three sisters sick. My cousin Imre come to meet train in his cart with big wheels and horse to pull it. Cart rolls on bumpy road and we pass fields full of sunflowers—so big you cannot believe. Imre give me side looks. He was four years more than me. He turn off road into small wood where he make love to me. First time for me. Bad for me by old gypsy code, because after I'm no good prospect for marriage. You never guess what happen.''

Magda paused for effect. Athena felt charmed by her stories as Suzie obviously was.

"Bee sting him on buttock. I pull sting out of him. So mad, he never speak to me. Next year, he go traveling."

Suzie laughed, then put a hand to her head. Athena laughed softly so as not to aggravate her wounds.

Ben Silver was standing in the doorway with a wide smile on his face. He'd probably heard Magda's words.

"Laszlo is ready to go home, Magda. He's still under strong sedation. I'll take him to the van in a wheelchair and might need your help."

"I come, Ben." Magda gave Suzie a kiss on the cheek. "Good-bye to good friends who hear old lady talk about long ago."

Magda's stride was peppy. Suzie looked sorry to see her leave.

"Magda is incredible. So is Laszlo. I love them to death."

"Let's talk about you, Suzie. I'm glad you're back in action."

"I lost a week somehow." Suzie put her hand back up to her bandage as if she didn't understand why it was there.

"How do you feel?"

"A little weak. A little dizzy. They want to have me walk the line and take a few tests, so I guess I won't get out until tomorrow."

"Peggy and I cleaned up your place for you."

Suzie frowned. "Was it that bad? I know I'm not the world's best housekeeper, but..."

"We wanted you to feel good when you get home. I'll explain later."

"Peggy sent beautiful flowers from the garden." Suzie gazed with obvious pleasure at the two vases on her bedside stand.

"They're lovely." Athena had been anticipating this moment. "I'd like to ask a few questions. Can you handle them?"

"Why not? Fire away. I can remember Hungarian words. That's pretty good, isn't it? What do you want to know?"

"Can you recall asking me to come to Aston on an emergency basis?"

"I did that? Why would I do that?"

"Do you remember the feud in the psych department?"

"Psycho ward. I like working there. Ginger's a good friend."

Confident she'd responded to the question, Suzie waited for another.

Athena hoped Suzie's head injury wouldn't impair her mental functions like Josh's did. "Did you get odd messages on your computer?"

"How could I? Don't play tricks, Athena. That's not like you."

Athena sighed. "Do you know why you're in the hospital?"

Suzie licked her lips. "Aunt Beth's picture fell down. I wanted to put it back. I guess I fell and hurt myself, but I don't remember falling."

"Was anyone in your house that night? Did you have a guest?"

Suzie shook her head and then made a face. "Ouch! I forgot to be careful. You look pretty strange yourself, Athena. What happened?"

"It's a long story. I'll tell you before I leave for Portland."

"We didn't catch up yet. Don't go so soon." Suzie looked tired.

"We'll have a good chat. Time for a nap."

Suzie agreed. "*Fáradt vagyok.* That means 'I'm tired' in Hungarian."

"Amazing that you know that." Athena adjusted the bed and pillow.

"*Köszönöm, drágám.* Thank you, my friend."

Athena watched as she closed her eyes and fell into regular breathing patterns. Recovery takes time, she told herself. If Suzie remembered Hungarian, all was not lost.

Ironic that she thought of herself as Suzie's savior and avenger while Suzie didn't recall a thing—even the emergency call that brought Athena speeding down from Oregon. Suzie's lack of outrage in no way canceled Athena's determination to find out who had injured her and why. She wouldn't quit without answers to all questions, answers to protect her friends from danger.

EIGHTEEN

ATHENA FOUND RUSS alone in the computer room. He was inputting from sheets of small, tight writing.

Missy wagged her tail from her prone position in the hall.

"So, how's the great detective?" Russ said.

"I need your help..."

"I read somewhere that all crime expresses a desire for dominance, an assertion of 'I deserve better' or 'I'm better than you.'"

"Where do you stand?" Athena asked. She had a feeling he was trying to slip away from any direct confrontation.

"I study all things human. I'm also grabbed by the idea that different historical periods have different patterns of crime, and that murders in different cultures tend to spring from different motives—for example, the British murder is done in a planned, calculated way. Italians murder for passion. Americans seem to excel in unpremeditated, even random murders."

"I'll make a note of that." Athena took a steno pad out of her purse. "You obviously have an interest in crime."

"Just trying to stay a step ahead of the mob."

"Are you admitting you're one of them?"

"No more than the average man," Russ said.

"Do you have a criminal record?"

"Let's talk about something interesting, like myths. Do you know that California was named for a woman warrior?"

Athena shook her head. "That's irrelevant."

"You listen to my story, and I'll listen to yours," Russ said. "Let's get a shot of caffeine at the coffeehouse."

Athena agreed and tucked away her steno pad. She'd have a hard time getting a fair hearing when he played all over the board.

Russ took the time to shut down the computer and stow his

papers in a scruffy old backpack. It reminded her of the renegade backpack with bomb materials. "Beware of the Magician," Magda had said.

As they walked down the hall and out into the sunshine, Russ cleared his throat, stopped to take a bow, and spoke as if onstage. "In the early sixteenth century, a Spaniard named Montalvo was recopying a knight's adventures and added a new section to the original tale. The book with the California myth was a best-seller in Spain. Explorers knew the story, and Cortez knew it too, since he named this area California. Montalvo told the story of Queen Calafia, who lived with a band of women warriors on an island named California. He described a place with steep, rocky cliffs and abundant resources. All women warriors wore armor made of gold. No men lived with them, because they'd trained pet griffins to tear men apart on sight."

"An interesting idea." Athena laughed.

"It didn't last," Russ continued as they crossed the quad in step.

"What spoiled their Utopia?"

"Being pagans, Calafia and her women warriors went to join the Moslems fighting the Christians in the Holy Wars."

"Did Calafia win battles?"

"As a matter of fiction, Calafia was defeated because of her love for a brave and handsome Christian knight."

"It figures." Athena spotted Missy chasing a dog that was chasing a Frisbee.

"She and her women warriors converted to Christianity and married."

"Sacrificing their strength and freedom. What a letdown."

"Not entirely. Calafia, her husband, and followers went around the world, fighting side by side for just causes."

"Equals! Still a Utopian vision."

"A tale of romance conquers all. Just what women like." Russ smirked.

"What do you think it takes to become a woman warrior?"

"One moment, please." Russ held up his hand. He seemed to move inward, as Magda did when she was seeking answers, maintaining complete stillness until he spoke. "Like a hero, the heroine faces a series of dangers. With each obstacle overcome, she advances, until after proving herself through many trials, she transcends the original self to reach new levels of being."

"Bravo!" Athena said.

They were inside the student union building and heading for the coffee urns.

"How do you know so much about myths?" Athena asked.

"I did an independent study. Then, I traveled all over the U.S. in search of myths and stories." Russ pushed the button for some Vienna Roast.

Athena served herself a cup of Irish Creme. "In libraries?"

"Hardly. For three years, I roamed the U.S. and Canada to gather stories from the elderly and the homeless in remote areas. I've got quite a collection, which should be publishable once I've put them all on computer. I'll send out samples soon to see if anyone bites."

They paid for their coffee and went to an outside table so Missy could join them.

Athena was impressed by the scope of his plan, if what he said was true. "What are you doing at the institute?"

"I'm a grad student. Laszlo could only offer me the last of his research assistant funds, which amounts to fifteen percent instead of the usual fifty."

"I don't buy it. You seem too out of place here."

"Here or anywhere else." Russ looked at her with resentment. "You're from a middle-class family and majored in something like art history."

"French." Athena hated to be typecast. "How did you find Laszlo?"

"I snuck in on a conference at Columbia where he was speaking. The man has style, wit, wisdom. He could have been a lawyer, politician, or leader of some kind. He chose a lesser branch of psychology and has made a name for himself. I've watched him in class and in his office, trying to reason with people who disagreed with him like the troublemakers in his class. He treats them all with respect and patience."

"Sounds like he's your hero."

"Okay. If you want to put it that way. What I'm really doing here is writing a book about Laszlo. I believe he deserves it. I take notes. I've studied his research papers and biographical information."

"Are you psychic?" She'd thought of asking him if he was gay, but the tension between them indicated a mutual attraction.

"Not a trace."

"You looked like you were in a trance after I asked you about becoming a woman warrior."

"The inner voice. You can learn to reach yours too."

"Tell me, is it more than just the usual self-talk?"

"It's more. You frame a question, right? You hold it in mind a moment. Then you observe complete stillness—no words, no thoughts, no images. You black out mentally. After a few minutes, you click on and you've got your answer from deep inside. You'd be surprised."

Athena wrote down his formula, intending to try it. "Now that you've led me around the barn several times," she said, "can we get to my story?"

"Your turn." He crushed the coffee cup in his hand as if he were ready to go.

"It requires a return to the real world where people get injured or die because someone doesn't like them and wants to get rid of them."

"The mean streets," Russ said.

"In this case, the psychology department at Westcott. I have specific questions, and I'd appreciate specific answers to the best of your ability."

Russ burped. "At your service," he said with a wink.

"I've seen you out walking your dog in the evening."

"Objection," Russ said. "Invasion of privacy."

"No, you invade other people's privacy. I want to know what gives you the right to peek in windows."

"Oh! Now I'm a voyeur fulfilling sexual fantasies by watching nude women through the window. Or a thief planning my next heist."

"I want to know why you do that. People inside hate to see someone staring at them from outside."

"Now you're referring to the time you chased me down the street. What right do you have to intimidate a pedestrian taking his dog for a stroll? My dog likes looking through windows; is that my fault?"

Athena saw that she was getting nowhere.

"I arrived in Aston on April 29 to find that someone had hit Suzie Frazier, a friend of mine and neighbor of yours, very hard on the head. I want to know if you passed her house the night before and what you saw."

"I saw the police and an ambulance outside, and then you came marching out of the house."

"That was the morning after. What about the night of April 28?"

"I don't remember." Russ was looking somewhere beyond the trees.

"Make an effort," Athena said, losing patience. "You were more likely than anyone to notice something going on there."

"What do you mean by something going on?" He shifted position in his chair.

"Did you see Suzie through her window that night?"

"I did not." Russ had his fingers interlaced and he pushed his thumbs against each other, as if they were struggling.

"Did you see anyone in the vicinity?"

"No. I think we went to West Aston that night to look in windows."

"You're as frustrating as Gerald Derring," Athena said angrily. "You don't know a thing, but you're guilty as hell."

"Wait a minute!" Russ sat up straight. "Don't compare me to that dildo."

"Then don't act like him. I need answers to real questions. No games."

"Whatever you say, almighty goddess." Russ threw pieces of an abandoned bagel to a motley bunch of birds, and they went for it with gusto.

"Have you told me exactly what happened on April 28 so we can go on to other matters?"

"Yes, ma'am."

"I'm not just working for Suzie. I'm looking out for Laszlo and Magda."

"If you want to know what's up, they're trying to exile Laszlo permanently. The idiots overrate themselves."

"What do you know about it?"

"Derring's hobby is plotting what he's going to do to Laszlo. There's a lot of bluster, but I'm not sure how far he'd go."

"I wonder too. Is he chief of the whole show?"

"An interesting question."

"Suppose someone more powerful is behind this whole anti-Laszlo operation."

"You're hot on the trail." Russ stood up.

"Do you know where the trail leads?"

"You find out and tell me."

"I need someone to tell what he knows."

"I've never aspired to be an informer. Listen, I've got to see someone about a dog," Russ said, moving away.

"Good-bye." Athena didn't thank him for his cooperation.

PUZZLING OVER HOW to pry more information out of Russ, Athena decided to pay him a visit. The walk from her apartment to his place wasn't long. The blue house with white shutters never seemed to change. The blinds were pulled down tight. She saw the mailbox stuffed with mail and enough unopened newspapers to amount to a week's worth. It was obvious that Russ didn't live in the main house. Perhaps there was a cottage behind.

She walked to the back and saw no additional buildings. Returning to the front, she noticed that the garage was detached with its own door. She knocked at the door. No response, so she opened it.

Russ' living quarters consisted of an unconverted garage space with a small, grimy window set in the door. A full-sized tattered mattress lay directly on the floor. A folding chair stood beside a card table. There were two goosenecked lamps in the whole place.

Several books were propped up with bricks as bookends. On the large metal sink, typical of laundry rooms, were hung drying briefs and T-shirts. Next to a big bowl of water lay a brush full of dog's hair. A large bag of dried dog food sat on a shelf. The only human food in sight was a box of crackers and a jar of peanut butter. Near the wall, a hot plate rested on top of a few bricks. The whole scene suggested a kind of grinding poverty, the bare minimum, that Athena had never experienced directly herself.

A row of cardboard boxes drew her attention. Each was full of hundreds of sheets of paper covered from top to bottom with the small, cramped handwriting she'd seen before. So, maybe he was the writer he claimed to be. These were his stories. She hoped they were good enough to sell. No one should have to live like this.

She took a quick peek at book titles and saw George Orwell's *Down and Out in London and Paris,* Studs Terkel's *Working,* and Colin Wilson's *The Psychic Detectives.* The last title especially piqued her interest.

She had just closed the door behind her when she saw Russ and Missy coming up the sidewalk. Russ was furious. "Get lost!" he yelled.

"Russ, I didn't mean..."

"Damn your curiosity and middle-class everything. Get the hell out and leave me alone!"

He walked past her to his door, then turned and leaned against it with his arms folded. His eyes were full of contempt and hurt pride.

Athena walked away, feeling a bit shell-shocked herself. Any insight into Russ exacted a price. His poverty looked real, but magicians were skilled at conjuring up smoke screens. She couldn't get rid of the impression that he wasn't what he pretended to be.

NINETEEN

ATHENA'S MIND teemed with imagined conversations with Russ. "Look, I've got a job to do. You're a major suspect and you won't clear yourself. How can I get through to you?"

She didn't have the power of the police to demand explanations. She didn't have any power at all. Evidently he'd noticed her from the first morning when she'd noticed him. At the one point where she'd seen a chance to breach the barrier, she'd failed, and her impromptu house call had canceled the chance to communicate.

After a restless night, Athena got up at six a.m. She decided to go for a walk and put the Russ fiasco behind her. He was probably not a major player, though he'd been well situated to observe. As a long-term student of Laszlo's, Robert knew more and was ready to tell.

Good news: Suzie would be coming home today. Bad news: The upcoming debate. No doubt, Laszlo was at a severe disadvantage. How could he do his best thinking after the recent trauma? The timing of the attack gave him no chance to recuperate—a strong indicator of foul play.

She was walking past a gift shop in the downtown area when she heard someone call "Athena!"

She turned at the sound of her name to see Russ and Missy closing in on her.

"Hey!" Russ said. "Sorry about last night. Being nosy is your job. You've got to poke around, looking for secrets in all the wrong places. This time, I'll forgive you, if you do the same."

"A deal!" Athena said with a smile. "I'll ease up on questions, if necessary, but I can't stop wondering what choice bits of information you're withholding."

"I can put doubts permanently to rest. I'm starving. How about you?"

"I'd like coffee. Any place open around here?"

"There's a good one a few blocks away."

Athena noticed that the little café had the lowest prices in town.

"Do you object if I order the Farmer's Breakfast?" Russ said.

Athena read the description: three eggs, bacon, sausage, hash browns, beans, pancakes, and coffee.

"I don't know how you eat it all, but go ahead." She picked an egg, over medium, and an English muffin. Small breakfasts were best, she thought.

"About windows," she said. "I confess that I like to see how other people live...how they decorate their walls and arrange their furniture."

"Typical middle class."

"Don't start that. How'd you like it if I said 'macho' every time you opened your mouth?"

"Touché. Here goes. In order to unburden myself of guilt at the feet of my favorite goddess—"

"I thought men usually preferred Aphrodite to Athena."

"It depends on whether they're ruled by their minds or their cocks," he said cheerfully. "In defense of my walking addiction, I plead a case of culture shock. I've never spent time in a town like Aston before...getting to know every street, every house...all nice, no run-down hovels off-limits to respectable citizens. Astonians have money to burn...cars outside, furniture inside, and expensive doodads for decoration. Blows my mind."

Their breakfasts arrived, and Russ dove in enthusiastically.

"So, you're a connoisseur of Aston lifestyles, searching for the pulse of the middle class?" Athena said. "Didn't your mother tell you it's rude to look in windows?"

Russ choked on his beans. It took him a minute to get his breath back. He wiped his mouth on the back of his hand and gave her a look of disgust. "You just keep hitting below the belt, don't you?"

"Macho! Pardon my middle-class blunder, but what did I say this time?"

"'Mother' is a dirty word in my vocabulary. My mother, whoever she was, left me in a garbage can when I was a few minutes old. I cried and was found, like Oedipus on the hillside. Oedipus later wished he'd never been born."

"Were you adopted?"

"In Brooklyn I lived in a series of foster homes, each worse than the last, until I took to living on the streets with friends or friends of friends with temporary floor space—whatever it took. Then I spent years touring the country by jumping trains."

"A seasoned traveler."

"I wanted to leave the mean city streets behind."

"Did you?"

"I can't shake them off completely. My biggest concern when I was in school was whether I'd make it home without getting beat up by gang members, who routinely scared the shit out of me. I never had protection. Aston people have protection from the day they're born to the day they die. They don't worry about crime. They go to the store, the campus, or do whatever they like at any time of the day or night."

"The attack on Laszlo was a noteworthy exception," Athena said. "If your background was as you claim, how did you get a university education?"

Russ tapped his head. "Photographic memory. I can often ace exams whether I've read the book or not. I worked my way through as a waiter, construction worker, loading trucks for delivery, et cetera."

"You're resourceful."

Russ grinned. He was making inroads on the pancakes. Syrup trickled down his chin.

"Why take notes on what Laszlo says?"

"I don't. I'm rewriting his comments for a book about his life and ideas."

Athena was impressed.

"Now, I'll tell you what Aston does to me. Seeing a family through a lighted window puzzles me. I don't know if 'family ties' and 'love' and all that middle-class shit really exist or if people just fake it like actors and actresses until they fool themselves too. Can a man and a woman be happy together? I think *love,* that used and abused word, is just a form of manipulation. When I hear fighting, raised voices, or screaming, it sounds real. That's what I understand."

Aston resembled a small fragment of Portland and lacked the contrasting neighborhoods, cultural diversity, and elevated crime rate of a large metropolitan area. It was a university town, no more, no less. What startled Athena was Russ' bleak view on life. She sipped coffee and took the last bite of her English muffin. Talking with Russ was like walking on a minefield with sudden explosions possible.

"Aston's so 'picture perfect,' it makes me want to puke," Russ continued. "Tree-lined streets, freshly painted houses, well-kept lawns—a poor man's vision of heaven. Astonians don't even know it. Of course, I also see them trapped in pretty little cages forever. They salute the rich and famous and try to imitate them, while avoiding the gutter and pretending it isn't there. My book of interviews restores the voice to neglected people in this society. They have stories too."

Russ mixed his eggs and potatoes together and dug in. "You think I'd harm Suzie? She found me a place to live." He took a huge bite. "So that's who I am and what I'm doing, Ms. Dick. I'll always be an outsider, looking in, but I'm no criminal. If I were into crime, I'd live high."

He gulped down a few more bites, then slipped a sausage and a piece of bacon into the folds of a napkin. His plate empty, he downed the last of his coffee and looked satisfied.

"And there you've got the whole can of worms. Now your sweet little middle-class heart will pitter-patter in sympathy like in the romance novels. Surely you'll pay for the poor man's breakfast, because I haven't got a dime." He pulled his pockets inside-out to prove his point. One of them had no seam at the bottom.

Athena couldn't help laughing. He was such an expert at turning her head and her feelings around. "You're exasperating!"

"I may be a genuine bastard, but I make it a practice not to ball ladies even when they're dying for it."

"For your info, I don't hop in the sack with every prick who comes along." Athena'd had three boyfriends, each long-term.

"You'd rather kick them in the balls, right?" Russ grinned.

"Only if they deserve it." Athena grinned back.

"As I see it, sex feels good because our species is driven to reproduce like rats, cockroaches, and other vermin. This world does not need more miserable bastards running around."

"To further your education, I will say that love is not a dirty word. It's more than sex. What you missed was the pattern of caring and sharing, including mutual respect, support, and understanding. That's what I received and what I expect in a relationship. My father died in Vietnam, but I was lucky because my middle-class mother was always there to encourage me, and my uncle Ted stepped in to act like a father."

"Thank you, Barbara Cartland. I never understood your fame."

"You may mock it, but love makes us human."

"Athena has spoken. What I know is: Missy loves me. Therefore, she must be human. Now I'll give her a morning treat to keep her satisfied. Thanks for breakfast, *ma chère.*"

Athena laughed all the way to the cash register. She'd been taken in by a trickster. What other tricks did he have? Next time, she'd be on guard.

ATHENA CALLED the hospital to see when Suzie could leave. Ten o'clock, they told her. When she arrived, Suzie was ready to go home. On the way, they stopped at the grocery store to buy bread, milk, and other necessities. Noticing how slowly and deliberately her friend moved, Athena did the legwork while Suzie stood in line.

"The doctor said not to do too much," Suzie said. "I'm going to stay home a week, then go back half-time."

"I worked at your desk for three days. Your job is demanding."

"The people are nice, though."

"Vicky won't be working there anymore," Athena said, once they were in the car. "Ginger sent her away."

"Poor old Vic. She's bedeviled by every complex in the book."

"You're very kind. She drove me nuts."

"Well, I've had my devils too," Suzie said.

"You were good at hiding them. I saw the video that Robert made." Noticing Suzie's blank look, she continued. "He interviewed you about your psychic experiences."

"Oh that! It doesn't matter now."

"When I watched you talk about what happened to you, you convinced me that some people really are psychic. I never suspected you."

"I thought I had an incurable disease...constant disturbances, some frightening."

"You didn't show any signs of it in Paris, except I remember you crying out in your sleep. I thought it was a nightmare. I have those too."

"Remember the pickpocket? I knew he was going to pull that on you before he even saw you. You wouldn't have understood, if I'd told you then."

As Athena pulled into the driveway, she realized Suzie was right. Three years ago, she wouldn't have accepted it at all. They carried the grocery bag in.

"I haven't been much of a hostess," Suzie said. "When we go to Europe next year, we'll have good times again."

Athena was glad that she recalled their plans for future travels. "How do you feel?"

"Sometimes I feel weak, but I'm going to be better than I ever have been." Suzie was putting the cold items in her refrigerator.

Athena had noticed a new lightness in her eyes, though she wasn't sure what it meant. "I always thought you were fine, Suzie."

Spook came into the kitchen to greet them with loud meows. Suzie didn't have to bend over; the cat jumped into her arms.

"I'm cured now. I can live like a regular person."

"You're getting over that knock on the head."

"No more voices. No more bad dreams. It's wonderful."

Athena suddenly realized what she meant. "No more psychic insight?"

"Not a trace." She persuaded Spook to jump down, then put a few cans of soup on the shelf.

"Does it bother you that someone hit you on the head with intent to kill?"

"If someone did, it brought a miracle. I'd thank that person. After living so long with information overload, I can say 'Ignorance is bliss.'"

"I'm glad you're feeling so good, but I have to warn you that someone tried to kill you. Be careful. Keep your door locked."

Suzie went into the living room and collapsed on the couch. "Time to rest."

"Will you be all right by yourself?"

"Peggy promised to come often. She makes good casseroles."

"I'll check on you too. Keep your door locked at all times. *Capisce?*"

"*Capisce.*"

Suzie always perked up at foreign words. It bothered Athena that Suzie didn't take the danger seriously. She needed to see the photos of herself and her house, but Athena thought she'd give her a few more days to recuperate.

Next stop, Laszlo's house. Athena parked in the driveway behind his black Lincoln Continental and went to the door. Magda met her, but not the same Magda. This time, no flamboyance. She wore a black dress as if in mourning, and it aged her many years. Laszlo's ordeal was taking its toll.

"Thank you again, Tina. You save Laszlo's life," Magda said as she invited her to sit down on a couch with an orange cushion.

"If Laszlo hadn't run so fast, I could have protected him better."

"You are power woman." Magda was too low to be jealous. She wore only one ring and bracelet, as if she'd given up her armor.

"I took Suzie home this morning. She's going to be fine."

"Suzie lose power," Magda said sadly. "I teach how to use—*boom*—it go away."

"Have you seen that happen before?"

"She lose great gift. I lose part of mine by giving public readings. Too much use, it goes. Also, power grow weak without exercise...like muscle."

"How are you and your signs?"

The older woman shook her head slowly. Magda was more depleted of energy than Athena had ever seen her. "Time runs to end."

"Don't let it."

"The moon sheds its shadow, then returns."

"Will you return, Magda?"

"If you keep memory. When I come, no one know me."

"Suzie and I can never forget you, Magda, but I won't let anything happen to you."

"Life is death, and death is life. You're too young...not understand. Force carry you very fast when time comes. Don't worry for me. I know what to do. Now we talk of other things. Tomorrow the institute is open. At noon is party for Laszlo. Please come."

"Do you need help for the party?" Athena realized with a jolt that the debate would take place tomorrow night. Too soon!

"Robert and his group do everything."

"May I see Laszlo?" Athena asked.

"I tell him you're here, Tina." Magda got up with difficulty.

Laszlo's face was so swollen that he couldn't open his right eye. He tried to turn the left side of his face toward her but winced in pain. Impossible to recognize the most handsome, well-dressed gentleman on campus. His nose was swollen out of shape, perhaps broken, and there were bandages everywhere. The cast on his left leg protruded from the covers at the end of the bed.

"Hello, Laszlo," she said. Other useless phrases popped to mind—"It shouldn't have happened," "We've found the guys who did this," "I should have stopped it sooner."

"Sit down," he said in a muffled voice.

She seated herself in the chair beside the bed.

"I didn't thank you yet," Laszlo said. "The man you hit was pulling a knife out of his pocket. I think he intended to cut my throat. Your blow made him drop the knife. That's when he decided to run."

Athena had not heard his account, since he'd been in no condition to talk that night.

"I've been thinking...about the insitute. I dreamed every detail...for years before I had funds. When we opened the door, I thought...my dream had finally...materialized. A permanent research facility...legitimizing all those who've shared my interest...a place for up-to-date research."

"You've accomplished that. I've heard your institute is the best. Would you like something to drink?"

"I've reached my limit of tea, coffee, soup, and fruit juice. Magda is my guardian angel."

"Are you ready to go on with the debate? You haven't had time to mend. Ben Silver can do the job...he said he would."

"Nothing can keep me away from the debate. Let them laugh, if they choose. It's not my looks, but the message that's important. The ego gets fearful of looking foolish, but beyond the personal, there's a larger purpose involved. I must be there."

Athena took Laszlo's hand, which was partly wrapped in a bandage. "I wish you the power and the strength to do what you need to do." She feared that he was reaching beyond his means.

"You are my Katya, even if you don't admit it."

"Perhaps I am." Athena hoped to speed his recovery.

A tear oozed out of the corner of his eye. He tried to smile but couldn't, so he squeezed her hand. As a thoughtful sister would do, she dabbed his tears with a tissue. Inside, she raged at the perpetrators.

TWENTY

On her way to the meeting of Psychics Unlimited, Athena saw Josh sitting on the back stairs. He was wearing the green sweater Vicky had made, one of a kind. It struck Athena how nice Vicky was to give Josh the sweater. Not many people gave custodians special consideration. The temperature wasn't cold enough for a sweater, but Josh seemed to be shivering. His gaunt face was a picture of despair.

"'Lo," he said, woefully, when she put a hand on his shoulder.

"How are you?" Athena asked with concern.

"Bad tum. Can't eat nothin'."

"Have you seen a doctor?"

"Nothin' they can do. Pernent damage, they say. First the bomb messed me up, then Agent Orange got aholt of me and been playin' with me ever since. I'm the last one. The others died long ago. They were lucky."

"Well, everyone needs to eat."

"Boy, I sure did eat in the old days. Nobody ate more 'n me."

Athena glanced toward the skull and crossbones on the custodian's door and realized that Josh had accurately outlined his own skull.

"Where you been? I missed you."

"I have a different job now."

"You're gone—I'm gone. Tomorrow's my last day."

"You're leaving?"

"Can't hold up. I'm countin' sunsets now for sure," Josh said, using his broom and the handrail to help him stand.

"You'll be missed. Thank you for the coffee, the sunsets, the computer victory, and the little deer, which stands on my table."

"You're extra nice. Knew that first time I saw you."

"Take care. Hope you feel better." Athena looked at her watch.

"Prob'ly not," he said, shuffling into his office. "See you soon."

She hated to be late for a meeting, so she rushed along the hall, turned the corner, and went down the other wing to the main staircase. So many flights to the tower room. She saw Russ and Missy at the bottom of the last and steepest stairs.

"Missy can't go up," Russ said. "She's got to stay here."

"Do you go to these meetings regularly?"

"I'm not hot on these people. Don't know if I'll stay for this one."

Athena climbed the stairs after him. In the tower, all desks had been pushed aside and a large circular table occupied the middle of the room. Candles were burning and reflecting on the panes of glass. Through the dome, a light purple sky dotted with early evening stars was visible.

Russ chose a seat close to the exit, and Athena sat down beside him. She was determined to find out more about Steve's death and wanted to see Russ' response to the meeting. Robert waved at her. He looked stiff and formal, even in khaki pants and a striped sports shirt.

"You have an admirer," Russ smirked.

"Not a plus," Athena whispered.

Only twelve people were present, including Russ and herself. Athena recognized a few faces, but most were new to her. Some unknowns were dressed like hippies of the sixties.

Robert stood up. "Last night, Laszlo was attacked while jogging near the river. Although he's in pain from multiple injuries, Laszlo plans to go on with the debate. He'll need your support more than ever. Please sign one of our petitions requesting that the university keep the parapsychology program. Now for our regular program...Steve Linstrom should be here with you tonight. I'm acting in lieu of Steve, our newly elected president and one hell of a guy. None of us will forget his remarkable efforts to familiarize the wider public with psychic concerns. I'm sure all who knew him share my grief and admiration for a smart and thoroughly nice person."

"Hear! Hear!" shouted Dan. Others clapped.

"Choke! Gag! All lies!" Russ whispered. Athena studied his profile and wondered about his antipathy. How far did it go?

"Steve was also a member of the death prep club in which we practiced ways to keep the ego intact and able to cross the border of death. We are hoping that Steve is capable of communicating with us. Alexandra, whom many of you know, has joined us tonight for that purpose."

All eyes focused on a stunning blonde, dressed in a long blue dress with a low neckline. A gold belt and gold shoes caught Athena's attention. Alexandra nodded her head with the studied elegance of an actress. She reminded Athena of a blend between a prom queen and a Las Vegas performer. Her elaborate eye makeup included painted swirls at the corner of her eyes and glitter above her eyelids.

"A genuine fake," Russ whispered.

"We're going to form a chain with our hands," Alexandra announced in a vibrant voice. "You two by the wall, please join us at the table."

Athena was curious enough to join, but Russ declined the invitation.

"All those present must participate in our effort to reach Steve," Alexandra said majestically. "Come!"

Russ moved his chair to the table and sat down beside Athena only when it was clear that everyone was waiting for him and would not proceed without him. Clasping hands with those on either side of her, Athena noticed that Russ' hand was callused and strong. Immediately she felt a current flow. Whatever it was, there was binding power. The group seemed to sway as they sat around the table.

When Alexandra requested that they clear out all earthly matters and become openly receptive, Athena allowed her mind to go blank. Alexandra focused on each person's face until satisfied that they were complying.

"Breathe deeply and evenly. You are each an empty screen, receptive to Steve Linstrom."

"Manipulator," Russ hissed.

"That means you too, Russ."

He gave her a dirty look.

After a few more minutes, Alexandra spoke, her voice becoming more stagey by the minute. "Steve, your friends are here to welcome you. Together we call you, Steve, wherever you are, to come to us now. We are waiting... We are waiting..."

Still, she seemed to fall deep into her self-induced trance. "We call you, Steve. Our hearts and minds are open. Come and be with us tonight. We are waiting to hear from you."

Alexandra's body was starting to shake, and her words became more and more slurred. Athena was wondering how such a bad actress would achieve something believable.

When a few clear words emerged, the voice was deep and husky. "Come, Steve. Come!"

Sweat trickled down Athena's forehead. The energy flow reminded her of a live snake, which they were fastened to and couldn't let go of. The room seemed to be in motion, making Athena feel slightly seasick.

Alexandra moaned and then a deep voice shouted so loud that it echoed strangely. "Greetings, friends! I have traveled far to other realms and back at your request. You will join me someday and learn different ways. There is fluidity and movement on a scale you have not dreamed. The Self you wear now is a mere shell. You do not need it. Other worlds and ways of being coexist with your own. You do not see them nor do they see you ordinarily. It could be good here, but I'm not satisfied. Restless and angry sensations hold me in a spiral when I want to be free. Earthly matters are still unresolved. I had a goal. I planned to rethink and revise the scope of Western psychology. The fire of genius burned within. Someone ruined my grand design for petty reasons. The message I leave is—*I was murd...murder... murdered. I was murdered.* Until my killer pays, I'm caught in muck I wish to leave behind. Set me free! Please set me free."

Steve himself suddenly grew above them, seeming to hover over them. His presence was faint enough to see through, but three-dimensional like a hologram. Impressions bombarded Athena of blond hair, wide shoulders, plaid shirt, hiking boots, a gesturing hand. How did they do it? The illusion lasted only a few seconds and then faded.

Strangely white beneath her makeup, as if drained of blood, Alexandra put her head down on the table. Contact broken, an awed silence followed. Then sounds of cautious movement and hushed comments could be heard.

Russ was squirming beside her. Athena felt as if she'd been either scorched or frozen inside, an unpleasant sensation. Had she imagined Steve, been tricked, or had Steve really been there? Russ was leaving. Athena wanted a breath of fresh air. Turning, she saw Josh standing at the edge of the room, his mouth open and a tear suspended from one bloodshot eye. He'd apparently seen the apparition without being part of the circuit.

Robert put a hand on Russ' arm as he started toward the door and said, "You should stay for our reintegration exercise. It will make it easier to go back into the world."

Russ shook his head and continued out the door, just barely escaping a tumble down the steep stairs. Athena stayed right behind. Missy was pacing restlessly. Had she sensed something or was she reacting to Russ' reaction?

The ground seemed fluid rather than firm beneath Athena's feet. Something had happened. She didn't know what and didn't like it in the least. But something had happened, even if the event was staged.

"We've got to talk, Russ," she said.

Russ was walking ahead of her, weaving slightly as if drunk. She had to run in order to keep up with him.

"Who do they think they're fooling? Idiots." Looking angry enough to punch through walls, he kept walking at an accelerated pace. Missy followed closely without any explorations on the side. Athena jogged along, recalling that Laszlo made a better partner because he was considerate. They crossed campus, which was relatively deserted.

Athena was wearing the wrong shoes for jogging. She could feel the blisters rise but was determined to get more out of Russ. If she let him go now, she might never find out.

They'd gone at least a mile in tandem and were in a neighborhood on the edge of town where Athena'd never been. Russ halted beside an all-night diner near the freeway.

"Two choices," Russ said. "Either you stand guard while I raid the Dumpster or we talk inside and you pay."

Athena chose the second option. She'd been set up again, but considering she could barely walk, she craved relief.

"Do you always chase suspects with dogged determination?" Russ said in a mocking voice.

Athena didn't answer. She was looking around the diner, which seemed totally devoid of atmosphere. From the big rig outside and parking space for more, it was obviously a truckers' stop.

At the moment, Athena felt pissed, to use one of Ted's words. The psychic event had caused her more anxiety than a real situation, in which she'd have found ways to cope. Russ' long walk with her running along made her feel like a fool, as well as a cripple. The current dump did not appeal to her middle-class tastes.

"Can I order?" Russ asked.

"Whatever." She'd rather say "Drop dead," but he might come back to haunt her.

The coffee was good and strong. From the way they greeted each other, Russ obviously knew the waitress well. He ordered a steak sandwich and French fries. Athena ordered a piece of cherry pie with a scoop of vanilla ice cream.

Her feet were literally killing her. She slipped off her shoes to observe three blisters—two sizable and one small.

"Well, well," Russ said. "Isn't this cozy?"

"Like a dream."

When her pie arrived, she felt instantly better. The food was ample and good. After skipping dinner, she needed a boost.

"Tell me about Steve," Athena said at last. She had to wait until Russ took several mammoth bites of his enormous sandwich.

"Steve was a flaming genius in addition to a flaming asshole.

An instant success everywhere he went. You've heard people talk about him."

"What do *you* say about him?"

"I say Steve was smart and savvy enough to play both sides of the field and get away with it. A classic con artist. No matter how devious, no matter how slick, he had everybody fooled."

"Specifics, please. I know you dislike him, but I want to know why."

"I saw him kiss Reyna Briggs smack on the mouth in her office, and she didn't push him away. The same day, he had his arms around the skinny one in the office. What did he see in her?"

"Did you know that Vicky is Dean Conway's daughter?"

"No!" Russ looked surprised. "It makes sense. He didn't do a thing that didn't have 'advantage' written all over it. He was one of those guys who could lie and cheat outrageously and still win the popularity contest with his toothpaste smile."

"More, more," Athena said.

Russ emptied half a bottle of ketchup on his fries. "He was just playing at being in Laszlo's camp, but he had them fooled. More than once I heard him leaking information on the phone. I don't know who he was talking to, but he shouldn't have been giving out inside stuff to anyone."

"Couldn't you tell on him?"

"Who'd believe me?" Russ said with a scowl. He poked a few fries in his mouth. "Everyone orbited around him, even Laszlo."

"You hated his guts."

"Damn right. What bothers me most is that people like him walk away with the prizes. Even though he talked out of both sides of his mouth most of the time, his image remained shiny bright. He could pull off anything."

Russ' assessment explained contradictions between Vicky's and Reyna's comments.

"What did you do about it?"

Russ paused. "Had a few run-ins with the guy. Sometimes we got along; sometimes we didn't. What *if,* and I'm saying *if,* I messed up his brake line, what would you do about it?"

"I didn't know Steve, and I don't care for people like that. I'm more concerned about how his death ties in with Suzie, Magda, and Laszlo."

"Everyone was singing Steve's praises when they should have ditched him. I couldn't stand it."

"Did you take steps on your own?"

"I'd like to make one thing clear—*if* I loused up Steve's brakes, I'd do it to teach him a lesson, not to kill the jerk. I'd want him to be riding along congratulating himself, lose control, bash a few parked cars, and face consequences for a change."

"I've picked up inconsistencies in Steve, but I don't agree with what you did."

"I didn't say I did it; I said *if* I did it. I'm not guilty, even of thinking about it, because I don't know much about cars. I've never owned one or taken an interest, unlike the guys tinkering with old wrecks on blocks where I've lived."

Just as Athena pinned him down, he slipped out. He sat there, looking at her with a raised eyebrow, and she wanted to punch him in the nose.

"One possible perpetrator is Vicky," Athena said. "She was starting to see through Steve's facade, and they were separating."

"The dean's daughter. You're looking in the right direction."

"Damn it! That's not enough. I want specifics. Do you know who tampered with his car?"

Russ looked at the ceiling. "I saw the person."

"Then tell me, Russ. I need a breakthrough."

"It won't make a bit of difference." He shrugged. "Believe me."

"I'd like to be the judge."

"The perp was an untouchable," Russ said.

"I doubt that."

"Okay. I'll tell you what I saw. That night, I'd been working in the computer lab. Missy and I were crossing the parking lot when I saw this tall, thin guy move away from Steve's truck. He had a streak of grease on his face. Didn't know who he was, so next time I saw him, I asked Dan, who said, 'Dean Conway.'"

"Why didn't you tell someone what he did?"

"Who'd take my word against the dean's?"

The transient versus the respectable administrator would hardly make a case, Athena was sure. Suddenly things made sense. Dean Conway argued constantly with Steve and loathed his connection with Laszlo's institute. Maybe he wasn't expecting the result to be so final. Maybe he was simply trying to prove some point they'd been discussing.

"Looks like what happened to Steve's truck might have been on the level of a prank—like fraternity guys play, which can end up in murder."

"By Jove, Athena! I think you've got it."

The dean's apparent guilt opened another avenue.

"I saw Dean Conway with Gerald Derring and other members of the new bunch," Athena said. "Is he a major player against Laszlo?"

"As clear as a day in May."

"Is he the top of the pyramid?"

"Good question. I know for a fact that it goes higher."

"Conway is just an assistant dean, so that leaves the dean."

Russ pursed his lips and frowned.

"Who's the Big H? I heard Derring mention him."

"Not the dean."

"Do you know who Henry is? Briggs dropped that name... The president?" she said on a sudden hunch.

Russ nodded.

Athena sighed. "Laszlo lacks support in higher places, does he?"

"Unfortunately, President Hennessey considers parapsychology a trivial pursuit and a disgrace to the university."

"There isn't much hope for Laszlo, is there?"

Russ shook his head. "Only if he can outmaneuver them."

"Does Laszlo understand the bigger picture?"

"He does, but he won't accept it. Presidents come and go. This one is hot to bury the old and jerry-build new programs all over. He calls himself 'the innovator.'"

"Would he take legal risks to dump Laszlo?"

"If I read him correctly, he's most concerned with appearances and would condone nothing that tarnished the university's image. Derring is blowing in the wind."

"And the debate will go on. We've got to prevent more catastrophes."

"I'm with you on that."

Athena was exhausted. "Finally a few answers. I thought you knew more than you were telling."

"Actually, you put it together. I didn't have my eye on the overview."

"There are still missing pieces, but you've helped a lot."

"Anything for a square meal in good company." Russ winked at her.

He'd saved some steak for Missy. When he told the waitress they were leaving, she gave him bones wrapped in butcher paper for the dog.

Athena didn't put her shoes back on. She called a taxi to take her to her parked car way across campus.

"What happened at the meeting tonight, Russ?" she asked as they stood outside the diner.

"Damned if I know," he said. "It appeared to be some kind of projection, but I don't know how they'd set it up, and Robert wouldn't stand for trickery. His life's purpose is convincing people that psychic intrusions occur in our everyday lives. According to him, they're so common, we take them for granted. He's writing a thesis on the subject."

"What if the apparition in the tower was real? Shouldn't we help release Steve from his spiral?"

"I'd say Steve has found justice in the next life. Limbo is where he belongs."

"You're not the judge."

When the taxi drove up, Athena got in, and Russ and Missy walked away toward the country. Russ was the free man, no strings attached, the traveler, the trickster. He'd given information that meshed with other details she'd picked up. Russ was an unlikely Magician. Who then was the enemy she had to fear? Who was masquerading? From what Athena had seen, Magda had a good record at predicting trouble, but maybe this time the cards had lied.

TWENTY-ONE

"LOOK!" SUZIE SAID with delight. Two hummingbirds hovered near a feeder designed especially for them. Athena caught glimpses of green and red, but they moved so quickly it was hard to get more than an impression.

They were sitting on lawn chairs in Suzie's back garden. Earlier, Peggy had brought them a tray with fresh-brewed tea, slabs of Scottish shortbread, and oatmeal cookies filled with apricot jam. They were chatting with her when Yuki suddenly shot through the gate, barking hysterically at the new mail carrier. Peggy went to calm her and apologize to the woman, who was on her first rounds in the neighborhood.

The general atmosphere at Suzie's was of a kind of lazy peace and calm. Athena was glad Suzie showed no interest in the psych department and was willing to miss Laszlo's party and the debate. The new Suzie radiated a deep tranquillity that made all squabbles and frustrations seem trivial. On the other hand, Athena couldn't tell her yet about Vicky's dance on the balcony rail, or the attack on Laszlo, or Steve's apparition at Psychics Unlimited, or the plotting of the dean and president against Laszlo, or how she found Russ physically attractive but his behavior repellent. She was left with more to say than she could ever remember, but no one to share it with. This led her to admit her involvement with people and events in the psych department. She felt she'd been there for months instead of a week and a half. One person would want to know the details—Ted. She could count on him to tune in and ask questions until he'd lived through it all with her.

"When you go to Hungary, you shouldn't try to outdo the regular tourists," Athena commented. They'd been comparing Magda's Hungary with Laszlo's Hungary.

"This time I'll be satisfied with bus tours that don't require walking. One thing I want to do for Magda and Laszlo is take quality photos of places they remember, so I can give them enlargements.''

''Magda said you'd put off your trip 'til later. You'll have more stamina then.''

''I'd lose too much money. This trip, I'll sit in sidewalk cafés or near the river and watch people and boats go by. It's so quiet inside my head now. I don't have to race around and do a million things to escape intrusions. You have no idea what a difference it makes.''

Suzie beamed at her. Athena felt relieved to share Suzie's pleasure in such small things as hummingbirds in the garden. She hoped it would last.

ATHENA NOTICED a lone woman sitting on a bench by the fountain in the courtyard. Overweight, she had brown curly hair and was dressed in baggy old clothes like a street person. She didn't turn her head right or left but kept her eyes fixed obsessively on the institute.

Robert and his crew had gone all out for the institute party. The table in the front room was laid out with plates of paté and cheese, various crackers, fresh-cut vegetables—which the French called crudités to Athena's amusement—small sandwiches, chips, dips, cookies, candy, bottles of soft drinks, fruit juice, and champagne. A movie screen was set up in front of several rows of chairs at the far end of the room.

Thirty or so people milled about. Ginger was there, as was Ben Silver. Magda wore the black dress that Athena thought should be put away permanently. Suppressing her joie de vivre, her special ingredient—the paprika, she'd called it—made Magda more vulnerable. Did advance mourning allow something to happen that wouldn't otherwise? Athena wondered. It made her uneasy. Laszlo himself was nowhere in sight.

Athena noticed that Russ was loading crackers with paté while Robert watched him contemptuously from a distance. Russ looked up and winked at her. Robert caught that too.

Robert came over to tell her about the meeting of the Psychic

Protection Squad at 2 p.m., when the party was over. It was important, he said, because they'd cover strategies for dealing with potential problems during the debate.

Russ was suddenly at her elbow, offering her a glass of champagne, which she accepted gratefully. Leaving Robert and Russ covertly snarling at each other, Athena went to join Ginger.

"I think the party should come after the debate," Ginger said. "Then we'll know whether the department pulled through in one piece or crashed on the rocks and broke apart."

Athena could feel Ginger's tension. When she wasn't actively talking to someone, Ginger's face betrayed the extent of her fatigue and worry.

"Who's the woman in the courtyard?" Athena asked Ginger. Through the glass door, they could clearly see the woman looking their way. "Do you know her?"

"That's Cheryl," Ginger said with a sigh. "She's the one who blames Laszlo for her sister's suicide."

"The hate calls," Athena said.

"Looks like she's going to be around for the debate. I'm glad you'll be here, Athena. We've all come to rely on you to help us in a pinch. If we survive the debate, I'll breathe again."

More subdued than when Athena had seen him last, Ben Silver called for everyone's attention. "Laszlo is going to give a short talk. This will be a trial run for the debate. Please sit down near the screen. I'll bring him in." He hesitated as if he wanted to say more but turned and opened the door to Laszlo's office.

Russ handed Athena another full glass of champagne. There was a general silence, as if no one knew what to expect. Silver came out, pushing Laszlo's wheelchair.

Tragic! came to mind for Athena. Laszlo did not have as many bandages as she'd seen the day before, but with the cast, the swelling and bruising, he was a living caricature of himself. Athena's bruise was changing color, from deep purple to a more reddish hue. Laszlo's swollen eye was far worse than hers, probably because he'd been hit in the same spot a number of times.

As Silver stepped in front of the screen, Athena noticed that Dan was moving about with a camcorder. A tape recorder was running nearby. Russ had come up with pen and notebook to put down each word in his tight script.

"With tonight's debate only hours away," Silver said, "Laszlo wants to take this opportunity to address the harassment issue and basic differences that have led to the need for a public airing of ideas."

At a nod from Silver, Robert turned on the overhead projector at the back of the room, flashing one of the insults on the screen:

1. Voodoo King holds ceremonies every Wednesday evening at 7:00 p.m. Bring your personal charm or fetish to share with the group. Refreshments of chicken blood and sheep eyes will be served.

A titter of laughs and comments rose from onlookers, but an uncanny silence fell when Laszlo began to speak. The strain in his voice was obvious.

"For several years now, I have been under an insidious attack by people who attribute the worst motives to my life and work. What you see before you was posted on public bulletin boards all over campus. I wish to address the nature of these assaults.

"First, there is the term 'Voodoo King.' Within the Caribbean culture, voodoo functions as a belief system that protects believers from enemies and the unknown and controls dangers to their survival. More specifically, 'voodoo' practices include sorcery, rituals, fetishes, and communication through a trance state with ancestors, saints, and animistic deities. In this context, I am being accused of questionable practices comparable to those in a preliterate society.

"Likewise the mentions of 'fetish,' an object believed to have magic powers, and 'chicken blood' and 'sheep eyes' point to what are, by Western standards, primitive rites of sacrifice, implying that I conduct substandard operations out of touch with current scientific specifications and practices."

Laszlo coughed and struggled for strength to go on. He had

never been less photogenic. Athena noted that Dan did not aim the camcorder at Laszlo but had it roaming the room to catch listeners' expressions.

"In response, I'd like to point out that my accusers don't know how I teach my classes or conduct my research. Fully aware that parapsychology stands precariously on the borderline of science and psychology, I never make unsubstantiated claims and exercise the utmost care in both the design and execution of experiments, adhering to the strictest scientific principles and utilizing the most updated equipment available. For these reasons, I have earned respect from those who are familiar with my work.

"Shifting the focus back to my accusers, unidentified but doubtlessly of a behaviorist persuasion, I would like to know truthfully when someone last reviewed their methods and statistical results with a critical eye. When was the last time a colleague painstakingly duplicated an experiment to verify its accuracy? The behaviorists study rats and primates. What could be more primitive? Their studies take them back to the prehuman era and focus on nonhuman habits, which they then apply to our species. When finished with an experiment, these scientists and others like them 'sacrifice' the animals because unless they can be reused, they are no longer worth the cost of keeping them alive. The accusers are the ones who ritually kill and have bloodstained hands."

Applause followed as Robert projected another taunt on the screen.

2. Laszlo Honvagy died of Ridicule on April 1. His last words were: "The more I peered into the unknown, the less I saw." An international gathering of fortune-tellers, palm readers, and mediums will take part in the funeral procession at 9 a.m. Friday. All generous donations will go to Muddy Concepts Unlimited for continued research in the supranormal.

After pausing for a moment, Laszlo continued. "In reference to the obituary notice, I will say that ridicule is an effective way to destroy a person. However, claims that Laszlo Honvagy was too weak to bear the brunt of these sophomoric attacks and chose April Fool's Day for his demise are plainly absurd. I can assure you that he is alive and well and knows more today than yesterday.

"What is most objectionable about this announcement is what it says about those who share my interests—the so-called 'fortune-tellers, palm readers, and mediums.' The names given them do not correspond to their social standing, for they are scientists, graduate students, and citizens interested in the findings of my studies and research. The fortune-tellers and their kin are fraudulent claimers of psi powers whom I have long discredited. My fellow explorers of psi are more open-minded than the followers of that most recent religion, *Science,* which dogmatically predetermines what one will study and how, drawing much of the pith out of learning with narrow limits on the scope of research.

"A final word about 'Muddy Concepts Unlimited'—where would physicists be if they studied only observable phenomena? Without a theoretical component, no field of inquiry can thrive and extend its boundaries. Theory has always been hard for the 'show-me' mentality to grasp.

"I've been fortunate in finding funds for my projects, to the rage of my detractors, because others recognize the importance of my efforts. No one questions the study of the 'abnormal' or the 'normal.' Why shouldn't there be studies of the 'supra-' or 'supernormal'? Finally, I'd like to ask: Why are they so afraid of me that they spend their time concocting absurdities, which reveal more about them than about me and my work?"

Applause and whistles followed as Robert switched off the overhead projector. From the front of the room, Ben Silver spoke up. "This gives you an idea of grievances to be discussed. We hope you'll come to the debate and show your support. Professor Honvagy's ability to teach classes to the many interested students is threatened because some faculty members claim that his presence undermines the psychology program. Personally, I think there would be a noticeable gap in our program if we lose parapsychology. I have proof that Laszlo is one of the best instructors on campus. If you wish to keep Laszlo on the teaching faculty of the psych department and have not yet signed your name, please do so.''

Athena was glad that she hadn't skipped the party. After hearing Laszlo defend himself so eloquently, she was sure that he'd do well in the debate. His arguments were clear and logical, if he could manage to deliver them.

It wasn't easy to get close to Laszlo's wheelchair. Many people wanted to give him their personal encouragement.

''Good job!'' Athena said to him.

''Katya, *drágám.* I'm glad you're here,'' Laszlo said. He looked so tired. ''I still haven't decided how to present my views.''

Seeing Magda all by herself, Athena went to talk to her. ''I think he can do it.''

Magda closed her eyes. ''I pray he can. It mean so much to him.''

''Tonight I'm keeping an eye on you too, Magda.''

''You have heart, Tina.''

A few minutes later, Athena crossed the courtyard with Ginger. She wanted to show her the photos she'd picked up earlier. There was also something oppressive, even claustrophobic, about the atmosphere within the institute, because few people had contact with the rest of the department. Athena needed to see Marcia Praeger and Mandy, or even Josh or Derring.

As they passed Cheryl, Athena called out ''Hello!'' in a friendly manner. Cheryl scowled and gave her an intense look full of hate. Athena's heart accelerated the same way it had at the sound of Cheryl's voice on the phone. Her animosity was startling. Was the woman capable of hostile acts as well? From a distance Cheryl looked like a pathetic heap of mismatched, cast-off clothes. Hardly a serious threat as long as one stayed away from her.

In the main office, Emily and Sandy were joking with Praeger and making funny faces at the young chimp, who made faces back before hiding behind Praeger's shoulder. It was good to see.

Once in the privacy of Ginger's office, Athena gave her photos taken in faculty offices and explained their importance. Ginger agreed to identify campus phone numbers in Derring's daily notes and check on some of those in town, so there'd be a list of his contacts during the latter half of April and early May.

"Something like this will keep my mind off the debate," Ginger said.

"What I'm particularly interested in are any phone calls that might connect him to the Lopez brothers."

"If Derring was involved in that in any way, I don't owe him a thing."

"There's something in Derring's superior attitude that invites a person to bring him down," Athena said.

"I agree all the way."

After sharing the latest information with Ginger, Athena returned late for the meeting of the Psychic Protection Squad. Robert stopped talking until she'd taken a seat at the table.

"We now have over seven hundred student signatures in favor of keeping Laszlo on as regular faculty," he told the five people assembled. "So far we've received over sixty support letters from former students, and most of us have written letters also. I think we've got enough backing to block administrative maneuvers, no matter how high they go."

Words to verify what Russ had told her. Athena glanced toward Russ, who was busy scratching Missy's head and basking in her loving looks and appreciative licks. She noticed that Russ was wearing a length of rope for a belt.

"These excerpts are drawn from letters we received." Robert passed around copies. "I call these quality responses."

Athena read a few.

> Laszlo Honvagy always has time for students. I'd keep him and get rid of the rest.
>
> —Miriam Kalesh

I am indebted to Professor Laszlo Honvagy for showing me what psychology could and should be.

—Randall Ingersoll

The effort to discredit Laszlo Honvagy's work places a blot on the whole university system.

—William Holloway

Professor Honvagy taught psychology in breadth and in depth.

—Carlos Anza

"I've been in touch with campus security. This evening there will be two police officers, plus one from the city police, and five of us to monitor what goes on in and around the auditorium. Based on recent events, we find it necessary to do a quick check of handbags, sacks, backpacks, and any loose clothing that might easily conceal something. I'm afraid we're limited to looking for the obvious. Let's hope that suffices. No weapons or incendiary devices are allowed. Someone suggested that we keep a lookout for firecrackers."

"Also, rotten fruit or vegetables," Athena spoke up.

Robert assigned areas to each person. Russ was to stay close to the speaker's platform. Sam would guard the Research Institute, Nina the entrance to the auditorium. Dan would be videotaping the debate. Athena was glad to be designated as "free-roaming." All security novices, the psi squad needed veteran police officers on hand. She still hoped to see Coles there.

"I've checked out portable phones, so we can communicate with one another. Some of us will be outside the auditorium, some inside; some far front, others far back. We'll contact one another only if the situation warrants. It's a precautionary measure."

Athena complimented Robert on his foresight. Everyone present got a phone and practiced calling one another from different areas of the institute.

"No mental telepathy required this time," Athena said to herself.

TWENTY-TWO

ATHENA DRESSED FOR comfort and efficiency in black pants and a loose jade-colored blouse to cover her lumpy utility belt. She tied a black scarf around her neck to add a special touch, then tucked her portable phone in one of the belt pockets.

Robert had asked everyone to show up at seven o'clock. According to Ginger, the campus was usually quiet on Friday night. At that hour, it corresponded to her description. The only sign of trouble was Cheryl camped on the front steps of the auditorium with a large sign that said:

LASZLO HONVAGY IS A CHARLATAN.
HE KILLS STUDENTS.

Athena doubted that she'd prepared the sign herself. Cheryl stared into the distance without any indication she noticed the psi squad a few feet away, discussing whether to ask her to leave.

"Ginger says she's harmless, though very hostile," Athena said.

"She has a right to express her opinion, if it is her opinion," Robert said.

They decided to ignore her and hope others would do the same. With partitions removed, four classrooms became a single auditorium, which could hold about eight hundred people. A few rows were reserved with strips of red and blue crepe paper. Recalling all the flyers she'd mailed out, Athena realized the space might fill up.

"Great timing!" Dan said. "Look at this everyone!"

He passed around a copy of the *Aston Times* in which a feature article discussed Laszlo, his work, and the trouble in the department. The reporter had presented the information without flair or bias but with enough bait to bring some news-watchers to campus.

The campus police came about 7:15 and immediately did a check of the auditorium for any signs of trouble. Athena recognized the policewoman who'd come during the bomb threat and evacuation.

Gradually people started arriving, one by one and in small groups. Robert had taken up a station at one of the large tables with Dan. They were directing people through for a quick check of all large bags, packs, or sacks. Robert got in a heated discussion with one student, who was carrying a large brown paper sack. Athena could see them arguing about who would have custody of it. Robert apparently won.

"What was in the sack?" she asked Robert a few minutes later.

"Overripe bananas!" he said with disgust.

Several buses of seniors from Sacramento, Fairfield, and even San Francisco parked in the street beside Rimington Hall, proof that Laszlo had a wide following among the elderly.

After a break in the flow, people kept coming. Athena wondered if the spectators were there for information or for entertainment. She felt increasingly as if she were attending a circus performance where people she knew were going to perform high-wire acts without safety nets.

Athena recognized a few students from Laszlo's class and graduate students who'd stopped by the main office while she was there. Nancy Coles arrived in uniform at 7:40 and Athena went to greet her.

"Did you listen to the tape I left for you?" Athena asked.

Coles nodded. "Professors think they're above the law. They're especially hard to nail down with solid evidence."

"I have some recent photos to show you too." Athena got Coles' phone number. In case of an emergency, she'd call her first.

Athena kept circulating with eyes and ears alert. Nearby, a woman student was examining her eye makeup carefully in a small compact mirror while her leather-jacketed boyfriend talked to the guy sitting next to him. Bits of conversation drifted Athena's way as she watched for signs of trouble.

"Derring's my advisor and he said I'd better show tonight and clap like crazy or I'd never get any help from him in the future."

Farther down the aisle, she heard:

"Carly, I told her, you better get your ass in gear and start going to classes or you won't have any classes next semester. You'll be out on your ass."

A little later:

"Never had a class from Honvagy. Heard he was a dude with a message."

Professors entered, searched for seats, and conversed with colleagues. Several rows were cordoned off for faculty in the psych department and campus notables. Dean Conway and his wife took seats. Athena had wondered if Vicky would come but she wasn't with them. Harold Springer and his wife, a stout woman who looked considerably older, slipped in beside the Conways. Faculty members and spouses continued to dribble into the reserved section. They reminded Athena of high society folk attending a gala event so they could socialize.

Seeing Magda some distance away, looking small and withdrawn, Athena went to give her a hug. It shocked her to see only one simple ring on her finger.

"Magda, I want you to stay within my sight all night," Athena said.

"I don't like," Magda said. "Professors talk...so boring. I understand nothing. I come only for Laszlo, but I don't want to see what happen. Bad feeling tonight."

"I'm going to watch you, so please help me by staying here. No risks. Okay?"

Magda shrugged. "Not good for Laszlo here. Not good for me. I don't want."

Russ had arrived late, and Robert wasn't speaking to him. Athena saw Russ wave and come toward her. Russ had Missy with him on the rope he'd previously worn around his waist.

"I've got to talk to you after this mess is over," he said.

"Sure. I'll meet you by the main staircase at ten o'clock,"

Athena said. She had a question for Russ too. Inside the building, they'd have a better chance of avoiding Robert.

People continued to stream in. With the remnants of his unruly hair combed almost flat, Ben Silver, dressed in a black suit, was testing the setup to make sure the microphone worked and that the right number of chairs were on the platform.

Someone poked Athena's shoulder.

"We're right behind you," said Ginger's voice. "I'd like you to meet my husband—Ron Wagner."

Athena saw a short, balding man. He looked uncomfortable and unhappy to be there.

"I made Ron come," Ginger went on. "We usually go to the movies on Friday nights. He didn't believe me when I told him it would be better than a movie. For you and me, it's in the line of duty. Maybe we can claim overtime."

Athena knew Ginger was trying not to show the pressure she felt.

"We have things under control, Ginger," Athena said in a soothing voice.

Ginger moved closer, gave her an envelope, and whispered, "Your pictures. I tracked down phone numbers for you. Couldn't find all. There's one in Los Rios that's a construction company. They've been renovating Derring's house. I asked the manager if the Lopez brothers work there. He said, 'They do, but I wouldn't recommend them to dig a ditch!' The police have them in custody from what he said."

"Good job!" Their eyes met. Anything against Derring was cause to rejoice.

A few minutes later, Reyna Briggs and Derring himself were fussing around the platform to make sure it met their satisfaction. Briggs wore a short, tight-fitting black dress that accentuated her trim figure and very high heels, which added inches to her height. She seemed cool, very much in charge, but Athena knew from last week's showdown with Vicky that Briggs was not entirely the steel woman she projected.

Athena met Magda's eyes and nodded at her. Magda shook her head.

President Hennessey and his expensively dressed young wife entered and stood poised as if waiting for trumpets to sound. Athena recognized him as the man in the coffeehouse with Derring, Springer, and Conway. She'd found his photo in the university catalog after talking to Russ. Chairman Silver bounded up the aisle to escort them to reserved seats.

People kept coming. Every seat was filled and a few folding chairs were set up in spots where they would not block the aisles. Laszlo would be pleased with the high turnout if he were at his best.

So, the stage was set. A huge audience had gathered. Dan was in position with his camcorder to videotape the debate.

The large wall clock read 8:20, and the crowd stirred restlessly.

An audible sigh filled the room as Ben Silver pushed Laszlo's wheelchair up the ramp. Although prepared, Athena was again touched by the contrast. Gone was the suave, handsome man who could hold the audience entranced with words and gestures. With a black patch over his swollen eye, he resembled a prizefighter who'd gone down under a rain of heavy blows. The clumsy cast on his leg and foot was visible, and he held himself so stiffly in a sitting position that his pain was evident. Laszlo, the convalescent, looked old, even frail, as if he'd suddenly aged twenty years.

Silver placed a tall glass of water on the table beside him and sat down in the adjacent chair. Pulling the microphone closer, Silver began the introduction. "At times when rifts within university departments grow too deep and too wide for an ordinary healing process to take place, it becomes necessary to appeal to a larger community in order to regain balance and restore reason to our predicament. We have gathered here tonight to voice opposing viewpoints. The issues to be touched on actually have a wider scope than the psychology department on the Westcott campus, for they center around what constitutes a proper definition of 'psychology' and who can assume the title of 'psychologist.' At stake also are the questions of academic freedom and the right to engage in the research of one's choice. I will turn the floor over to Dr. Leo Dyshkin, a former student at Westcott and current president of the Association of California Psychologists. At the last moment, Dr. Dyshkin requested that he be allowed to participate in this discussion. We welcome him."

Dyshkin was of medium height with dark hair. He wore a pin-striped shirt, brown pants, and wire-rimmed glasses.

"Thank you for allowing me to make a few introductory remarks. Like many entering freshmen, I signed up for my first psychology class at Westcott in the hope of gaining a deeper understanding of life...my own and those of others. I knew that the word psychology came from the Greek word *psyche* for soul, or spirit, and expected to learn about aspects of personality and wisdom derived from human experience. The textbook definition of psychology as 'the science of human and animal behavior' was a taste of what was to come. The professor's lectures were as appealing as day-old pizza. As I listened to dry details, I could not help wondering—Where are the people? I can honestly say that if I had not taken a course entitled 'Alternative Psychologies' taught by Laszlo Honvagy, I would not be a psychologist today. Honvagy restored excitement to psychology by assuming that we are more than conditioned reflexes and networks of neurons. He emphasized that humans feel and think and that potential mental abilities exceed our everyday capabilities. Honvagy also placed great importance on the human need for the spiritual element in our daily lives."

Onstage, Derring leaned over to make wisecracks to Briggs, who kept a knowing smile plastered across her face.

Dyshkin continued, "Experimental psychology in the U.S. has long limited the scope of its focus and research in an effort to obtain the credibility of science. For science, mind is not different from—but an extension of—body. At present, psychology finds itself in danger of being annexed to biology. How did this happen? Early in the twentieth century, John B. Watson, founder of behaviorism, insisted that the only possible subject matter of psychology must be 'objectively observable behavior.' Led by Pavlov's demonstrations of conditioned reflexes in dogs, Watson and his followers performed endless experiments on animals to gauge the learning potential of rats prompted by electrical shocks and the maternal behavior of rhesus monkeys under captive conditions, to mention a few of the countless absurd and questionable experiments. As a result, human feelings and thoughts were declared off-limits to experimental psychologists. In the meanwhile, endocrinologists demonstrated strong relationships between hormones and aggression, sexuality, parenting, fear, emotion, and mood to create a new field of behavioral endocrinology. Neurobiology explores delicate and complex networks within the brain—the stuff of which thoughts and dreams are made—pointing to the possibility of neuropsychology. I'm saying that psychology is losing its domain, and we can't allow that to happen.

"Professor Honvagy understands what I'm saying. I learned it in his class, but I also believe it very strongly. Now, I'd like to turn the discussion over to Laszlo."

Laszlo cleared his throat and began to speak. At first his voice seemed scratchy from lack of use.

Knowing how hard it was for her, Athena looked at Magda, who had her head down and seemed to be picking aimlessly at the fabric in the skirt of her black dress.

"I come before you a changed man. Two evenings ago as I headed homeward from a five-mile jog, I was accosted by men who tried, with punches and kicks, to put me out of operation. My attempt to fight back may have increased the punishment. The results of that encounter are observable—a black eye, a broken ankle, broken ribs, and extensive bruising. At the very moment of attack, I was planning tactics for this debate. Like my body, my mind was altered on that riverside path by two strangers who worked me over."

Laszlo winced and slightly shifted his position in the wheelchair.

"You scientists, scholars, and students assembled here differ from those men with ready fists. We have passed beyond brawling to settle conflicts. I await the day when conflicts of interest are passé and verbal duels outmoded. For those of us gathered here, similarities far outweigh differences. Surely, with collective self-knowledge in psychology and sociology, with the vast pool of information available to us in private and public libraries, and with sophisticated methods and technology at our disposal, we can move together toward a more enlightened community where physical coercion and, equally damaging, mental torture and manipulation will lose all efficacy.''

Athena kept moving and checking the audience from different angles. The temptation to listen to Laszlo was strong. Russ was writing pages for his book as he listened instead of watching for danger signs.

''We in this room share a wealth of common experiences that we have never explored,'' Laszlo continued. ''At Oxford University, I chose to study PPP—physiology, psychology, and philosophy—with no idea of what that entailed. In practical classes, I dissected frogs and rats, set up research projects involving mice and fish, and at a more advanced stage, a team of us had a human cadaver, on loan from a medical school, to examine. In private tutorials, we were given questions to answer as opposed to the prepared information in lecture courses. I researched and wrote many papers, including one on biochemical reactions of the central nervous system and one on the physiology of learning. I acquired a first-rate education, for which I shall always be grateful, with an emphasis on physiology. I also participated in the track team, and running has been a great source of satisfaction until my encounter the other night.''

Laszlo's voice was noticeably fading. He paused to take a long drink of water. Silver looked increasingly apprehensive. Athena worried that Laszlo was wandering without making precise points. Would he be able to hold up?

''Having moved beyond the student stage, we have become scientists with a common goal of testing reality 'out there,' that is, outside our subjective minds. We seek recurrent phenomena to observe and measure, so that we might generalize about causes and effects, which we expect to produce particular results. Like you, I value the importance of careful experimental design and the necessity of repetition, control, and statistical verification. I have never tampered with statistics to enhance or solidify the positive results of my experiments. When necessary, I write up negative results and analyze why the experiment didn't work. This is common in science."

Athena thought of Derring's doctored statistics. At the moment, Derring looked like a well-groomed, rosy-cheeked cherub, awaiting his chance to deliver a message.

"In addition to being scientists," Laszlo continued, "we are educators, who seek to pass on what we have learned and kindle our students' desire to know. I'm sure all of us who teach can name students who suddenly stand out from the crowd. They wake up and tune into your message as if they've been waiting for what you have to say. As teachers, we must agree that the long-range goal of education is not imitation but discovery. Students come to psychology to find out more about themselves and others and to look for ways to cope with life's difficult experiences. What we can give them are useful tools drawn from alternative interpretations of human experience, including indications of the limitations in each approach."

Difficult as it was for Laszlo, he was getting through it, Athena was happy to note. If only the rest of the evening would go as smoothly.

"We all know that psychology is a young discipline, as our colleagues in physics and chemistry frequently remind us. Our roots go back in time, but the main body of our work is recent and still half-baked. Psychology is undergoing a process of self-discovery and definition, which leaves us vulnerable to the currents and tides of fads.

"Among our permanent landmarks, Freud created psychotherapy, involving a prolonged, deep, and often agonized confrontation between therapist and patient that lasts for years. More in keeping with the rapid pace of our contemporary lives, behavior therapy, by addressing actions and practices rather than problem origins, eliminates harmful fears and alters behavior within a few sessions. In other words, behaviorism discarded what lay beneath the surface of experience to investigate only observable behaviors, which can be traced to specific stimuli and yield predictable patterns. The simplicity in this approach brings immense satisfaction, for it means we no longer need to speculate about anything hidden from view. Humans are animals. We eat, drink, work, reproduce, care for young, get sick, and die, so that comparisons with other animal species can both illuminate and put our own activities into perspective. I can fully appreciate the behavioral approach because it meets all criteria of the scientific method and yields verifiable results. Many remarkable contributions have come from this source. Behaviorism's clear advantages lie in practicality, efficiency, and helpfulness in identifying and solving specific human needs. All these characteristics are consistent with your American cultural heritage."

Deathly pale, Laszlo reached for his glass and gulped more water. He closed his eyes for a moment as if trying to gather enough strength to go on, while Ben Silver leaned over with words of encouragement. Under the circumstances, he was doing a remarkable job. Most spectators seemed to be listening sympathetically, Athena noticed.

"Like many of you, I might have chosen to become a behaviorist. I did not. Armed with the training and dedication of the scientist, I chose to investigate hidden channels of mind—mysticism, spiritualism, psi, and altered states. The strong appeal can be explained by my Catholic upbringing, forced underground by the Communist-materialist takeover that I endured for several years before escaping. Everything in me resisted social conditioning. There had to be more to life and mind than ugliness, poverty, and Communist platitudes, so I had a secret garden where I cultivated forbidden fruits of spirituality. They were the only things that made life worthwhile and worth continuing.

"I tell you this so you can better understand my choice of specialty. It is true that science favors the material world, but there are some of us who have tried to explore the nonmaterial world scientifically. Our goal is to bring forth, define, and prove beyond a reasonable doubt the existence and importance of the invisible—the dreams, intuitions, and spiritual dimensions of human experience."

Laszlo reached into his pocket and extracted a tissue. He dabbed his good eye, which seemed to be tearing, and blew his nose. The formerly refined Laszlo would never do that in public,

Athena thought. He really did seem like a different person. Yet, his voice, in full stride, rang with a familiar tone and conviction.

"We are all students, educators, and researchers here. Our similarities are more significant than our differences. I understand and sympathize with the opposing position. All I ask is that you do the same for mine. Education is multifaceted and interconnected. None of us holds more than a piece of the larger mosaic. To chop off and discard any one segment detracts from the greater whole. We need each other. Let us admit that all our paths converge. Let us put aside all differences and join in our efforts to further extend the boundaries of human knowledge. How can we squander time and energy when there is so much to learn, so much to teach?"

Strong applause broke out as Laszlo sat back in his chair, almost in a swoon. At the same time, a rumble of booing and foot-stomping was heard from one area. At least the detractors were not in the majority, nor were they throwing hand grenades, Athena thought. As she clapped for Laszlo, Athena looked for Magda in the audience and saw that the seat where Magda had been was now occupied by a man. She experienced a chill. How could this happen?

Looking very calm and superior, Gerald Derring leaned toward the microphone on the table. "In these times of shrinking funds both for research and for education itself, I think we need to take a cold, hard look at results. I think we must consider which programs are worth preserving and which are outmoded in concept and outcome. If possibilities do not readily translate into provable probabilities, then what is the point of continuing to pursue that line of inquiry?"

Athena glanced at the entrance and saw Sam, who was supposed to be guarding the institute. She moved quickly up the aisle to his side.

"Why did you leave your post?" Athena asked him urgently.

"Magda told me she'd look after things over there. I didn't want to miss these talks."

"I'll check on Magda," Athena said. "She shouldn't be alone."

Words reeled through Athena's mind: "Find Magda. Before it's too late."

TWENTY-THREE

ATHENA HAD NOT seen Cheryl inside the auditorium. Concerned that the troubled woman might be a threat to Magda, she opened the front door and spotted her sitting outside with her back against the wall.

"Where is she?" Cheryl said in a low, threatening voice.

"Who are you expecting?" Athena asked.

Cheryl glared at her, so she repeated it.

"Vicky," she said. "She told me to come and said she'd meet me. She didn't show."

"Vicky couldn't come tonight." Athena left Cheryl to brood. At most, Cheryl was a hate-caller, but no agent of destruction.

Athena jogged down the hall to the courtyard exit. Rimington Hall resembled a giant tomb. She was the only one in that part of the building. The hall lights were dim, and the cement floor echoed dismally.

Through the glass door the institute looked as if it were cradled between the intersecting wings of Rimington Hall. Athena was out the door and running the moment she saw the brilliant flash inside the institute. She punched Coles' number on the phone and shouted, "Fire at the Research Institute. Woman inside."

The courtyard seemed to grow in length under her pounding feet, creating the sensation of running on a treadmill and getting nowhere. A dark sky, dotted with a few early stars, arched calmly over the makings of chaos below. A landscape so deserted and silent it seemed surrealistic, though sirens were starting up some distance away.

Moira, moira, that fate-filled Greek word, haunted Athena's mind. Could she stop it?

Finally arriving, peering through the glass into the institute, Athena saw fire extending down the middle of the hallway and speeding toward the entrance. She yanked open the door, which Magda had left unlocked. The heat of the fire and nauseating fumes of some flammable essence hit her physically in waves.

"Magda! Magda!" She yelled so loud, she thought it would split her head open. Only the hissing, crackling fire answered her call.

Suddenly, her eye caught a slight movement in the doorway of Laszlo's office beyond the advancing river of flames. Magda stood there, her skin glistening. For a split second, their eyes met across the blaze. Huge golden eyes, calm and resigned. "What did I tell you?" she seemed to say, though she spoke no words. Her arms were folded defensively across a file folder. Suddenly choking, Magda put a hand to her throat as thick black smoke billowed from the back hall and screened her from view.

"I'm coming!" It still wasn't too late. Athena pulled the black scarf bandanna-style up over her nose and stepped behind Magda's desk where a fire extinguisher was located. Breaking the glass with a heavy paperweight, she reached for the extinguisher. Knowing the fire retardant would protect for no more than a minute, she aimed the nozzle, pulled the lever, and swept it back and forth to create a pathway of light yellowish powder. Without hesitation Athena plunged through on the makeshift corridor, found the wall, hot but not smoldering, and moved right, almost tripping over Magda.

"I've got you," she muttered, as she reached under her armpits and pulled.

Small as a child, Magda's dead weight seemed double. To avoid smoke, Athena was crouching and bending, an awkward position for an effective use of her strength. Frantically, she tugged Magda onto the powdery path. She had little sensation of motion, though she shifted her weight from one foot to the other. "Quick! Quick!" She'd get them out. Not far to go when she tripped on the uneven carpet.

From a point below most of the smoke, Athena eyed a series of open doorways along the hall, etched in gold, with fire dancing and leaping inside as dark, sooty smoke wafted out. The loudest popping and crackling issued from the library where the fire had found an ample meal. Strange how flames down the hall were slightly blue in the center, but mostly yellow shades, in places golden like Magda's eyes, then bright orange at the edges. Glowing and hissing, the fire moved like a living thing. The hall carpet was melting into black liquid, and little rivulets ran along with the flames.

As if her mind had left her body, Athena saw Magda lying inert in funeral garb on the fragile powder path and herself crouched like a cornered animal. For an instant, she was a child with her mother, gathering wild flowers in a mountain meadow. Her favorite place, so far away in time and distance. Her mind seemed to refuse to join her body to create the necessary motion. Intense heat was scorching them. They were going to burst into flames any moment. Through her dulled mind a message flickered, "The fire wants both of you!" "No!" was the response echoing only in her head.

What ignited next was the ceiling along the hall, from back to front, with a sudden roar and a huge increase in volume. Knowing they'd burn, heat-stunned so that she was barely conscious, Athena pulled Magda and herself clear just as the place where they'd been reignited. Head down, Athena dragged Magda toward the door. Fire reached out with visible fingers, trying to catch and destroy. Athena could barely move fast enough. It was coming from the far side too. Soon the threshold would be blazing.

Suddenly, Nancy Coles was there to open the door and pull them out. Athena tumbled out the door with Magda, just as fire engines arrived. Fed by fresh oxygen, the fire gave a victory roar and claimed the entire front room in a giant gulp.

Two university fire trucks careened through the alley into the courtyard, barely clearing the walls of the two wings of Rimington Hall that extended partway across. An emergency vehicle followed.

Yanking the scarf off her nose, Athena gasped for air. Nothing else mattered. At first, she couldn't get enough oxygen to stop choking and coughing. She was vaguely aware that Coles was stamping out a sudden flame on Magda's skirt and then pulled her farther from the burning building before administering CPR.

The first medic to emerge brought air packs and a large water bottle, which he offered to Athena. She drank and drank, then gasped for breath, and drank some more. She thanked him and moved closer to see if Coles had Magda breathing again. Medics were putting an air mask over Magda's face and had a gurney ready.

"We made it, Magda," Athena croaked. Her voice was ruined. In spite of the shakes that seized her periodically, she felt an upsurge. They'd beaten the odds. The rescue, which seemed to take forever, had only been a matter of minutes.

Firefighters in yellow helmets had pulled out the hose lines and connected them to the truck tank and to a fire hydrant near the entrance of the courtyard. Though running, they seemed to be in slow motion. To Athena the whole courtyard was strangely like a movie set.

She was close enough to hear a red-hatted fireman, apparently the chief, speak into a radio: "Flames and smoke visible. Engine One lay lines into the building. Engine Two assist with lines and supply. I want someone on the roof and a line to protect Rimington Hall."

Moving closer to the emergency van, Athena accepted the mask offered her by the medic; she was still having difficulty breathing and needed to clear out her lungs. Magda, still masked, was now on the gurney and held out a hand to Athena, who clasped her hand. Magda nodded and squeezed her hand. She squeezed back and felt the vibrant energy, surging stronger than ever.

"You'd better come with us to the hospital for testing," said the medic, who'd supplied her with water and air.

"Impossible," Athena said. Much as she'd prefer to stretch out on the pavement and go to sleep, she had other things to do. She bent down to pick up the abandoned file folder and saw that it contained Adamian's research paper, the one Laszlo had asked Magda about. So trivial now, the only thing spared from the blaze. She thought of the museum, one of a kind, and of the library, the largest collection on parapsychology ever assembled, already up in smoke.

"OOOOOOOOOH!" The eerie noise accompanied a swarm of

people entering the courtyard to watch the fire. More and more people were pressing into the area, occupying space, standing on the steps and sitting on the low stone wall as well as on the rim of the fountain. Police were keeping the crowd out of the operations area.

"Flood it!" The chief roared, clearly aware of the new audience. "You from Engine One, move in. Take another line to the top."

As if in response to his command, the windows exploded and fire roared through the openings. Luckily, no one was inside yet. Athena watched as two firefighters with masks and breathing tanks kicked aside what was left of the door, crouched down and went in on their hands and knees, spraying a stream of water ahead of them.

She wished them luck. Nothing would induce her to re-enter that blazing chaos. From past experience, Athena knew she'd have nightmares about the fire, her most relentless and unpredictable adversary yet, for months to come. Her head throbbed, and pinpoints of pain flared up here and there. She shivered in the cool night air.

"Did you hear anything before the fire started?" the female campus cop asked Magda. Coles was right beside them.

"I hear *clink* and *whoosh*. I think cleanerman come," Magda said in a shaky, whispery voice.

Hearing yells from the other side of the courtyard, Athena spotted Josh, observing it all from the second-floor window of Rimington Hall and apparently staring directly at her, though it was too far to tell. Several people were scrambling out of the basin, and she noticed that the fountain, which hadn't worked in years, was gushing streams of water. A few were soaked. One jumped back in to stand directly in front of the water flow. Athena had a yen to immerse herself in water to ease an unpleasant sensation of a severe sunburn all over her body.

At that moment, she noticed the cortege of Laszlo in his wheelchair, guided by Ben Silver, and Russ and Missy flanking them. They had crossed the police lines and were coming closer. Athena went to join them.

Laszlo's good eye was wide with horror, contributing to Athena's overall impression that they were all characters in a monster movie. At the moment, nothing seemed real, even his grief.

"Gone... Everything I built over the years," he muttered like an old man. "This is the end, Ben. This is it. They got everything."

Silver's jaw was rigid with anger. "They'll regret this. They've just lost what they hoped to gain. I'll see to it."

They kept talking in low voices, Laszlo's anguished, Silver's reassuring.

Russ put his head close to Athena's and said into her ear. "When they announced the fire, Conway came straight over to Derring and asked what he knew about it. Derring said, 'There's some genius around here doing things right.'"

"That hardly convinces me of his innocence," Athena said with difficulty. Her throat was dry, and her head pounding.

The show continued to unfold. With the ladder partly extended, one firefighter was on the roof, wetting it down with a hose. Another was dousing the wall of Rimington Hall.

"What if the whole department burns up?" Athena said.

"Boomerang effect! Target someone and it destroys you."

So far, the water wasn't winning. The crowd was fascinated. The debate had turned into a circus after all, Athena mused.

"Off the roof!" the chief shouted. "It's going!"

The firefighter on top barely climbed back on the ladder when the roof where he'd been standing plunged down and flames leaped into view in ever-increasing volume.

Athena couldn't stand to watch any longer. "I'm going."

"Meet me at ten o'clock by the stairs," Russ said.

Athena checked her watch. That was half an hour away. "Right-o. I'm going to wash up."

Her arms and legs were smeared with ashy streaks. The smell of chemicals on her clothes was disgusting. She could taste it, along with the smoke in her mouth.

Russ looked her over curiously. "Now that you mention

it...you've got evidence to dispose of before someone notices. You look like hell."

"I got Magda out of hell." She left with three pairs of puzzled eyes on her.

On her way through groups of people to get to the door of the building, Athena heard random comments.

"Not bad!" a man said. "I was just about to leave before the sirens came."

A few steps away, Athena heard a chubby woman announce to those around her, "I heard he's divorced and lives in sin with his secretary."

"Worship the devil and see where it gets you," another woman said as Athena passed.

Mean words. Athena vaguely recalled reading about "the just world hypothesis," which resembled "blaming the victim," because people preferred to believe that guilt brought punishment rather than admit that catastrophes could strike anyone at any time. Laszlo deserved better!

Far away, she saw Ginger and Ron. Ginger's face was wet with tears. She kept holding a handkerchief up to her eyes.

In the bathroom, Athena looked in the mirror and saw that her hair was singed in a few places. It could have caught on fire. Horrible thought! She tried to wash the stains out. She was able to clean the stuff off her arms and was struggling to get it out of her blouse when she heard a *clink* in the hall, then another and another.

Opening the door cautiously, she could see Derring's office. He was placing shiny metal cans in the hall and making no effort to be quiet. Gallon-sized, the cans were perfect for transporting gasoline or another inflammable liquid. Any minute, someone would arrive to dispose of them, she thought. She closed the door quietly and reached for the psi squad phone in her utility belt. It might not be working, but she was determined to snare Derring. She punched Coles' number and was satisfied to hear a ring.

Coles agreed to come to the bathroom right away with the campus cop, whom she identified as Laura Mallory. It took about ten minutes, but Athena had time. She was scrubbing her pants and shoes obsessively when Coles and Mallory came in.

"You'll need to tell me what you suspect. What happens on campus is under our jurisdiction," Mallory said.

Athena met Coles' eyes.

"I've been telling her about the psychology department crimes as you described them," Coles said.

"We've been aware of trouble for some time, but we hear lots of gossip, including accusations and counter-accusations. You'd be surprised at how often hostilities come up in departments. It can go on for years with one side wildly accusing the other but no tangible proof of malfeasance. Aside from constantly attacking and undercutting each other verbally, they don't lead to injury or death," Mallory said. "What do you have to show us?"

"Professor Derring put six silver cans in the hall outside his office. I think you'll agree that they're perfect containers for the stuff used to accelerate the fire. Believe me, the fire was set. I can still smell it."

They trooped into the hall to inspect the cans.

"Gasoline, I'd say." Mallory wrinkled her nose after taking a whiff.

She knocked on Derring's door, and when a voice answered from inside, she entered and walked straight to his desk with Coles and Athena right behind her. Seated behind his highly polished desk in the middle of the spotless room, Derring raised his eyebrows at the sight of police uniforms but did not look the slightest bit alarmed.

"Sir," Mallory said. "We have questions in regard to those empty cans outside your door."

"Ladies," he said. "I can explain. I never saw those cans before in my life. They were simply in the middle of my office when I returned. I have no idea as to their original purpose or why they were placed here. I never allow clutter in my office, so I put them out for the custodian. I'm sure he'll take them away. It's his job, not mine."

"Those cans may be evidence connected with the fire in the Research Institute," Mallory said.

"We also need to question you about things that have occurred on and off campus in the last few weeks," Coles said.

Derring leaned forward on his elbows. "How could I possibly have started the fire? I was in front of the crowd. Hundreds of people could say where I was at the time."

Frowning ferociously, Reyna Briggs stood in the doorway. "I think you have a lot of explaining to do, Gerald. This time you've really gone too far. Maybe you didn't do it yourself, but I'll bet you had something to do with it."

"Would you be willing to answer questions about recent plans and activities of Professor Derring?" Coles asked.

"I would," Briggs said.

The thought crossed Athena's mind that Briggs wanted to be the new leader of the Young Bunch.

"How could you? We're on the same side." Derring bellowed, looking worried for the first time.

"There's a limit and you crossed it. I warned you more than once," Briggs said.

"I'm asking you now, Professor Derring, to stand up and come with us to the campus station," Mallory said. "If you do not agree to come peacefully, we'll have to use handcuffs."

Derring wanted to laugh it off, but his face grew increasingly contorted. He opened and closed his mouth, and his eyes darted to avoid confronting the four accusing women in front of him. He was becoming aware of possible consequences. A first for Derring, Athena was sure.

"You can't do this to me. I'm a full professor. I have connections."

Looking up at his bookshelf, Athena saw that Homer's Iliad was still in plain view. She reached into her utility belt and handed Mallory the packet of photos she'd taken in professors' offices. "I'll explain later, but you should have this evidence."

Derring glared at Athena and bared his teeth. *"You're fired for your insolence and incompetency, you sneaky bitch. This is a frame-up. I want a lawyer. You're all going to regret this. I'll make sure of it."*

As Mallory and Coles led Derring away with Briggs tagging

along, Athena couldn't help feeling jubilant. Even though she ached all over and had a splitting headache, it was good to know that justice was finally getting a shot at Derring.

Waiting for Russ by the stairs a few minutes later, she imagined telling him about Derring's arrest. He'd love it. She wanted to laugh wildly and hysterically to let go of pent up pressure. The expression "strung as tight as a bow" described the tension she still felt throughout her body.

Athena heard a slight noise behind her and that was the last she knew.

TWENTY-FOUR

ATHENA WOKE UP with the sensation that her head was expanding and contracting. A craving for cool, fresh water was persistent. While her eyes were closed, she was still seeing bright glimmers, afterimages of fire, but after opening her eyes, the darkness was dense and total.

Her immediate response was fear that she'd lost her sight, but by gradually clarifying the situation, she was able to partially calm the alarm. She was lying on her back, her wrists tied securely in front of her, her ankles also bound. Despite the restraints, she was able to touch her eyes gently and confirm that her eyelids were definitely open. Wherever she was, no trace of light was present to make outlines visible. Since no air stirred, she was probably enclosed in an as yet undefined space. Her utility belt with its handy phone was no longer around her waist.

In spite of residual smoke, she had a distinct impression that the air she was now breathing was stale and old. A scratchy blanket covered her. With her sunburn, she didn't need it. She shoved it off and heard it fall, though she wasn't sure how far. Beneath her was a thin, lumpy mattress, which she guessed was on some kind of frame.

Unsure what to expect, she stretched out her bound hands to test her surroundings. From what she could tell, she was not shut in a small, tight space such as a coffin. Where was she? From a bedazzling fire to the midnight black of nothingness in a short period of time. Total darkness was one of her childhood terrors. At home in Portland, she could not sleep without leaving a low watt light on.

Magda's prediction of danger through the tarot cards—this must be it. A second challenge to follow the first, which had almost overwhelmed her. She thought of Ted's words, ''Hesitating can be fatal.'' It almost had been. ''Sometimes, you've got to act on your gut level feelings.'' More of Ted's words. Those didn't help at present. Too many unknowns. At the gut level, she was terrified. A version of FDR's words, ''There's nothing to fear but fear itself,'' came to mind, and she repeated them like a chant.

Was it day or night? How much time had passed? She tried to reconstruct what had happened. She'd been waiting for Russ. There'd been a slight rustling noise, then pressure on her neck took her down. She'd had a vague sensation of being carried, even dragged. Then she'd lost consciousness.

''At least I'm alive.'' She ignored the prickles of anxiety that ran through her limbs. Her thoughts kept turning to water, desired by every cell in her body.

''Wouldn't you like a glass of champagne?'' Russ had brought her some at Laszlo's party.

''For you, Athena,'' he might have said. She imagined him holding the glass to her lips, tipping it slightly so she could sip. She almost felt refreshed.

''Thank you, *drágám,*'' she said out loud. The sound of her own raspy voice startled her. It echoed, which raised more questions. Too much to face after the other ordeal of fire. She was drifting into a shallow sleep state, shutting out all the unknowns.

Hot, hotter, hottest. At what point did the body reach its physical limit? Athena found herself trudging naked over hills and valleys of sand in search of water. Her skin was burning from exposure to the sun's rays above and intense heat rising up from the sand below. Each step required maximum effort, for she sank in and then pulled her feet up, one after the other, as she struggled toward the top and finally looked down. Sure enough, an oasis with a few shade trees and a well. Not much and not close, but survival depended on her getting there. Striding through the slipping, sliding sand, she covered some ground before looking for the bright promise again. No sign of it. A mere mirage. She was doomed.

Wrong setting. She was mountain-climbing not far from Portland, as she often did when she had time. The air was cool and fresh. Already high up, she was moving along the steep, familiar path. She already felt wrapped in clouds, which were giving her wet kisses, when rain started to fall. It soaked her clothes and soothed her chafed skin. She held out cupped hands, and they quickly filled with water, as if she were standing under a water spout in the basin of the courtyard fountain. She took a long, satisfying drink and felt restored.

She opened her eyes suddenly. This was no time for dreams; she had to plan. Even locked in a closet in an abandoned building or deep in a cave, she could take actions to free herself. One thing was clear to her, though she wasn't sure why. She'd let her mind do most of the work. In the dark hole where she found herself, there was no other choice. She visualized a ship afloat in an unknown location. No one would jump off a ship and swim for shore if no shore were visible. A gut-level feeling she chose to respect.

Russ had mentioned the inner voice, and Athena remembered the way to access it. Ask a question. Wait a few minutes with your mind blank. Then a voice comes from inside. She could use a guide now.

"How can I get out of here alive?" Athena focused all her attention on that question. Then she cleared her thoughts, trying to ignore the occasional shiver that passed through her. She wasn't sure how long she held that suspended state before summoning the inner voice. To her surprise, she got a response from a deep source she'd never heard from before: "Don't trust your host. Do not partake of the feast," said the voice, which was unmistakenly feminine but unfamiliar.

Vague. Who was the host? Where was the feast?

Given a choice, she'd order a small Caesar salad; a filet mignon, medium well; a baked potato sans sour cream; a glass of white Zinfandel, deliciously pink and frosty to the tongue; and perhaps an assortment of fresh fruit with a light glaze on top.

In Portland, she knew exactly where to find it any day of the week. It would be good to get back to her favorite city. She'd done what she could in Aston, though some questions remained unanswered. She'd wanted to ask Ted, "When do you know that you've done all you can and it's time to move on?'' Ted often said, ''Give it your best shot and then do a little bit better.''

Derring's downfall was a major coup. Though he'd probably walk away from it, he'd never forget it. She'd helped Suzie get back on her feet. She'd intervened on behalf of Laszlo, not a real triumph, but an honest effort to fulfill her promise. She'd pulled Magda to safety against the odds and in spite of her near fatal lapse, which she couldn't bear to recall at the moment. She had some info about the posters and computer messages, though it wasn't complete. There were more loose ends than she wanted to admit.

Behind it all in the shadows were the figures of Vicky and her father, Dean Conway. A strange pair. They were manipulative people, no doubt about that. Hard to imagine Vicky wielding a hammer, though her anger and spite toward Briggs had revealed a mind with no ability to draw limits according to social conventions. Vicky remained a puzzle.

Then there was Russ, to some extent a crippled genius, if he'd been truthful. He wanted to convey the image of an old-fashioned traveling man with books for baggage. Beneath that rough exterior, he was highly vulnerable, one reason for his unapproachability, Athena guessed. Why didn't he come to the rendezvous by the stairs? Why did he always seem to taunt her?

Her thoughts started to drift erratically: Springer ''springing'' around like a rabbit with a foolish grin on his face; Silver presenting Laszlo's case before a judge in a courtroom the size of Rimington auditorium; Briggs with remaining members of the Young Bunch planning to bring Big Henry down so she could take his place. Entertaining but she was losing her logic along with any sense of time, Athena feared.

Was she experiencing sensory deprivation? She saw herself suspended on Magician Laszlo's couch in the middle of a black cell. Others could see in, but she couldn't see out.

''Why didn't he tell me?'' she said out loud, which brought her back to the escape plan she was supposed to be working on.

''What are you doing, Athena?'' Spoken words made her feel

more real. She'd be both interviewer and interviewee to fill the void.

"So kind of you to ask. I'm waiting for the host."

"He's been delayed but will come as soon as he can."

"The sooner the better. I don't know where I am or who brought me here. I'm probably dressed all wrong for the occasion, because no one told me what to expect. If someone somewhere would give me a clue, I'd know what to do."

Finally, Athena heard a noise. It sounded like blocks of wood scraping together. Then there was a faint light somewhere down low, not far from the cot. A huge shadow was becoming visible on the wall across from her. Good to know that she could still see, though she had no idea what to expect.

A flashlight flicked on, and Josh was standing over her. From her prone position, he looked twice as tall and distorted by the odd light.

"Hi, there!" he said.

"Hello," she croaked, noticing how dry her tongue was.

"Sorry 'bout the hit I give ya," he said gruffly.

"Why did you do that, Josh?" Athena asked.

"For your own pertection."

"I don't need protection." She sat up awkwardly and tried to calm the whirling in her head.

Josh had on the green sweater Vicky had given him. He was looking at her far too amorously.

"Why do you think I need protection?" she asked, because now she knew Josh was the enemy. She'd tried to overlook his strangeness and had even felt sympathy for him. By being friendly, she'd encouraged him too much.

"Cops n' eggheads," Josh said. "Bad bunch! Hey, I got ya some grub."

He handed her a Taco Bell sack. Inside she found two tacos, two burritos, and a giant Pepsi. She really couldn't handle the food but the drink was something else. Athena started to sip through the straw before she remembered. She let the liquid back down through the straw, and it left an odd aftertaste. At least, she hadn't swallowed any, as thirsty as she was. To refuse her physical need required all her will power. The charade would have to continue with her pretending to drink but not really doing it, as with his awful coffee the first time they met.

Gaunt and troubled, Josh sat on a folding chair across from her.

"Wouldn't you like some?" Athena asked. "It's more than I can eat."

He shook his head and put one hand to his stomach. Finally he said, "We're friends, ain't we?"

"You've been a friend to me," Athena said, hoping he didn't mean more, "but friends help each other instead of hurting people."

Josh seemed to be brooding. A very alarming person. She really didn't know much about him or have any idea what his intentions were. Anything she said might provoke an unexpected reaction.

"Where am I, Josh?" she said when she couldn't stand the silence.

"Guess."

Athena noticed that they were on a small flat place with stairs above and below. If she'd tried to explore earlier, she might have fallen.

"In the walled-off place?" Athena said.

"Inside the wall by my office."

"I don't like it here. It's not a nice place. I want out of here, Josh." Athena had a quick thought of being confined for months without anyone knowing. The old walls were so thick. No one would hear her scream or call. "I can't stay here."

"You won't," Josh said with a shadow of a smile. "You'll be outta here in no time. I'm gonna take you to paradise."

Athena didn't like the sound of that either. At least she was near familiar things. Where was he going to take her?

"It was clever of you to fix this place, Josh."

"Not me. The fella before me. Had hisself a nice hidey-hole I jes' found it."

He got up to turn on the lamp. Athena stared at Josh, and he seemed to change before her eyes. His posture straightened up He took a bow.

"Introducing Alan Linstrom, formerly known as Josh."

"Josh is not your real name?" Athena felt like an idiot.

"No...my last drama-in-real-life role."

"You're an actor?"

"An amateur. Didn't you ever suspect that Josh was pulling your leg? As smart as you are..." His comments had a biting quality.

Athena nodded. "Only once or twice. I liked Josh."

"The poor, brain-damaged war vet. Well, I was in 'Nam and the wounds were real. The tattoos were a trick some buddies played on me when I was doped out of my mind. You wouldn't believe what went on over there. I'm still paying for it."

"Why did you come to the psych department?"

"A long story."

Athena felt a flash of anger. "Why did you bring me here?"

"You saw me tonight. I knew you'd figure it out."

"I saw you standing at the big window on the second floor but I didn't think anything of it. You're a regular."

"I'm flattered. You're the only one who saw me. I have to admit that I wanted you to look my way, making you either a tattletale or an accomplice, and I made the decision for you."

"That's ridiculous. An accomplice to what?" Athena was thinking hard. He seemed to believe she could read his mind. "You didn't set the institute on fire, did you?"

To her surprise, he nodded, looking self-content.

"Why did you do it?" Athena said. She was confused.

"*Revenge!*" Alan's blue eyes would not meet hers but stared at a distant corner of the room.

Athena exploded. "You destroyed Laszlo's lifetime work. You almost killed Magda. What did she ever do to you?"

White-faced, the former Josh had glittering eyes. "I didn't know she was there. That was an accident. The plan was to take one can of gasoline over every day in my basket and hide them in the library. The timing had to be right. I wasn't sure if I could keep going long enough to get the job done. Luckily for me, it worked. I did what I had to do, then I put the empty cans in Derring's office."

"Why there?"

Alan paused and then said, "Derring was an arrogant bastard. He told me to clean the parking lot around the Dumpster. That wasn't my job, but he acted like it was my fault that garbage trucks spilled things. He always wanted special services—his floor mopped several times a week instead of once. Never a kind word. He treated me like scum."

"Why hurt Laszlo and his people? They didn't offend you, did they? Did somebody pay you to burn the institute?" Athena looked at him defiantly.

"Nope," Alan said bitterly. "Thanks to the institute and that crew, I lost my son, my only child, Steve. Brought him up myself. He was so smart, so much better than I am in every way. I should have died instead of him. I've got nothing to lose. My wife left us. I wasn't the same after 'Nam, and she couldn't take it. What was I supposed to do with a kid? I was in recovery, with war wounds and emotional ones. I would pinch the little guy and punch him occasionally, but still, he would put his arms around me and look at me with those clear blue eyes. Before long, I was teaching him things. I had him reading before he was three years old. He always amazed me. What a kid! What a brain! In no time, he knew more than I did about everything. He ended up teaching me. I was so proud of my son."

Athena realized that Steve must have carved the wooden deer Josh had given her.

Alan shook his head. His voice got weaker and he looked like he could hardly sit up in the chair. Suddenly he put his hands over his face, and she could see his shoulders shake. Athena was stunned by his sudden revelation. She'd considered Josh an outsider with no department connections.

"He was the *only* purpose in my life. Gone, just like that." He clicked his fingers. "Everyone said he had a brilliant career ahead My life is ending but I thought he would carry on. Now, all I can do is punish the person responsible for his death."

Alan pulled a bottle of medicine out of his pocket and took two pills. He swallowed them without liquid, scratched his head and sighed.

"Good thing I don't care about living. Don't have much left."

"I've heard that Steve was very special," Athena said, trying to find the right chord. "A lot of people felt that way about him. You were lucky to have a son like that."

"I know...but why did I lose him? He was my reason for keeping on. I wanted to make sure he was on the right track and that I'd done everything I could for him. I've had several bouts with cancer—the aftermath of Agent Orange: 'First we spray; then we pay.' This time, it's taking me down. I told the docs not to bother anymore. They wrote me off years ago. One thing about Steve. He didn't feel any pain when he died. I've taken the pain for both of us."

Alan paused and Athena sipped some liquid in the straw and then let it fall back in the cup.

"Why burn the institute?"

"Latso filled Steve's head with nonsense about communicating with ghosts and fairies, then told him to prepare for death. Latso made him die. It was part of an experiment." Alan was shaking violently. "I hate the guy so much, I should have set him on fire. Vicky said to go for the institute."

"Vicky?"

"When Vicky came to the hospital to tell me what happened, I got up from my deathbed and knew I had one more thing to do."

"Why did you believe Vicky?"

"She was Steve's girl. She was going crazy. She wanted me to do what she couldn't."

"How did you get the custodian position?"

"We paid the real one to go on vacation disguised as sick leave. Vicky worked it out."

Athena was seeing all sorts of possibilities. "You drew the caricatures of Laszlo, didn't you?" She'd known when she saw the computer sketches, but it just didn't surface. "Did you send computer messages, supposedly from Steve?"

"Yes to both questions."

"Do you know who sent the other batch?"

"Redheaded guy."

Athena paused and kept her voice very controlled. "Did you hit Suzie Frazier on the head with a hammer?"

He hesitated and then shrugged. "I did. She saw Vicky and me talking, privatelike, and I knew she had ideas. Vicky said I'd better make sure she didn't interfere."

"You went to her house?"

"Stopped by for a little chat even though it was late. I had gloves on, because I planned to strangle her, but she offered another possibility. She was hanging a picture and asked me to pass her the hammer. I brained her with it."

"You sure did." Athena wondered what plans he had for her. This grieving father was capable of anything.

"You didn't know her. She wasn't like you. She told me to sweep in the corners. I couldn't do things right. She was nosy, and that's why we had to get rid of her. I made it look like a robbery. They'll never figure it out."

"How could you do that?"

"Vicky told me what needed to be done. When they sent her away, I promised her I'd finish the job."

"You hit the wrong targets."

"I completed my mission," he said. "I deserve a medal of valor. You don't know how hard it was to push that broom and cart around when all I wanted to do was lie down and die. I did it all for my boy."

"You did it for Vicky."

"She knew the right moves. I couldn't think clearly. There's a point after which right and wrong don't mean a thing. I had to do something for Steve."

Athena stared at him. She felt nauseated. He'd done all that without a pang of conscience. She dreaded to ask but faced the fear and went ahead. "What next?"

"I got a little job for you," Alan said.

Athena shook her head. "Not a chance. I have to go back to Oregon."

"This won't take long...two days at the most. I need your help."

Athena shook her head.

He went on. "I've got a cabin in the High Sierra. Steve loved that place more than anywhere else in the world. The sunsets are fantastic."

Athena listened carefully.

"I've got Steve's coffin in the back of my pickup. What we're going to do is take him up there and bury him. I dug holes for the two of us, side by side. I've long outlived my time. Now I want my boy and me to be together in our favorite place."

He looked at her, and she shook her head. "I can't help."

"I need a woman's touch," he said with difficulty. "You're an angel of mercy to forgive me for all mistakes my whole life through. You'll prepare my mind and my body for the final journey. I want you there with us, tuck us in nice, shovel the dirt on our coffins, then you're free. I'll leave the keys to my truck for you. I'll give you the truck. This is my last wish."

Athena's newly discovered inner voice warned her. "This man will never let you come back."

He closed his eyes, and Athena could see how sick he was. She was speechless at his request. He had caused so much havoc and he wanted peace of mind. He had suffered a lot, but he'd made others suffer too.

"I knew your dad over in 'Nam," Alan said.

"Don't," Athena said, holding up her tied hands. She believed he'd say anything to get her cooperation.

"You're coming whether you want to or not," Alan said. "The drug in your drink should take effect soon. If not, I got the ether pad right here."

That clued Athena that she'd have to fake it. Her mind was working fast on the best way to overpower him, but her hands and feet were tied.

Athena tried a little self-hypnosis and noticed that her head felt wobbly. The impulse to lie down was overwhelming. She'd be a dead weight, making it hard for him to take her out into the hall and she'd be waiting for the right moment to take control.

TWENTY-FIVE

"THIS IS THE MAN who almost killed Suzie and almost killed Magda. Have no mercy on him," Athena told herself. She had to build her resolve, because a trace of the friendly Josh lingered in the corners of her mind. Alan, the Magician, about whom Magda had warned her, had said and done the right things to throw her off guard, though he'd generously given clues she missed.

As Athena pretended to yield to a deep sleep, she clasped her hands together to make one large fist. If she could position herself to swing her arms in unison, she'd deliver quite a punch. If she had a chance to bend her knees up, she could kick with her feet. For the moment, she had to appear completely relaxed and lethargic.

She had no idea how strong Alan was in the advanced state of his disease. He'd managed to do things where a lesser man would fail, such as carrying and dragging her quickly down the hall and out of sight. From his track record, she knew he'd rise to the occasion when necessary.

Athena concentrated on slow, steady breathing. She could tell Alan was standing beside the cot and looking down at her. No, she could not peek, even the slightest bit, or he would know instantly. She expected him to lift her at any moment, but he did not.

His ragged breathing moved closer, and he started to touch—her hair, her face, her neck, her breasts. Nothing infuriated her more than "touchy-feely." At a cinema in France, a man sitting next to her had managed somehow to finger her under the protection of a folded raincoat on his lap. It had felt like cockroaches or a little mouse running up her leg. When she realized the real source, she elbowed his arm so hard he yelped and moved to another area. Alan's fingers were moving over her in that infuriating, exploratory way.

Now, Athena kept her mind focused on not tensing up when everything in her wanted to react. One wrong move and she could be on a trip to the mountains with Alan at the wheel, Steve's coffin in the back, and no guarantee of a round trip.

Evidently he was in no rush to drag her down the hall. Alan unbuttoned her blouse and put his hands on her breasts, fondling and squeezing them.

A woman's touch! She'd like to give him a woman's touch such as he'd never had before—clobber him good. He had no right to be pawing over her. No one touched her without her consent.

Gradually he was moving downward. When he started to tug on her pants, trying to pull them down, she flinched—a giveaway. Opening her eyes a crack, she saw his eyes only a foot away.

"Looky here," he said. "She's only playacting."

Turning, he moved back slightly and was reaching for something in his pocket when she let him have it. Athena bent her knees and kicked her feet into his chest as hard as she could. Choking, he backed away. She sat up and moved her back against the wall to give herself more support. He made a noise that sounded like a roar. She saw the fury in his eyes. He had the ether pad in one hand and a rope in the other. Lifting it up, he lashed at her. She didn't feel it. As he lunged toward her, she delivered a two-footed kick to the groin. He bent over but kept on coming. She hit with a two-handed karate chop to his neck and then shoved him as hard as she could. This time he staggered backward to the edge of the landing and fell down the five steps to where the old entrance had been before it was cemented out of existence.

She was up in an instant, looking for some way to cut the bonds on her hands and feet. If she didn't get them apart, she didn't have a chance. There were no sharp objects in view, just an empty beer bottle by the chair. She lifted it and smashed it against the wall. Even with a clumsy cutting edge, it was taking too long.

Alan had used her own scarf around her wrists but twisted and knotted it to make a strong bond.

That was when Alan started to moan and cry out. It was an inhuman, animal sound that rose from low to high and echoed off the walls and high ceiling of the enclosed space, giving her goose bumps. Was he really in bad shape or trying to get her help—at which time he'd overpower her again?

As far as she could tell, he was sprawled there on the lower level, seemingly helpless. She couldn't tell the extent of his injury. He kept on emitting the horrible sounds—lonely noises of a beast in agony.

First things first. She had to get unbound. Sitting on the cot, Athena tried with her hands to untie the knots in the rope around her ankles. Alan knew how to tie knots right. She couldn't get them undone, so she cut again with the edge of glass. This time, it went faster. She had just sawed through the cord when she heard a muffled noise at the custodian's entrance.

A snarling, furry beast came barreling through. It flew toward Alan, grabbed his pants leg in its teeth, and started shaking vigorously. Alan's noisemaking ceased.

Athena was glad to see Missy, especially since Russ was right behind. It took him a minute to crawl through the opening. Russ went down to join Missy and evaluate the situation.

"Hey! Cut me loose!" Athena said.

Russ pulled a penknife from his jeans pocket and sliced through the scarf in no time. He looked at Alan, who lay still with his eyes closed.

"Don't believe what you see," Athena said.

"Did you knock him down?" Russ asked.

"He fell down the stairs," Athena said, realizing that her blouse was open and buttoning up quickly.

"Your phone is out in the other room. I saw your belt on the counter."

Russ took the rope from around his waist and went slowly down the stairs. Missy stayed right with him, her eyes fixed intently on Alan's body. Russ prodded Alan with his toe, and the man groaned. When he tried to turn him over, Alan struggled.

Russ punched him a couple of times in the face, and Missy had a fresh hold on the leg of his jeans.

Athena crawled through the opening just as Russ was tying Alan's hands behind his back with the rope. She saw her phone and punched Coles' number. With no idea of the time, Athena waited, then tried again. Coles finally came on. She was at the campus office with Laura Mallory, still on duty, and they would come back right away.

"I have the man who bashed Suzie on the head and started the fire tonight," Athena said, realizing just how tired she was. She told her how to find the custodian's office.

"How come *you* make all the breakthroughs?" Coles asked with good humor.

Athena went back into the hellhole with reluctance. Russ was sitting in the lone chair. Missy had her nose in the Taco Bell bag and was devouring its contents with enthusiasm.

Alan had propped himself up against the wall below. There were red areas on his face where Russ had hit him. He started to moan again. "Can't stand the pain. Get me a pill. Please get me a pill."

"Boy, am I glad to see you," Russ said as Athena sat down on one of the steps that went up. She wouldn't go near the cot. "I checked all over—Suzie's, your apartment, back to campus. I made the circuit, because I knew something was wrong."

"Thanks for not giving up on me."

"I'd never abandon Athena in distress, but you had things under control."

Alan's moaning made it impossible to talk.

"Where's the pill, Alan?" Athena asked.

"Top pocket," he said with another moan.

"I can't stand this," she said.

Russ went back downstairs with her. Alan looked up adoringly as Athena put her hand in his shirt pocket. There was a pill there, a big white one, a real "horse pill," as she'd always called the ones that seemed too large to swallow.

"Thanks, honey," he said with special emphasis on the words. His eyes didn't leave her as she held out the pill. He opened his mouth like a giant fish. Would he bite? she wondered. Then she slipped it in his mouth. She took a minute to brush the thin strands of hair back off his forehead.

"For Josh," she said and backed off.

Alan closed his eyes. "You gave me a real gift," he called out as they went back upstairs.

Missy was having trouble coordinating her movements. Athena stroked her ears. "A real champ," she said. "I'm afraid Alan doped the food. Missy may be out for a while. I should have warned you."

Russ sat down on the cement landing beside the dog. Her breathing became very slow, the state Athena had tried to emulate.

"Missy kept stopping at the custodian's door," Russ said. "She probably smelled the food. I didn't pay attention the first couple of times. It was only when I heard the ugly sounds that I let her come in."

If the lower panel had been in place, no sounds would have been audible, Athena guessed.

"We'll load Missy into my car to sleep off the aftereffects," Athena said. "What time is it?"

"I don't have a watch, but it must be midnight or so," Russ said.

"Is the institute still burning?"

"They finally put it out. They've cordoned the area off with yellow tape. It was total."

"Alan set the fire," Athena said in a low voice. "He put empty cans in Derring's office, so the police took Derring in for questioning."

Russ laughed. "Guilty in thought if not in deed. Did he pay Alan?"

"Do you know who Alan is?"

Russ looked at her and raised his eyebrows.

"Steve Linstrom's father."

Russ whistled. "I remember one evening I was working on the computer. He was standing right behind me, watching. Then I saw him later, typing on one of the computers in the lab."

"He put messages in that were supposed to be from Steve," Athena said. "There were two sets—why did you do it, Russ?"

"The Code 3 messages?" Russ looked bothered. "You're too wise, Athena. Give a man a break. Laszlo was so low after Steve's death. He started seeing his whole career as a failure. I wanted him to have the satisfaction of getting messages from beyond."

"That's fraud!" Athena said.

"I'm not a scientist. I'm a writer," Russ said.

"How did you figure out a way to do it?"

"Actually, Steve was showing off while he and I were in the computer lab one day. He told me he'd altered the program for the computer in the main office while his girlfriend was in Ginger's office looking for a classified file he wanted. His adjustments made it possible to send messages from the computer terminal in the lab straight into the office computer while it was on, regardless of what the operator was doing at the time. He'd fixed it so he could confuse Suzie when he felt like it. Steve showed me how. He knew all about computers. I just know basics."

"Did you make up the messages?"

"Steve showed me what he planned to send, supposedly from a disembodied spirit, sending messages from afar. I just made up a few in that vein."

They both heard Alan slide against the wall and looked to see what had happened. His body had gone rigid and toppled over. He'd turned even more pale and ghastly looking. Athena knew before she checked. Alan was dead.

"The pill," she said. "I gave him the pill that killed him."

"You did him a favor."

Athena felt sorry for the Vietnam vet and the grieving father. She did not mourn the criminal, who used battle tactics in Aston.

"He bashed Suzie and almost killed Magda. Vicky asked Alan to get revenge for her and smoothed the way for him. Any way you look at it, Vicky was central to the disaster. She has a knack for causing trouble. Like father, like daughter, as Ginger told me in the beginning. They should both pay, but the dean may be protected by rank, and she can plead insanity without a blink."

"The way of the world," Russ said.

"I'm going to tell Mallory and Coles everything I know and see what they can do. Ben Silver wants all evidence I've gathered. He'll get lawyers to look it over. Any idea what Laszlo will do without the institute?"

"He and Magda will go back to Europe. I've heard them argue about the possibilities."

"Terrible that he lost his library collection."

"He didn't. Robert got a grant from some psychic society to duplicate Laszlo's documents. He and Dan worked on it all last year. They have copies in storage somewhere, so Laszlo can start over, though I think he might retire and write books."

"What are you going to do?"

"I'll be here for a month or so to get my books on computer. I'll submit the one on Laszlo to Shambala Press, the collection of personal stories to some other publisher, and then I'm off and traveling again."

"Where do you get your mail and messages?"

"A friend in New York City lets me share his P.O. box and his answering machine. What I really want to ask you about is Missy. I'm worried about her." He paused. "I found Missy by the road. She'd been hit by a car and left to die. I flagged down a guy who helped me get her to the vet. She's an excellent dog. The perfect companion."

"You two are inseparable."

"She's the best friend I've ever had," Russ admitted. He was stroking her gently. "I want her to have a good life...without me."

"Her life is with you. She loves you."

Russ looked troubled. "I can't let her hop trains, and this time I plan to take ships to distant harbors. Missy deserves a good home."

He stared at Athena intently.

"There are lots of nice middle-class homes in Aston. Surely you could find someone to give her tender, loving care."

Russ shook his head. "She's a working dog. She likes to be part of what's going on, not exiled out in someone's backyard all day long. She could be an asset to you in your work. Someone trained her to attack and harass on command."

"I live in an apartment where dogs aren't allowed," Athena said. "My uncle Ted has a little house with a yard."

"Do you think it's possible?"

"Ted had a dog named Ari—short for Aristotle—a golden retriever who died last year. He misses him, so maybe I can persuade him to take Missy. I know he'd love her, she's a doll." It occurred to her that through Missy she might keep in touch with Russ. He'd have the address, phone number, and an open invitation to stop by.

They both heard sounds in the adjoining room.

"In here," Athena called out.

Coles and Mallory came through on their hands and knees.

"Well, well," Coles said, once she was on her feet. "Isn't this quaint?"

"I'm afraid the perpetrator died," Athena said. "He took a pill he called a pain pill, but I believe it finished him off. His name is Alan Linstrom, Steve Linstrom's father. He was seeking revenge."

The two policewomen checked the corpse and put in a call for an ambulance. Then they were emptying Alan's pockets and comparing observations.

"You'll come to the campus station for questioning tomorrow morning at ten o'clock?" Mallory said to Athena. "We have lots of questions. Do you know, for instance, who D.C. is?"

"Sounds familiar. I'll be there. Also, you should find a pickup outside with a coffin in the back. It contains Steve's body."

Coles whistled.

"Alan wanted me to bury both him and his son at their mountain cabin."

Everyone was staring at her.

"Let's get out of here." Athena loathed the prison where she'd been held. "Finally I can say the worst has come and gone, and good friends survived."

"You're amazing," Russ said. "Are you going to stay with the P.I. work?"

"I learn more every day," Athena said, touching the area around her eye, which still showed signs of bruising. Ted would give her hell when she described the incident with Alan. "You let down your guard," he'd say. "Emotions clouded your judgment." He'd show her a dozen ways she could have done things differently.

"Let's go get something to eat," Athena said.

"Best idea I've heard recently," Russ said, pulling Missy's body to the opening. The way she would have been dragged if Alan had succeeded, Athena thought.

"When I was lying here in darkness," Athena said, "I called up the inner voice the way you said. To my surprise, I got good advice. It saved my life. Do you understand what the inner voice is?"

"All I know is—there are more things inside us and outside us than anyone can measure," Russ said.

He reached out his hand to help pull her through to the other side.

TWENTY-SIX

ATHENA HAD PACKED her car and was ready to leave, but Suzie had insisted on breakfast at Laszlo's.

"Magda has something for you," she said.

Although eager to get on the road and start her journey home, Athena agreed to go.

Magda looked animated and seemed to charge the air around her with energy. Her dress was a riot of bright colors, and she wore many rings on her fingers. A few minor burns on her legs were the only sign of the ordeal she'd been through. She had prepared a concoction of mixed fruit, including slices of nectarine, strawberry, banana, papaya, and kiwi, along with plain yogurt. A baguette of French bread looked inviting.

As she poured freshly brewed coffee, which emanated steam and an enticing smell, Magda said, "I have news. I have news."

She kept them waiting while she put the coffeepot back on its hot plate, sat down, and served herself some fruit.

"Laszlo and I go back to Hungary this summer," Magda said finally.

"Will you be there while I am?" Suzie asked. Her eyes lit up, her mouth turned up, and she was her old self again.

"Yes. We go late July, and we stay. Two years ago, Laszlo apply to Hungarian government for property that belong to his family. He want to live again in his grandfather's house and have guests with interest in psi. Maybe he have research institute or museum there. We hear nothing yet, but if we're there, they pay attention."

"Sounds good," Suzie said. Once Athena had updated her Saturday on all happenings, she'd been very worried about Laszlo and Magda. "We'll all get together."

"We will. We will. What I love," Magda continued, "is apartment in Budapest. We spend part of year in city. I can't wait."

"Don't take that mirror with you," Athena said with a smile.

"Aaaach! I get rid of mirror yesterday. Sell to antique dealer in town. Get some money back. You know, Suzie, that Tina save my life?"

"Athena told me about so many things that happened when I was 'out of order' that I thought she must have made them up," Suzie said.

"She save Laszlo too." Magda got up and went to pick up an envelope from a small table nearby.

"I guess she saved mine as well," Suzie said. "Even when she showed me pictures of me and my house, I thought it must be a joke, but Peggy confirmed that it was real."

"I know it's hard to believe, but do you think I'd play tricks on you about such serious things?" Athena said.

"Not you," Suzie said laughing. Of the two, she was more prone to play tricks.

"For you, Tina," Magda said.

Athena opened the envelope. Laszlo had written: "You will always be Katya to me. Please come to Hungary in the future." The fancy card was signed by Laszlo and Magda both. The check, signed by Laszlo, was for $5,000, the most she'd ever earned at one time.

"Thanks, Magda." Athena knew Ted would be pleased that she returned with a healthy bank balance. He often complained about how clients forgot to pay once a job was done. "Where's Laszlo?"

"He go with Ben to campus to inspect damage." After a pause, Magda said, "Do not forget your psychic potential."

"I realize now that in my type of work, we sometimes use intuition—what we call 'hunches'—but, like my namesake, I rely strongly on reason to put pieces in sequence. When my mind is working on problems, it feels good. I'm not the one you were looking for. The goddess Persephone concerns herself with psychic, mystical, and spiritual things."

"But you see psychic skills are important, yes?"

Athena thought of the surprises—Suzie's confession, Steve's appearance at the séance, the inner voice. "I've learned a lot. There's certainly more to it than I thought."

"After seeing how native cultures used psychic powers, Margaret Mead fully supported parapsychological studies," Suzie said, always well equipped with facts on any subject.

Athena had finished her fruit and was sipping the last of her coffee. "I told you this would have to be short."

As they left, Magda gave them both a hug and a kiss. Again, Athena felt the current of energy, which she'd decided might be Magda's strong heartbeat, and savored her exotic cinnamon and spice perfume for the last time.

"You come to Hungary, Athena," Magda said.

"I will." Athena envied Suzie, who'd see them that summer.

"I still can't believe that so much happened while I was out of action," Suzie said on the way to her house. "I should have been there, helping you out."

"Next time," Athena said.

In Suzie's driveway, they chatted a little more.

"I hope Ben Silver can get Dean Conway and Vicky for all the trouble they caused," Suzie said.

"I am writing a detailed report on everything I found out and everything I suspect," Athena said. "Silver thinks some action might be possible because of Derring's incriminating comments and the physical evidence, though scanty."

"I'll send you any news articles on the subject," Suzie said.

There was a tap on the window. It was Peggy, holding two small tin boxes. Yuki was jumping against the car door as if she wanted to get in. Athena rolled down her window.

"I want to thank you for helping Suzie and giving me a chance at finding that hammer," Peggy said. "I've got scones and Scottish shortbread for you to take on your trip."

The boxes had lovely pictures of English gardens with paths, gates, and abundant multicolored blossoms.

"Thanks for the treat," Athena said.

After a few more minutes of friendly chat, Suzie said "*Au revoir,*" and, arm in arm, she and Peggy waved as Athena drove away. Barking ferociously, Yuki ran along the sidewalk until satisfied she'd chased the car away.

Athena stopped one block over to pick up Missy. Ted had enthusiastically agreed to take the dog, once he heard she had special training.

She knocked at Russ' door. He didn't invite her in. From the look in his eyes, he hadn't slept much last night.

"Here's the address and phone number of our business," Athena said. "Come by and see how she's doing."

"I won't. I don't look back." His words were clipped, his voice broken.

He had put the slip rope around Missy's neck. He sat down for a moment in his doorway to give the dog a mammoth hug. She licked the tears off his face.

"You could bring her to us in Portland." Athena preferred it that way.

He shook his head, clung to Missy tightly, and then let go. "You two take care of each other," he said with difficulty.

Russ stood up and held out a hand to her. She shook it but moved in closer to give him a quick kiss. She could feel how tight his muscles were, the outsider who'd never let anyone in, unless he let go of the chip on his shoulder.

"I'll watch for your books," she said.

He gave her a half-smile as he held out a large sack containing the plastic dish, brush, and dog food.

"Go, Missy!" he said, pointing down the sidewalk to the car. "Go!"

Partway down the sidewalk, Missy looked back, and Athena did too, but he'd already closed his door.

"We have a lot to talk about," Athena said to the dog as she opened the car door and Missy jumped into the passenger seat.

FREE BOOK OFFER!

Dear Reader,

Thank you for reading this Worldwide Mystery™ title! Please take a few moments to tell us about your reading preferences. When you have finished answering the survey, please mail it to the appropriate address listed below and we'll send you a free mystery novel as a token of our appreciation! Thank you for sharing your opinions!

1. How would you rate this particular mystery book?

1.1 ❑ Excellent
.2 ❑ Good
.3 ❑ Satisfactory
.4 ❑ Fair
.5 ❑ Poor

2. Please indicate your satisfaction with The Mystery Library™ in terms of the editorial content we deliver to you every month:

2.1 ❑ Very satisfied with editorial choice
.2 ❑ Somewhat satisfied with editorial choice
.3 ❑ Somewhat dissatisfied with editorial choice
.4 ❑ Very dissatisfied with editorial choice

Comments ______________________________

______________________________(3, 8)

3. What are the most important elements of a mystery fiction book to you?

____

______________________________(9, 14)

4. Which of the following types of mystery fiction do you enjoy reading? (check all that apply)

15 ❑ American Cozy (e.g. Joan Hess)
16 ❑ British Cozy (e.g. Jill Paton Walsh)
17 ❑ Noire (e.g. James Ellroy, Loren D. Estleman)
18 ❑ Hard-boiled (male or female private eye) (e.g. Robert Parker)
19 ❑ American Police Procedural (e.g. Ed McBain)
20 ❑ British Police Procedural (e.g. Ian Rankin, P. D. James)

5. Which of the following other types of paperback books have you read in the past 12 months? (check all that apply)

21 ❑ Espionage/Spy (e.g. Tom Clancy, Robert Ludlum)
22 ❑ Mainstream Contemporary Fiction (e.g. Patricia Cornwell)
23 ❑ Occult/Horror (e.g. Stephen King, Anne Rice)
24 ❑ Popular Women's Fiction (e.g. Danielle Steel, Nora Roberts)

WWWD98B1

25 ❑ Fantasy (e.g. Terry Brooks)
26 ❑ Science Fiction (e.g. Isaac Asimov)
27 ❑ Series Romance Fiction (e.g. Harlequin Romance®)
28 ❑ Action Adventure paperbacks (e.g. Mack Bolan)
29 ❑ Paperback Biographies
30 ❑ Paperback Humor
31 ❑ Self-help paperbacks

6. How do you usually obtain your mystery paperbacks? (check all that apply)

32 ❑ National chain bookstore (e.g. Waldenbooks, Borders)
33 ❑ Supermarket
34 ❑ General or discount merchandise store (e.g. Kmart, Target)
35 ❑ Specialty mystery bookstore
36 ❑ Borrow or trade with family members or friends
37 ❑ By mail
38 ❑ Secondhand bookstore
39 ❑ Library
40 ❑ Other ______________________________ (41, 46)

7. How many mystery novels have you read in the past 6 months?

Paperback ________ (47, 48) Hardcover ________ (49, 50)

8. Please indicate your gender:

51.1 ❑ female .2 ❑ male

9. Into which of the following age groups do you fall?

52.1 ❑ Under 18 years .4 ❑ 35 to 49 years
.2 ❑ 18 to 24 years .5 ❑ 50 to 64 years
.3 ❑ 25 to 34 years .6 ❑ 65 years or older

Thank you very much for your cooperation! To receive your free mystery novel, please print your name and address clearly and return the survey to the appropriate address listed below.

Name: ____

Address: ______________________________ City: ____________

State/Province: ____________ Zip/Postal Code: ____________

In U.S.: Worldwide Mystery Survey, 3010 Walden Avenue, P.O. Box 9057, Buffalo, NY 14269-9057
In Canada: Worldwide Mystery Survey, P.O. Box 622, Fort Erie, Ontario L2A 5X3

098 KGU CJP2 WWWD98B2

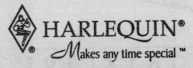